Certified Human

Dieter Lüske

Books

LU Books - Australia

Books

LU Books — Australia

Copyright © 2024 by Dieter Lüske

Cover Design by Giselle www.gallerygiselle.com

Edited by Lynne Lloyd at Lloyd Moss Publishing www.lloydmosspublishing.com/

Author website: www.DieterLuske.com

A huge thank you to my wife, Giselle and my son, Marly; this book would not have happened without their love and encouragement.

I LOVE YOU

1

Looking in the mirror, Blake Newcome saw a young-looking 38-year-old happy guy. The mirror image didn't do him justice; it was not large enough to show his 6-foot-fit figure. He hand-combed his full head of dark blond hair back away from his high forehead and smiled at his reflection. How could he be so smitten by a girl he met just a few weeks ago?

Having skipped shaving for a couple of days, he lathered up big-time. Blake was proud to be old school. Being retro was his thing. In 2033, wet shaving was out, and that wasn't the only behaviour that differentiated Blake from his contemporaries; he also had an intense interest in cooking at a time when society had switched to household service robots and ready-made meals. Cooking had become decidedly an old-school interest.

Service stations had transformed into brand-spanking e-car charging ports and ready-made meal pick-up stations. High-tech hot or cold packaging ensured the food was in pristine condition, and there was an overwhelming range, even for the most discerning taste buds.

Blake too had sampled the designed ready meals probably way too often. He was particularly partial to the organic butter chicken, but not today; today was special. He had driven straight home after charging his e-car, a DIA-Move, from a company called DIA-International, short for Digital Inversion Autonomous. His investigative journalist mind had its own idea of what DIA stood for, secretly thinking that inversion autonomous meant to turn life on earth on its head automatically. Was he onto something?

Blake had arrived home early, a rarity. Being a journo often prevented early homecomings, but today, he prioritised. He had to be early, not only because he needed a shave but also because he had planned an elaborate dinner with a stylish candle-lit table setting. He had carried a few bags of food items up four floors to his Brisbane West End unit, hardly ever taking the lift. Everything went as planned.

Super smooth shaving out of the way, he was close to being ready and set up to cook his unique recipe for a scrumptious spaghetti meal. But first, his bachelor unit needed a clean-up. The open-style living room and kitchen were messy with crumpled-up sheets of paper of unfinished articles, books he promised to read one day, plates with leftover butter chicken, and empty beer bottles.

He grabbed a large black plastic rubbish bag from a kitchen cupboard and raced around the room, stuffing it with everything not worth keeping. He rearranged or straightened up furniture, fluffed up pillows, and, as a final touch, raced one more time around the living room with his stick vacuum cleaner.

He should have tidied up before showering. Never mind, he can have another quick shower after cooking.

From his kitchen vantage point, he cast a last look around. It looked reasonably respectable. Bookshelves with hundreds of books were loaded close to breaking point. A comfortable leather couch and chairs were placed neatly around a low set table, and his prized possession, a high-quality record player, the newest model Technics AI-2000RE, accompanied by hundreds of LPs, alphabetically sorted on the overhead shelving. What was not to like?

Something was missing on the dining table: flowers. Where can one get flowers at this late hour? How could he have forgotten? He had bought candles, even napkins, but no flowers. Walking to the balcony of his unit, he eagle-eyed the lower-ground surroundings. Yes, he spotted what he needed: bottlebrushes with a few leaves would be a thoughtful Australian table arrangement. He made his way downstairs, scissors at hand. Anyone looking? No. A few snips and the deed was done. It was getting late; he had to get his gig together.

Back to the kitchen, boiling water for spaghetti. His Bolognese departed from the usual sauce. Instead of beef mince, he used chicken and a greater variety of vegetables accompanying the usual tomatoes and onions. It would be like a hot stew, with chilli and garlic included. He also had a special touch for the spaghetti; once cooked, he tossed it around in a frying pan with lots of olive oil.

Surely, his thoughtful plan would convince his new girl to stay for breakfast.

He was moonstruck when he first saw her a few weeks ago while interviewing a couple of brokers at a prominent Wealth Management, Stock Broking, and Financial Planning office in Eagle Street about an apparent share fraud.

She sat in the background in front of a couple of computer screens and overhearing Blake's questioning; she looked straight into his eyes. He stopped breathing for a second, taken off guard, and stumbled over his question to Dave, his broker friend.

"Are you alright?" Dave asked. "Something wrong?"

"No, sorry mate, something occurred to me, never mind. What was that initial share order again?"

Blake's brain was, at best, half in attendance; the other half was hopelessly preoccupied with that striking, model-look-alike girl at the computer.

"Have you noticed any inflated orders from other broker firms or individuals using software and AI within the last few months? I need any info that is not in line with accepted limits. Has there been any unexplained offloading of shares? Anyhow, you know what I am looking for; let me know when you come across something."

"Sure thing, Blake, don't worry, I'll keep my eyes open."

"Thanks, something else; who is the lovely brunette over there? I have never noticed her before."

"That's Jess. She's new. She started a couple of weeks ago. We hired her for her expertise in blockchain and crypto security applications," Dave answered with a cheeky smile.

"What are you smiling for?"

"I don't think you are interested in her computer skills."

"OK, you got me. Is she having drinks with you guys after work?"

"Yeah, most days, happy now?" Dave couldn't stop grinning.

"Your usual watering hole?"

"Yes, what else would you like to know, her shoe size?"

"Married?"

"No, get out of here now; I am busy."

"Talk soon, catch you later for a drink."

Dave was more than a good mate to Blake; he was a reliable and trustworthy friend. Their friendship had roots that stretched way back to their pre-school days. During their university years, they shared a unit. Blake knew, without a doubt, that he could always count on Dave.

As he made his way out of the office, he glanced back, having a fleeting look at Jess. She looked straight back; no doubt, there was a connection. Not sure how to react, he managed to give a little nod and continued his way to the lift, pressing LG2, hoping it was the correct parking level where he had left his car. It was; he saw his car within walking distance of the lift. He sat down and leaned back in the driver's seat, asking himself, *now what*?

After a few minutes, he drove off, returning to his unit and home office. The newspaper he wrote for, the 'Fact File News,' had no brick-and-mortar office in Brisbane anymore; Sydney was the solitary office, and everything else was online. However, it has become one of Australia's most prominent news outlets over the last couple of decades.

There was still time to write his share fraud article and send it to his smart-intelligent-looking 35-year-old boss, editor, and special friend, Frances. He didn't see her as a boss; he considered himself freelance; even so, he had been writing for the Fact Files for years.

Frances was his primary working contact, editing his stories or sending him on a chase for tech scoops. Most of all, he valued her connections and that she found him reliable sources for his quests.

They had a love affair when their working relationship began while she still worked from the Brisbane office. Still, somehow, being busy, always chasing the next story, they hardly noticed they had drifted into the friendship zone with the occasional benefit or rekindled fling. Eventually, when the Brisbane office closed, Frances moved to the head office in Sydney. They met up a few times per year when Blake stayed at her place before returning to his turf.

Two hours later, he had finished his piece about the latest share fraud scam involving identity theft, offers to buy shares at a discount, and selling them with exaggerated profits. He hit the send button. Ten minutes later, Frances replied with her approval: the story would be up the next morning. A PS was asking when he would be in Sydney again. Blake thought briefly before replying, "Soon," adding a smiley face. He still had undiminished feelings for her.

What was the time? He checked his vintage Rolex Submariner: 4:30 pm, enough time to drive back into the business precinct to join Dave and his team for a drink and hopefully catch sight of Jess.

Shortly after 5 pm, he walked through the doors of the Port Office Hotel on Edward Street and spotted Dave and the other guys.

"What a coincidence; what are you doing here?" Dave asked, grinning again.

"The story will be out tomorrow. I thought you wanted to know," Blake said, waved at the barman, ordered a beer, and cast his eyes around the joint but couldn't spot Jess.

"Jess wouldn't be here, would she?" he asked Dave.

"No worries, mate, she's in the lady's room."

Blake had taken a sip of beer when he saw her returning, joining the others. At Dave's office, she was sitting down, glancing from behind her computer screens; now, he saw her walking towards the bar, tall and stunning, with an aura of confidence and a figure suggesting hours of strenuous gym workouts.

"OK, here we go, now or never, and don't make a bloody fool out of yourself," Blake murmured to himself.

He walked over to her and said, "Hi, I saw you at Dave's office. You must be new. I'm Blake."

"Good to meet you, Blake; I'm Jess, but I have the feeling you knew that already."

"Yes, I confess, I knew; I asked Dave about you; I am always looking for new perspectives on possible cyberspace spam and stories. Dave mentioned you are into crypto and blockchain applications."

"Is that all you are interested in? That's disappointing," she laughed.

"Actually, I am starved and haven't had time to eat. Can I invite you for dinner?"

"That sounds better; let's get out of here."

Pretty forward, that lady, Blake thought. They walked to Blake's car, deciding to have dinner at Southbank. There was no warm glow of the setting sun bathing Southbank in a golden hue, but it felt like it. The evening exceeded his expectations. They didn't just click; they resonated. The conversation flowed effortlessly, with no awkwardness at all. Their chemistry was undeniable. It was clear they were falling for each other; no need for the usual dating games.

Their meetings became more frequent over the next couple of weeks, mainly for drinks or dinners. They loved to talk and discuss their favourite topics: high-tech inventions, artificial intelligence, crypto, the banking system, and even politics and how it could benefit from an online voting system. They had kissed, and there was a tangible desire for more intimacy. It was time to step it up a notch. Blake knew there would be no objection when he invited her to his place. He called her; he had decided to cook for her.

"How about coming to my place on Friday night for dinner? I would love to cook something special for you."

It was a loaded question; he had more than cooking on his mind, even though he was a passionate hobby cook. He spent way too much time cooking, planning to cook, and serving it up to his close friends, Dave included.

Her answer came without hesitation: "Love to, can't wait. What can I bring, red or white?" She knew he loved cooking; had she anticipated being asked for a home-cooked meal?

That was it; it was a date, and he looked forward to it.

The video intercom rang; he sprinted to the door and buzzed her in: "Hi Jess, take the lift to the fourth floor; I am on the right side when you come out of the lift."

He waited in anticipation and couldn't believe his nerves. *Come on, man, I am thirty-six; what am I nervous about?*

The lift door opened; there she was, in all her beauty, with a bottle of wine at hand. It was not the wine that excited him; it was her figure-hugging pencil skirt, the see-through dark blouse, and something tiny underneath, faking it as a bra.

"You look so beautiful. What are you trying to do to me? Come, let me show you around."

"Thanks, you are not looking too bad yourself," Jess replied, touching his clean-shaven cheek and adjusting his shirt collar.

"Great unit. Have you lived here long?"

"Nine years already; I love it here, village atmosphere with enough privacy; no one is bothering me."

Jess walked around and inspected the bookshelves, commenting on some of the book titles, "Who is Buckminster Fuller?" but didn't expect an answer. She walked towards the couch setting and smiled about the fluffed-up pillows. "Did you clean up before I arrived? It looks suspiciously clean for a bachelor pad."

Blake grinned at her, "I don't have to tell you everything".

"Where is your bedroom?" she asked.

"Down the hallway." He couldn't believe it; she was checking out his private domain.

"Dinner is ready," he called out. Jess came back, slowly moving towards

Blake, touching his face, kissing him, and looking at him.

"Can't wait, comfy bedroom."

They sat down; Blake poured the wine and served his spaghetti dish. The atmosphere was electric. Jess ate in slow motion, touching Blake's legs playfully with her foot.

"It's the best spaghetti I ever had," she said after finishing. "Maybe we could have the dessert later." She lifted herself out of her chair and leaned over the table.

Blake, confronted with a view into her loose hanging top, raised his glass. "Cheers to that," he said, taking a sip, stood up, and walked around the table. Jess took his hand and pulled him towards the bedroom.

Blake had his fair share of interactions with women. He possessed a certain handsomeness that effortlessly drew the attention of the opposite sex. However, Jess was something else. She was refreshingly open, forward, and in control. That, and her flawless beauty, had attracted him to her in the first place.

For the first time in his life, it wasn't him who took the lead.

The fact that he hadn't been with a woman for a few months may have intensified his surrender to what followed: a night of unrestrained pleasure.

He didn't even have a moment to arrange the perfect mood lighting and music.

"Leave the light on; it's more fun that way," Jess said, stripping off her top.

It was shortly after 8 pm, Blake noticed on his bedside alarm clock. The next time he looked, it was 3 am, and Jess, with her immaculate naked body, was using Blake's bed as a trampoline.

"Keep hopping; I can watch you forever," he said.

"I don't think so," she laughed and replied, "Catch me if you can." She hopped off the bed and ran across the living room to the balcony.

No choice, Blake rolled out of bed. He would have run after her a few hours before, but now he was spent. He was puffing when he made his way after her.

I need to do more exercise, he thought.

It's hardly the time to come up with good intentions.

When he came around the wall and into the living room, he saw her doing yoga stretches on the balcony. *Boy, could she stretch.*

"Please, Jess, come back inside."

"No, it's so nice out here, clean, crisp air. Come out and do some deep breathing."

He stepped closer, softly speaking, "Please, Jess, don't scare the neighbours."

"It's the middle of the night; your neighbours are sleeping," she said, moving closer to the balcony railing and stretching out her arms in salute to the moon.

"Please, Jess, as beautiful and tempting as you look, please come back in."

"You better come and get me then," she teased, sitting on the balcony railing.

Blake, naked as well, ventured out to the balcony, stretching out his hand, "Come now, please come down; it's dangerous."

She playfully held her arm towards him, only to pull it away, laughing, teasing him, and holding out her arm again. That time, Blake gripped her wrist quickly, "Got you; come down now." Frowning, he wasn't looking happy anymore.

"No, I want to be here for longer," she laughed and forcefully pulled her arm. Blake kept holding her. She released her arm tension, then quickly and firmly pulled her arm free, losing her balance. A second later, she was gone – no scream, not a sound, until Blake heard a dull thud.

He jumped to the railing and looked down in horror. His brain stopped functioning. Jess was lying on the ground, a glimmer of moonlight on her exquisite naked body.

"No, no," he ran into his bedroom, pulled out a pair of shorts from the wardrobe, slipped them on, and raced from his unit towards the lift, hitting the ground-floor button. He stopped. *What am I doing?* He dashed back to fetch his mobile. Back out again, the lift had arrived; he pressed ground and rang Triple Zero while waiting in agony for the lift to make its slow descent. When he hurried out of the lift, his call was answered.

What could he say? "Emergency, please quickly send an ambulance; my girlfriend fell off the balcony." He passed the lobby and ran around the building to where the balconies were located.

"Sir, is your girlfriend breathing? Can you do CPR?"

"I haven't reached her yet ..."

There she was, so beautiful, lying peacefully on the grass. Not a scratch, no blood, nothing distorted, a perfect human being. He bent down. Was she breathing? He couldn't hear anything and tried to find a pulse on her wrist, nothing. He felt for a pulse on the side of her neck, nothing.

He heard the distant sound of the ambulance siren. Although he had never performed CPR in a real-life situation and could hardly remember the specific sequence, he closed off her nose and blew into her mouth several times. No reaction. He pumped her chest hard and rhythmically, continuing with brief pauses for mouth-to-mouth breathing.

The siren stopped. His numbed-out mind vaguely registered the sound of footsteps, running and stopping. Someone gently pushed him aside. "Please, sir, move away." He was barely aware of what was happening, stunned in disbelief, watching everything in slow motion, devoid of emotions.

The defibrillator appeared to make no difference; her body was not even moving when the charge was applied.

A concerned ambulance officer bent down to Blake, who was sitting on the grass, his head between his knees. She touched his shoulder. He looked up to her, still hoping. "Sorry, sir, we couldn't revive her. We are going to take her with us. The police have arrived. They will let you know about the next steps."

"Thank you." *Why am I thanking her?* He asked himself.

He felt dull. He wasn't quite with it and wondered why he felt no sadness. The whole three weeks with Jess were a blur and seemed unreal now. He had been a journalist long enough and had watched countless crime stories on television; he knew what came next for him.

Slowly, he felt panic rising from the pit of his stomach; fear and anxiety took hold of him. Tears squeezed out onto his cheeks; he hadn't cried for years. Crying came hard for him; laughing was his forte. He knew he wouldn't be able to laugh this one off. The police surely would accuse him of manslaughter. His life wouldn't be the same ever again.

Someone tapped him on his shoulder again; this time, it was the police.

"I am Detective Inspector James Moorhead. Can I have a word?"

Blake glanced up. A tired man looked down on him, holding a serious, questioning stare. "Perhaps we could proceed to your unit. We will need to conduct a thorough investigation, you understand?" His words were polluted with alarming ambiguity.

"Yes, sure." Blake stood up slowly; he felt a hundred years old. He wouldn't have made it if not for the inspector's helping hand.

They made the way up to his unit, the inspector holding his arm. Was it to help Blake or to make sure Blake didn't do a runner?

2

Sydney – The formative years

E ven as a young boy, Blake exhibited his inquisitive nature and drove friends and parents mad with his constant questioning, revealing the qualities of a journalist in the making.

Everyone said so, particularly his mates he had known forever. They first met at pre-school, living in the same neighbourhood. A year later, primary school, mingling with the big kids. Their friendship survived despite a few hiccups at high school.

That is where it started for Blake; he founded the first school newspaper. Teachers were delighted. They never had a dedicated group to put up a school paper lasting the distance. It needed someone like Blake and his teammates to pull that off.

There was young Blake, cheeky and inquisitive, squeezing worthwhile topics out of pupils from every grade, free of fear or consequences. Blake's writing developed quickly, never shy of controversy.

The team behind him consisted of Dave, the go-getter, forever scheming how to make an extra buck; Jake, who knew he wanted to be a police officer like his dad; Oliver, shy and always with his head in the books, fascinated by politics, law, and the environment and the team's go-to person for answering even the most tricky questions; and Mark, the sporty guy who wrote the sports section and surfed whenever time allowed.

But their bond wasn't always smooth sailing. The emergence of romantic interests, often in the same girls, had been a source of tension. Yet, even this couldn't break the bond they had forged over the years.

Mark was something of a rascal. He had blond, nearly white-washed hair from surfing, strong physical abilities, and charm galore, and he developed into a girl magnet.

When it came to parties, Mark was the guy who invited all the pretty girls; the other guys were a bit slow to catch on.

Oliver seemed not to have noticed that girls existed; even at parties, he brought a book. Being pale and less sporty, Mark's choice of girls had no impact on him.

A few years later, at university, Oliver had developed his persona which he had most likely modelled on a 1960s high school teacher. He wore checkered jackets with leather elbow patches and carried a pipe around but didn't smoke. He surprised them when he moved in with his girlfriend, Mona, from the outside, a complete opposite: short, spiky blond hair, fine angel-like features, a porcelain complexion, black suits, ties, and crazy pattern shirts. Despite her eccentric looks, she suited him like a glove. And, of course, they both studied law.

Blake went on to study journalism; what else? Dave decided to pursue an economics degree, and Jake couldn't wait to get his bachelor in criminology to become a criminal investigator.

Mark did the unexpected. He wasn't focusing solely on competing for surfing titles and becoming a professional surfer; he placed a bet both ways and added a physiotherapy degree to his goals.

Sydney – December 2019

By the end of 2019, Blake, Mark, and Jake had finished their degrees, and it was time to party.

Mark lived in a house he shared with another couple and, of course, his girlfriend. He and everyone else called her Bidi, but her real name was Bianca. They had been going steady for a year, and where else would they be living than in Bondi?

They had met sitting beside each other on their surfboats, waiting for the next wave to catch.

She had studied computer science, specialising in algorithmic processes and artificial intelligence. Besides being sporty, Bidi qualified as a computer geek without looking like one. With her raw beauty, freckled cute face, snub nose, blond hair, and impressive 5 foot 7 slim but muscular physique, no one would have thought her hobby was 'hacking'.

Planning the party came naturally for Mark and Bidi. The housemates joined in; everyone was invited, and most brought food and drinks.

Blake and Jake, less domesticated, put their money on the table for pizzas and some famous chicken nugget delivery for the extra base load to manage their drinking.

The party took off on a Friday; some arrived as early as 5 pm, hoping for free pizza. By 3 am, the party had taken its toll.

New couples getting to know each other occupied the bedrooms, and way too many guests had too much to drink and were lined up before the one single toilet, hoping that vomiting would relieve their pain. To top that mess, the dream team had decided they needed to cool off and headed down from Sandridge Street to Bondi Beach for a late-night swim.

They should have known better; Oliver and Mona called for caution, but to no avail. They always did everything together and stayed well back in shallow waters. The other guys went way too far out. It was too much fun to resist. Luckily, they made their way back, body surfing.

They had sobered up and laughed about their stupidity. Except Mark, who must have thought he was invincible. Had he swum out even further to catch a better wave? Everyone had returned safely, but Mark was still missing. Bidi, as well as the others, looked out over the dark ocean. Where was he? Surely, he was safe, being a strong swimmer and great body surfer. He was the guy who understood Bondi Beach; he could read the surf like a book and knew what to do if he got into trouble.

They waited. Did they wait too long? After waiting for a slow 10 minutes, they realised something must have gone wrong and called triple zero. They had to wait much longer—an agonizing whole night.

Mark must have been unable to catch the wave he wanted. He didn't come back at all, and rescue services searched the rest of the night and into the daylight.

Police found his body at sunrise on the other end of Bondi Beach.

The boys and Mona stayed with Bidi at their shared house after the police left. All had grown up instantly. Life would never be the same. That day, they mourned and cried together; nothing helped, a moment marked into their memories forever. They felt utterly alone, and all they could do now was to support Bidi, who lay curled up on the couch, crying. Dissolved in tears, the sweet IT consultant wouldn't consult anyone for some time.

Eventually, it was time to go, leaving Bidi to grieve alone, but not before they strengthened their team pack and invited her to join.

In a last act of being like teenagers, they swore to stick together, always, come what will, being there for each other, supporting each other, even if they would live in different cities and have different interests. They had a strong bond, Mark's death, which they could come to terms with if they stayed united.

3

Detective Inspector James Moorhead wasted no time.

"Let's sit over there, and you tell me what happened," pointing at the couch.

Blake sat down first, looked up to the inspector, and paused for a moment to collect his thoughts. He had nothing to hide, nothing to leave out.

"We had a great time. Everything went well, and we stayed in bed until around 3 am when Jess danced around, teasing me, and then ran towards the living room, wanting me to follow her" Blake paused and raised his hand, "I need a glass of water or something stronger."

"Sure, go ahead," the inspector didn't look bothered.

Blake had emerged from his dazed state. He knew he had to be careful not to say something that could be misconstrued. He poured himself a whisky, waiting for its calming effect to chase away the butterfly in his stomach while he drank it. "Like one?" The inspector shook his head.

Blake knew he needed to continue with a clear head: he walked over to the kitchen sink, collecting his thoughts as he filled his glass with purified water and returned it to his seat.

"Where was I?" his voice stronger now.

"Your girlfriend wanted you to chase her," the inspector summarized, putting his slant on the story so far.

"Yes, that's right. Jess ran around the couch and table setting a few times, laughing, dancing, and teasing me. I followed slower behind but urged her to return to bed. Instead, she ran out to the balcony."

Blake sipped on his water, clearing his throat. The inspector waited, stern-faced, watching Blake.

"Then what happened?" he asked.

"I pleaded with her to come in; what would the neighbours think? After all, she was naked." Blake paused once again and calmed himself before describing the final bit.

"She hopped onto the balcony balustrade. That worried me even more, and I moved closer to grab her arm, but she pulled it away. It must have been at that moment she lost her balance and fell. I was like paralysed for a moment before I called for an ambulance and ran down. You know the rest." Blake finished, his voice trembling with a hint of guilt as if he had told a lie, even

though he didn't do anything wrong. He stared at the inspector, waiting for a reaction.

"I think that's all for the moment, but I need you to come with me to the station and put your statement in writing," he looked at Blake and added, "Should be easy for you as a journalist." Was he mocking Blake?

"Why is that? I haven't done anything wrong; I can write my statement here?"

"I fear it needs to be more official; I have to follow the protocol. I would also like to keep you overnight while we await the forensic report."

"What has forensics to do with it? We all know how Jess died?"

"Don't get too concerned; it's protocol, eliminating any other factors," the inspector stressed.

"I have no idea what needs to be eliminated?" Blake questioned, half talking to himself.

"We will find out soon, but now we have to go," the inspector said, gesturing for Blake to follow. His voice carried a firmness that tolerated no argument.

Blake wasn't happy. He considered asking for the one phone call a suspect was meant to get, but he stopped himself in time. It could direct more suspicion to him.

He wasn't an anxious person, but he had no trust in the police anyhow, and in his case specifically. He didn't trust John Moorhead, the inspector, who seemed determined to turn that sad but innocent event into a murder investigation.

The other police officers had finished investigating his unit and left. Blake asked permission to dress more appropriately than in shorts, locked up the unit, and followed the inspector to an unmarked car.

Would the inspector push down his head when getting into the car, as seen on TV when a crook is transported off to the station?

No, it was pretty casual, like getting a lift from someone.

Blake had never been into the inner sanctum of a police station, but he wasn't surprised when led into a sparsely furnished room with empty walls and a lonely-looking desk with two chairs. And yes, there was this black window in the wall that had no pretty view to the outside. He knew what that was about.

Still, it was a casual atmosphere; the inspector didn't even lock the door when he left after giving Blake a clipboard, pen, and paper.

Blake went to work; after all, writing was his forte, and he may as well make it into a good story. *Funny,* he thought, *I am not even thinking about Jess. Was it an aberration, and now I am waking up again?*

His mind flipped back to his journalistic self; it was like he watched himself writing a report about his experience. He felt better and less anxious and sure everything would work out.?

It must have been a couple of hours or more before the inspector returned. Blake had fallen asleep. The inspector sat down; he looked tired and less assured. Blake slid his written statement over the table to him.

"Thank you, Mr. Newcome." That was a new one. Blake was addressed formally. Was that a good or bad sign? Blake sensed it could be good.

"There has been some development regarding the deceased. I need to ask you to stay a bit longer; we have prepared a cell for you to catch up with a couple of hours of sleep. We will know how to proceed in the morning. Let me say you have nothing to worry about, but we have to clear up legal issues and wait for the appropriate government response. That's all I can tell you at the moment," the inspector said.

Blake's mind was overwhelmed with conflicting thoughts, unsure of what to make of the situation. Yet, a spark of curiosity ignited within him. Could this be the story he had been waiting for? Was he being callous in his eagerness? "Thank you, and yes, I wouldn't mind having a sleep; hope you serve a good breakfast."

The inspector smiled warily, "I'll see you in the morning."

4

Every year for the last five years, Blake and his friends had come together to commemorate Mark.

Life had changed. They had all finished their education, worked in their professions, and survived the Covid epidemic. As a group, they were disgusted and deeply saddened by the invasion of Ukraine. How could something like that happen in 2022? Peace was undoubtedly a better option, saving lives and much cheaper.

Bidi and Blake had become more than friends, not in the love department, but in their working relationship and political philosophy.

They shared a passion for new technology, cyberspace, artificial intelligence, and robotics. Bidi, with her specialty in cyber security, hacking, and crime, was a great source of the latest tech information. Meanwhile, Blake worked out how advances in AI and robotics could be misused and warned in his articles about it.

Dave, the handsome Porsche-driving stock broker with slick, combed-back black hair and tailored suits, provided Blake with information on the stock market, trading, and related fraud.

Oliver and his wife, Mona, both now practising solicitors, had become significant assets. Over the years, they had helped Blake out of legal problems. They also regularly supplied him with information about people who had lost money through scams.

Occasionally, Blake received discreet tip-offs from Jake, who had worked undercover for a couple of years. He had risen in the ranks to become a detective sergeant and would soon be an inspector.

Jake was Blake's secret informant, never to be named in his articles.

No wonder they called themselves the Dream Team; everyone supported everyone.

One more person held a special place in Blake's circle of friends despite not being a direct member: Frances, Blake's editor boss. Living in Sydney, she was a constant source of news topics for Blake. Their infrequent meetings couldn't hide the fondness they had for each other.

So far, the team had met in Sydney every year to remember Mark, but this year, they met in Brisbane at Blake's brand-new unit in West End.

Mark was foremost on their mind as they raised their glasses in his honour. What followed was a prolonged catch-up session and too much to drink.

Mona and Oliver received many toasts; they had ensured everyone was legally protected. Outspoken as everyone was, they had needed Mona and Oliver's help over the years.

All had become painfully aware of changes in society and were not afraid to call them out and, in Blake's case, write about them. Blake took up any opportunity to be a voice for his friends' grievances, mainly in the field against tightening government control or limiting individual freedom without the general population noticing.

They agreed life had become too regulated for their liking. That fact intensified after the worldwide Covid pandemic, and even more so when Russia invaded Ukraine.

Blake updated his friends on his interests, which were as diverse as they were intriguing. While he was fascinated by international politics, he didn't write much about it. His focus was fraud and scams, with occasional incursions into the Australian political scene.

He had worked on a few cases where people had lost minuscule amounts of money from their bank accounts but needed to figure out how it had happened. It was an ongoing investigation that consisted mainly of collecting details provided by Mona and Oliver about a few of their clients who had lost small amounts of money from their bank accounts, which were too small to worry about, but nevertheless concerned that the amounts could increase. Investigations so far had delivered no result; it felt like a lost cause.

Bidi was also involved; she worked with a cybersecurity agent on similar cases. They suspected money was extracted from bank accounts using sophisticated software capable of harvesting login details and personal data remotely from someone's computer.

They hadn't come any closer to solving those cases, so they decided to continue collecting details and using AI to find possible connecting data. The question was, what did all those cases have in common?

Again, no results except the obvious: They all had computers, bank accounts, and mobile phones, but nothing else obvious.

Talks continued into the early morning. The main topic had shifted to the forever-increasing influence of artificial intelligence.

Everyone agreed that artificial intelligence should have been regulated better when it started. By now, that ship had sailed. AI was everywhere; no one knew what was real, and everything seemed to be replaced by AI-generated content, including people one saw on social media or magazines.

AI-deep fakes could replace voices and steal whole identities. There was nothing AI hadn't touched. No one believed the news anymore, which was where Blake's articles stood out.

It was not long ago that the future had passed them by. Did anyone even notice the "tipping point"?

Blake had written about it when the world was rudely disrupted, and probably not many people were aware of it, or at least didn't pay much attention, but the 19th of March 2016 is a date to remember.

In his article, Blake warned in no uncertain terms that it was the day the world had changed forever and artificial intelligence became a reality.

For the first time, an AI-generated computer defeated the world champion of the ancient Chinese board game 'Go'.

Considering that 'Go' is probably the most complicated game ever invented, with apparently more possible moves in a game of 'Go' than there are atoms in the universe, it was a big deal. Not that any of the friends had ever played 'Go'; chess was the game they were more familiar with.

It was the day computers learned to think and out-smarted one extremely competent human brain. That friendly computer was called AlphaGo, and as Blake said at the time, "That computer could beat me at any game."

His article pointed out the enormous benefits that AI could achieve. It also recognised the scary part: technology is disruptive and artificial intelligence could cause unexpected hazards.

As one can imagine, the article caused a stir, particularly when Blake recommended that safety concepts and regulations needed to be developed now, not when AI has developed to an even more advanced level.

Blake stressed that the progress of AI was so fast that if let run free, it may not be able to be contained. The future came at them faster than the speed of light; it had already passed.

One global company, DIA-International, had sent him a personal message ordering him to retract some of his claims; they argued his article sounded like a conspiracy theory.

Blake refused, of course. Their objection was not unexpected; the company in question was developing AI next to their manufacturing and development of electric cars and robot technology.

When discussing those topics, everyone on the team had their own experiences with the continually progressing advances in AI and related technologies.

At the end of the night, they vowed to continue their fraud-related technology research and for Blake to keep publishing his articles.

In subsequent years, the group's meetings became more intense. Everything they had discussed over many years had come true and even went further than they had imagined.

Not every article Blake published created a stir. Most of them were of an informative and alert nature.

Everyone had become more measured in their critical responses to the world around them; no doubt, they had grown older and wiser.

One thing they had kept up was their yearly meeting. It had become less about remembering Mark and more about catching up for a night of good food, drinks, and deep discussion.

It was the September 2033 get-together when discussions became heated, with Blake revealing that he and Dave had discovered a possible share market fraud. Why did some people lose money without apparent reasons, and why were some politicians' wives' share portfolios allocated with shares before they were even floated?

5

B lake woke up exhausted. The bench bed had been comfortable enough, and he had fallen asleep instantly, not bothered by the spartan décor of his sleeping chamber, but vivid dreams had kept him on edge.

"Wake up, Mr. Newcome, time to get up," the inspector shook Blake's shoulder.

Blake reluctantly opened his eyes. He wasn't ready to face the world yet. It took him a while to recollect his thoughts from last night.

"Morning, what's up, inspector?"

"Time to go home. We have cleared you of any wrongdoing, and we would like to thank you for your cooperation."

"Thank you, and what was the long hold up? Did you think I chucked my girlfriend off the balcony?"

"As I explained before, it's protocol, nothing personal. We can't know what you have done or not; we need evidence."

"I would like to see Jess and say my goodbye."

"Unfortunately, that will not be possible; she has been collected already."

"Collected that early, by whom, her parents?"

"It's not under my jurisdiction to give further information. The case has been closed."

"Fair enough, but have the parents been notified, and have you got their address or mobile number? I want to give my condolences."

"I'm sorry, that will not be possible." The inspector looked to the side, not making eye contact, and Blake thought something was off.

"Please sign the papers, and you are free to go."

"Does that mean you will keep me if I don't sign?"

The inspector, looking more uncomfortable by the minute, didn't answer.

"What are you not telling me, and why do I need to sign something? I haven't done anything wrong." Blake grabbed the paper and started reading; it was a non-disclosure agreement.

"That's crazy; what am I not allowed to talk or write about?"

"Read on, and sign the damn paper." The inspector loosened his collar. "There's nothing to it; it just prevents you from making it into one of your stories."

"You can't do that; I want to know what's going on; I am sure you have no right to force me to sign this. If you do, I want my solicitor."

"You will get into real trouble if you write an article about your girlfriend, and there will be no way I can protect you. It's way above my pay grade."

"Let me get that right. You don't want me to write anything about Jess, you don't give me her parent's address, and I am not allowed to see her. You better let me know what the heck is going on here." Blake threw the paper back onto the small plastic table.

"Fine, I warned you, it's up to you now. I don't take any responsibility for what you will hear next." He paused, took a deep breath and came out with it. "All I know is Jess was not human."

"What the fuck are you talking about? I can vouch she was human alright; after all, I slept with her, and we weren't sleeping."

"According to forensic evidence and outside sources, all I can do is to repeat what I have heard. Jess was an AI-controlled robot, a very advanced prototype with real skin and everything. They called her a humanoid or android, which is all I know."

Blake interrupted, "This is bullshit, no one would believe that crap."

The inspector continued his speech, "There is one more thing: if you sign the paper, the company will not press charges against you for damaging their android. The potential cost for you would go into the millions." The inspector wiped his forehead, relieved everything was out in the open.

"If you publish anything about this affair, they will sue you for damages. They claim they have papers to show you leased the android for your pleasure."

Blake jumped up, "What? Sounds like I am in deep shit; still, I will not sign the paper, and I will go now; I have better things to do than to listen to stupid accusations." Blake moved towards the door, then turned back to the inspector, "What company is that supposed to be anyhow?"

"Nice try, Blake. I can't reveal that, but I am sure you can work it out yourself. There wouldn't be many companies that could pull off something like that."

"It's DIA International, isn't it? Blake tried again.

"I am not at liberty to say," the inspector responded.

Blake left the police station, remembering he had no car to drive home. A long walk and some breakfast at West End might do him good.

The walk failed to clear his head but brought a sense of stability to his disrupted life. He looked forward to his usual breakfast at his favourite café: a comforting combination of scrambled eggs on rye, avocado, and Camembert, served with a mug of black coffee.

Relieved, he arrived at the café after the long walk, being greeted by the waitress, feeling at home again.

"Hi Blake, you are late; what can I bring you?"

"The usual, please."

While waiting for his breakfast to arrive, he tried to unravel the bits of information he had about AI and robots.

He knew about the mind-boggling advances made in robotics and artificial intelligence; after all, that was his topic, and he delivered at least one article per week on it.

Household robots, once a novelty, had become a part of everyday life.

In the 2020s, and even earlier in Japan, they became affordable as support or companion robots for pensioners and health-impaired people, bringing comfort and assistance to those in need.

The waitress approached with his breakfast, "Enjoy."

"Thank you, and I think I will need a top-up of coffee later on," he began to eat slowly, enjoying every bite as if it was his first meal in a long time.

His mind intruded on his pleasure, leading him back to face the facts about androids and robots.

Japan's robot industry alone equated to over U.S. $7 Billion even 10 years ago, a testament to its technological prowess. China, on the other hand, had an even bigger market. In 2018, spending for industrial robotics was estimated to surpass 6.4 billion U.S. dollars, a staggering figure that showcases China's rapid technological advancement.

Blake didn't have all the figures, but he was sure that personal computers were also developing at light speed. When it came to the development of AI, the U.S. was the leader, with Silicon Valley being the global hub for technology innovation.

But none of those gigantic markets had yet developed an android with the look and capability of Jess, the android he had been confronted with.

The spot of breakfast had helped; he had settled and felt human again despite the fact that he had no idea what to do next.

He stared at his coffee cup in his hands and still found it difficult to accept the possibility, the reality, that Jess was an android. The thought triggered emotional turmoil, taking him away from the facts and leaving him grappling with his understanding of what it meant to be human. AI was already bad enough at faking humans, but androids that can't be differentiated from humans opened a whole new box of problems.

His deep thoughts were interrupted by the waitress, "More coffee?"

"Yes, please, top it up," he answered before continuing his contemplation on industrial robots and the shift toward adopting automation for packaging and transport that had been growing out of proportion with people losing jobs left, right and centre.

No one knew to what degree people were replaced, controlled or monitored by robotic and AI technology. On the other hand, he believed that personal care robots were a vital addition, particularly for the elderly.

Japan's utilization of personal robots was driven by a pressing need to cope with its changing demographics. Rapid population aging and the shortage of caregivers have spurred the government to promote the use of robots in nursing homes and for personal use, highlighting the crucial role of technology in addressing societal challenges.

Blake had nursed his coffee for over an hour by now, but he still couldn't shake off the nagging thoughts and consequences of Jess being an android.

As he prepared to leave, a fundamental question lingered: *How many androids already exist within our society, and what are they attempting to do? Have androids replaced politicians?*

Over the last few years, Blake and his friends have discussed society's changing nature way too often. The curious part was that even with robots and AI expanding into every niche of human life, society appeared to have somehow settled down, with less aggression and, one could even say, a degree of complacency.

Blake hesitated as he arrived at his unit; a wave of unease washed over him. He opened the door slowly, looking carefully; he felt butterflies invading his tummy. Were there androids lurking in the dark? Why did he feel he was returning to a crime scene?

Was it a crime scene? A crime committed by whom? Not by him, but what about Jess? Did she or did it commit a crime?

It slowly occurred to him: was he a target of a crime? Why had he been meeting an android? Surely, no one wanted him to find out Jess was an android. There must have been another reason, and Blake promised to find out.

He wandered around his unit, Jess's perfume lingering in the air. Looking to the balcony, his mind flashed back to an image of Jess falling over the balustrade. He closed the balcony door; he wouldn't sit there for a while. For the next hour, he cleaned and tidied all the rooms, made the beds, and cleared everything away that reminded him of Jess.

He was tired, but there was one more thing he had to do: call Jake, who was now a detective inspector stationed on the Gold Coast. Would Jake be able to find out what happened at the Brisbane morgue? Someone must have been responsible for picking up Jess's body. And who was the pathologist who undertook the forensic examination? He would have received a shock.

Blake wondered if Jess had any internal organs. A forensic pathologist would remove all organs, from the tongue to the reproductive organ, including the brain. How quickly did the pathologist realise Jess was an android?

Something else had crossed Blake's mind: *How would he and others ever differentiate a human from an android?*

He wouldn't get the opportunity to interview the pathologist, but he hoped to find out the name of the Forensic Mortuary Technician. He or she could be more willing to spill the beans.

A post-mortem examination is always done if the cause of death is unknown or unnatural. According to that, he was sure that the staff in attendance did the initial forensic examination that night.

Blake wanted to know what occurred after the post-mortem team had overcome their initial shock. Would that reveal who was behind the ploy to hook him up with a perfect android as his girlfriend? Who had the staff notified, and who arrived to pick up Jess?

Blake's mind was relentless, and no rest was in sight.

Pouring himself a cup of tea, he sat at his kitchen island, notebook at hand, calling Jake's private mobile.

"Blake, what's up? Anything special? I am working."

"Yes, sorry, mate. I'm onto something huge. I can't tell you on the phone. Is there any chance you can come to my place tomorrow morning, maybe around 11 am?"

"Sure thing. Saturday is good for me; it sounds major."

"It is; in the meantime, if you have any connection to the Brisbane morgue and Detective Inspector James Moorhead, find out what you can about a corpse called Jess, why it disappeared yesterday, and who is behind it."

"Sounds mysterious. Is there anything else you can tell me?"

"Not yet; it's a long story with many follow-up questions and even more consequences. It is bigger than anything we have seen for a while. Anyhow, see you tomorrow."

Blake felt better. Jake would be vital for his research into androids; he needed all the help he could get.

Next on the list to call were Oliver and Mona. They were constantly going in and out of the Queensland Police Service headquarters, which was located at Roma Street, not far from their office. Blake talked to Mona. She knew Inspector James Moorhead and promised to look into it. She couldn't wait to hear more on Saturday.

Blake jotted down more notes and grabbed his mobile to call the rest of the gang.

Everyone was free to come to Blake's unit on Saturday. It was close to the day to remember Mark, making it a reunion of sorts, and everyone looked forward to it.

He called Bidi last; she would know which company was most likely manufacturing robots. Bidi's office wasn't far from his home office, so he asked her if she could come after work. She usually knocked off at 4 pm on a Friday, and Blake asked her out for dinner.

They met at Southbank at an Italian restaurant and secured a corner table for privacy.

Blake ordered red wine for both; he knew Bidi's taste.

"What is the big secret? The suspense is killing me," Bidi laughed.

"Yes, I know. Sorry about that, but what I want to tell you is difficult to convey. Let's have a drink first. Cheers," Blake said, lifting up his glass.

Blake had a second sip before putting down his glass.

"OK, here we go; I mentioned I had met someone when we last spoke."

"Oh my God, you are getting married."

"No, no, far from it. We got on like a house on fire, but it ended tragically."

Blake explained what happened up until just before Jess fell off the balcony. He paused to give Bidi time to adjust before he continued with the rest of the story, up to where the inspector wanted to let him go.

"Tell me, how come he let you go without further charges?" Bidi asked.

"That comes now; have another sip from your wine. It will be too hard to believe," he paused. "I'll tell you straight, like he told me. Are you ready?"

"Yes, sure, let's have it."

"She is not human."

"What," Bidi interrupted, "What do you mean? Don't tell me she was an alien."

"You could say that, but no; she was or is an android, a robot, totally mimicking a human, and let me tell you, I know, there was nothing robotic or artificial about her."

"You must be kidding me; that can't be true; I can't believe it."

"Yes, I know, it's too hard to come to terms with, but that is why you are here now, and we're all meeting tomorrow to get to the bottom of it."

"As you can imagine, once you get over the shock, many questions arise, and I hope you can answer some of them."

Blake stopped talking to take a few bites of pizza.

"Here is one question you may be able to answer: who or which company would be most likely able to create a fully functioning android? It would be one that manufactures robots already."

"Absolutely, if possible, I can think of one, a global company, and you know them as well; you bought their car, Digital Inversion Autonomous, DIA-International. You joked about their name, remember? You said inversion autonomous meant to turn life on earth on its head. Your joke was prophetic if it is true that Jess was an android."

"Yes, that's what I thought. DIA sound like a conceivable candidate. How can we investigate them? Do you know anyone working there?"

"I did cyber security work for them a few years ago at their Melbourne factories, protecting their household robots from being hacked and used for criminal activities. By now, those robots have become a regular retail item, affordable for all. Not sure if you know, but you can pick up their best-selling robot, called Bengo, for $3500." Bidi took another sip of her red wine and leaned back in her chair before continuing.

"Those household robots are equipped to handle a wide range of manual tasks and offer support. Thanks to AI, they have the ability to learn, adapt to its owner, and respond accordingly."

"I hadn't realised they had become that cheap," Blake said.

Bidi continued, "I wanted to talk to you about that topic anyhow. Those robots work on Wi-Fi. They connect to the owner's computer and probably collect vital personal data, including banking details and passwords. They don't need to be plugged in to recharge; they are charged wirelessly by electromagnetic induction."

Blake nodded, "And what did you want to talk about?"

"Yes, it's coming now. I am sure DIA-International has access to the data collected by their robots. Any Internet-connected gadget you have could theoretically spy on you and transmit details to whoever is in charge of the gadget. That would include robots, mobiles, computers, televisions, radios, and possibly even your robot vacuum cleaner, fridge and other automatic online ordering systems. It may answer your question about why people lost money from their bank accounts without knowing how it happened. They may all have robots or similar devices collecting their banking details."

"That's what you mean, good thinking. You are right about how people could be losing money without noticing it. Do you have data on how many people in Australia have a personal household robot like Bengo?" Blake asked.

"I don't have figures, but DIA has saturated the market within the last ten years. Any other robots coming on the market, even the ones from Japan, can't match the low prices of the various models from DIA-International. They have a monopoly. I am sure DIA is manipulating the market by selling the robots at cost to dominate the market."

"I wonder how DIA can afford that; maybe the answer is by extracting money from their customer's bank accounts?" Blake interrupted.

"The Australian market had been much slower in the uptake of household robots than in Japan, but once it started, there was no stopping," Bidi said.

"Why has the Japanese market always been stronger on robot-associated topics?" Blake asked.

"I think it's the Japanese mentality and attitude towards innate objects and the world around them. They have a different origin in their philosophy from Shinto, their official national religion. Japanese don't believe that humans are superior and robots could become a threat like we do in the West. They believe that nature doesn't belong to us; we belong to nature, and spirits live in everything, including rocks, tools, homes, and robots. Their robots become part of their family; they may even dress them up and build bonds with humanoid robots more enthusiastically than any other." Bidi explained.

"That is interesting. I have never looked at this specific aspect. I base my natural suspicion on the Western attitude; even so, I share the philosophy that we are a part of nature. All my articles are directed towards caution, confirmed by all the scams and political and corporate business dishonesty we have been experiencing." Blake finished his wine.

"Let's go. If you like, you can stay at my place tonight, crash on my couch, and be ready for the guys tomorrow. I wonder what they'll think about my android experience."

"Thanks, I will do that. Even so, I'm a bit worried about another android paying your unit a visit," Bidi said as she stood up and followed Blake out of the restaurant.

6

S aturday morning began harmlessly enough: breakfast with Bidi in the kitchen, where we talked about the consequences of androids living among us.

Blake felt nervously energized. He knew he was onto a significant story, probably the story of a lifetime, but he had no idea what he would discover or how it would turn out. The path ahead remained shrouded in mystery.

Sometimes, reality is confusing. Blake sat with Bidi, having scrambled eggs on rye. The sun was shining, and the world was perfect. At the same time, something huge was brewing with unknown consequences. He remembered what a coach told him years ago: 'You can't change the past, and you can't control the future; the power is in the present.'

Deep in his gut, he knew his future would change soon, and nothing would be the same again. He wasn't even sure he had power over the present; people much more powerful than him might already have control over his present.

Jess resided vividly in Blake's thoughts, an unsettling development. Strangely enough, he slowly developed empathy for the android. Did that mean she was influencing his present? It seemed so, her past actions shaping his life, not in person, but through the ripple effect of her choices and the consequences Blake was now experiencing.

The intercom rang, and Blake snapped out of his philosophical ruminations about life, androids and humanity.

"That must be the guys coming," Blake called out to Bidi and pressed the buzzer to open the door to the foyer.

Moments later, Oliver and Mono walked in, followed by Jake and Dave. Blake's espresso machine was running hot.

"What's all this suspense about?" Dave asked. "Anything to do with Jess, your hot new girlfriend? What is Frances thinking about that?"

"You leave Frances out of it. It's a long story; that's why I had to get you guys here. I will need your help. Dave knows something about it. I was preoccupied the last couple of weeks with a girl, Jess, I met at his office. Before I go on with the story, Dave, was there anything you noticed about Jess, in retrospect, that was out of the ordinary?"

Dave thought for a moment before he replied, "She only worked the last few weeks for my office, but as you asked, yes, she was peculiar, nearly too perfect. She arrived punctually, 5 minutes before 8 am, sat down at her computer and worked till noon without leaving her desk once, not even having a drink of water or going to the toilet. If you addressed her, she was polite, friendly, and gave direct answers. At 1 pm, she was back on her desk, without getting up till 5 pm. I'm not sure what it was; maybe she was obsessed with her work."

"Thanks, Dave. That's a great observation. Even though I met her at your place, I didn't know her work behaviour. I found her to be amazingly straightforward, and I loved it. No silly games; it was like she knew things about me already. Thinking about it now, I feel she targeted me for whatever reason, and the way she was always straightforward could have been a lack of social skills." Blake glanced over to Jake.

"Did you learn anything about the morgue and the missing body?" Blake asked.

"Not much; the body was Jessica Brindly. She had an accident; there was no foul play suspected, and an undertaker collected her on the instructions of her parents. That's pretty much it; I know the names of the pathologist and her technician if you want to talk to them."

"Nothing suspicious at all?" Blake pressed him.

"Not really. It was odd. However, when I wanted to talk to James, the inspector, I was informed he had taken a long service leave and couldn't be contacted. I'm not sure what that was about; no one ever takes leave before the Christmas season. Even more strange, I was informed I will be transferred to Brisbane."

Oliver and Mona looked at each other with a hint of raised eyebrows.

"Come on now. What's this all about?" Oliver urged Blake on, sucking on his cold pipe.

"OK, as you know, I met Jess at Dave's office two weeks ago. We hit it off, and everything was fine till Friday, when I invited her for dinner. We had fun; it was a great night, and she played 'Catch Me If You Can' early in the morning, around 3 am. The fun stopped when she ended up on the balcony, naked, by the way, and sat on the balcony balustrade. It was dangerous. I caught hold of her, but she pulled her arm away and fell to her death."

Dave interrupted, his eyebrows peaking and his mouth dropping open,, "Are you kidding me? Is that what happened?"

"No, I am not kidding. That's exactly how it went down, and it's getting worse. The police brought me in, and I spent the night in the slammer, courtesy of Inspector Moorhead, who now seems to be missing. Anyhow, I was free to go the next morning, but I was asked to sign a non-disclosure paper, which I didn't do. I also demanded to see Jess. That's when he told me she had been collected. I asked for the parents' address to give my condolences, but no such luck; he couldn't give it to me. It was all pretty odd sounding, but then came the bombshell. Brace yourself, he told me she was not human; she is an android." Blake had finished giving his speech and looked at his friends and their stunned facial expressions.

"Yes, I know. I didn't believe it either, but by now, I am past the shock and believe it," Blake said and sat down.

Jake stood up, "Sorry, mate. I can't believe it. Yes, I know our world is flooded with robots, but I am not aware of anything like you described, and of course, my police-trained mind needs evidence. All you have given us are some odd behaviours and circumstances, but nothing else. Now I know why the inspector has taken leave; he is probably in a mental institution."

"Maybe you are right; it hasn't even occurred to me that his statement could be false. On the other hand, why was I not allowed to see Jess or her parents? Why the non-disclosure paper? The whole thing is suspicious. The more I think about it, the more I am sure Jess is an android, and someone wants to stop the truth from coming out. Please, Jake, I need to find out more. Try to speak to the technician; the pathologist may not want to say anything to protect her job." Blake turned to Oliver and Mona.

"You've been quiet. What are you guys thinking? " Blake asked.

"We did some initial investigations. We found out her surname and also where she worked before working for Dave. It's the company you know, DIA-International. Obviously, we do understand Jake's need for evidence, but we are open to the concept of Jess being an android." Oliver said for the both of them, pointing his pipe at Blake.

"Bidi also thinks that DIA-International is the one company capable of producing androids," Blake said, acknowledging Oliver before continuing, "There are a few more things I haven't mentioned. In my conversation with Inspector Moorhead, he made it clear that someone had a signed document stating I had rented the android for my sexual pleasure. If I was to publish articles revealing Jess to be an android, they would sue me because I have destroyed their million-dollar robot. This is so weird; they confess that Jess was an android, but not why I was the target. Who in their right mind would pursue me with a multi-million-dollar android machine, and why?" Blake paused, observing the impact of his last words.

"Can we move past the doubt that Jess is an android and concentrate on more important questions?" Blake looked at his notebook before continuing.

"Was Jess a prototype, or how many androids are walking around amongst us? I don't think she was the only one; I can't imagine I am that important to be targeted by a prototype android; there must be hundreds." Blake finished his coffee before reading more from his notebook.

"How can we detect if someone is an android? There must be ways to differentiate between humans and androids." Blake asked, turning to Bidi for answers.

"That will be easy; there are many devices and possible applications on smartphones to measure radiofrequency, Wi-Fi or electrical current. There are even hand-held ultrasound scanners that can see what is under their skin," Bidi explained.

"Fantastic, we are getting somewhere. Even if they look human, androids surely need electricity to function. The cheapest detection may be an electric power and Wi-Fi finder app. How about we add those apps to our phones and start scanning? The ultrasound scanner could be too costly for the moment. Maybe Bidi could invent an android detection app?" Blake walked over to the coffee machine, "I need more coffee, anyone else?"

Having made more coffee, he went on with his speech.

"OK, bear with me; I need to get these worrying questions off my chest. Why would anyone manufacture human-identical androids? What is their end game? Why would someone keep androids a secret if not for questionable motives? I think the key may lay fair and square with DIA International. They already rule the market with their household robots, and that is where I have another idea to investigate.

Does anyone know of a forensic accountant? I believe DIA's robots are used to skim money from bank accounts; I call it 'nano skimming'. The amounts are tiny: cents, not dollars. It's a quantity thing; pennies skimmed off from millions of accounts amount to millions, if not billions." Blake paused again before spelling out his next theory in simpler terms.

"Some of my articles have shone a torch onto share market fraud, a topic I am investigating with Dave, which could be why Jess infiltrated Dave's office. The other articles of interest were all about ordinary household appliances that could potentially harvest bank login details, passwords and the like.

Most people have fridges connected to the net that order supplies when food items are low. That trend started when ready meals became the norm, not the exception. Think about it: your fridge is ordering and paying; what could go wrong?" Blake smiled at his last statement. He had finished; he laid everything on the table.

His friends stayed for the rest of the afternoon to discuss Blake's questions, mainly about how many androids have infiltrated society and how to tell them apart from humans.

Later, they headed off to a nearby restaurant. If someone had been listening to them, they would have assumed it was a science fiction movie they were discussing without realizing that fiction and the future had collided.

Were there any androids sitting close by?

7

*W*ho are the billionaires who could possess more power than even *top-level politicians?* Blake asked himself.

Blake met Bidi at their favourite coffee shop and filled her mind with what would be controversial questions for anyone else but Bidi. Her task was to investigate and identify likely billionaires who could be involved with DIA International and the manufacturing of androids whenever she had time free from her work.

It was clear to Blake that someone powerful with unlimited amounts of money was pulling the strings. Billionaires were the topic for his next article, and 'Billionaires and Power' was the headline he posted to Frances for approval. Bidi would be a valuable asset in helping him with research.

That morning, before he met up with Bidi, he had also called Frances and told her about Jess, leaving out his sexual escapades.

He felt guilty about cheating on her, even though they were not officially an item and only saw each other a few times each year. He realized he liked her more than he admitted; why else would he feel guilty?

Like the others, Frances was stunned to hear that Jess was most likely an android.

"Let me think about this for a while: the concept of androids that cannot be differentiated from humans is alien to me. I need more time to digest it. I am like your friend Jake; evidence would help me to believe. Something else, when are you coming down to Sydney again?" she asked.

"I was planning to come soon, to see you, of course, but also to ask for a few favours. You know influential people; I wondered if you could spy on them for me. I will explain more when I am down next week. I am flying to Rockhampton tomorrow, possibly staying for a day or two. After that, I will be able to come to Sydney."

"Rockhampton? What on earth is in Rockhampton you possibly could be interested in?" Frances asked.

"200 km west of Rockhampton within the old coal mining fields, DIA Industrial has a huge fabrication complex for robotics of all kinds. I am going to pretend or maybe even write an article about them. But my main reason is to snoop around to find something relating to my android story. By the way, with your connections, do you know who owns DIA International or is the main shareholder? Any names? Is it a person or a group? I own their e-car, but I know nothing about them. Bidi, who you met in Sydney, knows a few things. A few years ago, her job was fixing security issues with household robots, but that is all; we need more info."

"I'll keep my ears and eyes open and ask some people I know. I always can pretend that we will publish an article about them."

"Great, anyhow. I better go. I will see you soon. Take care." Blake ended the call without saying more; he kept the last words locked up in his mind: 'Love you.'

As he pondered over the call, a thought crossed his mind. *What's happening to me? Could the Jess episode have stirred something within me, something I've long kept hidden? More feelings for Frances than I've admitted?*

Blake finished his coffee and quickly asked Bidi one last question, "Why do you still keep your nickname?" He had often wondered about it. Bidi sounded too young and sweet; he thought it was time for her to reclaim her real and more powerful name, Bianca Brightworth.

"I like it," she said decisively, "Bidi is my greatest asset for investigations; people underestimate me and tell me things they otherwise wouldn't. Little girls get much more attention and information than they ask for, particularly from men." She smiled.

"That makes sense," he laughed. "It's late, and I have to get going. I must prepare for tomorrow and pack a few things for Rockhampton."

8

After getting up early and skipping breakfast, Blake took the train to the airport, arriving at the terminal in time to catch his flight.

He felt like a spy. He had loaded several surveillance apps onto his smartphone and even invested in an ultrasound pad that could be easily disguised in the palm of his hand. He was determined to test the equipment at any opportunity, keeping in mind that if there was one android, there would be more.

He was early enough to take his apps for a run, but he had to get close enough to someone.

He spotted a couple of support personnel close to the airline counter and addressed one of the women.

"Excuse me, is that the right section for flying to Rockhampton?"

"Yes, gate 7; your ticket and gate number are visible on your phone."

Blake looked at his phone and touched her arm. "Thank you; I didn't check for the gate number," he said.

He went to gate seven, 10 meters further on, still looking at his phone. The scan images showed up on his phone. Yep, definitely human, he thought. That was easy.

He went to gate 9 and played out the same scenario, again human.

Let's try a more likely candidate. A security guy seemed a promising option: "Excuse me, sir, I can't find a toilet. Is there one around somewhere?"

"Yes, not far, gate 7."

"Thank you," he said, his curiosity piqued when he touched the security officer's arm. He couldn't help but notice his phone vibrating; he had it switched to silent mode.

It wasn't a call he received; it was the WIFI app, indicating a hotspot.

Blake moved away quickly toward gate 7. He spotted the toilet, went into one of the cubicles, and checked his phone.

There was no doubt the security officer emitted a radiofrequency electromagnetic field (EMF); that's WIFI, he thought. But checking the ultrasound, he was dumbfounded; he had never seen anything like it. A quick look showed a human arm, muscle and bone, but looking more closely there was a net-like structure around the upper arm, where he had touched the officer.

That's it, he thought; that's clever; the net must have a similar action and purpose to a human's nervous system.

He had detected his first android. A voice announcement woke him up from his daze. It was time to catch a plane. He wiped the sweat from his forehead and hurried out of the toilet, walking over to gate 7 while looking for the security officer. There he was, not far away.

Blake quickly texted Bidi, 'Come to the airport, please. Domestic, gate 7. The security officer is what we are looking for a tall guy with good looks and sunglasses. Observe him for as long as you have time, and follow what he does, and if he does anything out of his usual routine, anything peculiar.'

9

Frances woke up drained, haunted by dystopian visions that had disturbed her most of the night. Her mind was restless after her conversation with Blake. The mere thought of androids infiltrating her world, or worse, having unwittingly interacted with them, shattered her usual trustful nature, replacing it with a chilling sense of paranoia.

She pulled herself together. After all, she worked for an extensive news network and had the resources to delve into the archives and uncover the truth about a company as significant as DIA International.

Having restored her confidence and having something to focus on allowed her usual efficiency to shine through. It was not long before she had found the first 12 articles about DIA International. She was in for a long and busy day.

Scanning article after article, she learnt that DIA International had been around for two decades. They hadn't started with robotics; it was a software and web-hosting company in the early days. Expansions, however, happened surprisingly fast. Something must have occurred in the early 2000s.

It took Frances another hour to paste all the information together to reveal a takeover of a relatively unknown entity, a company run by a low-profile software engineer. A cashed-up IT company took over that small company, leaving the software engineer a billionaire. He, in turn, took over DIA and renamed it DIA International. So, she thought, who is that mysterious new owner of DIA?

Frances wrote down his name; she was sure more research would allow for a deeper insight.

She couldn't wait to tell Blake the name. She had not been aware of that guy before, but surely, people in the software and artificial intelligence community would know who Derek Hampton was.

She felt like one of the many investigative journalists whose articles she frequently had to edit. Now, it was her turn, and she knew she would be successful. She knew heaps of influential people, and they knew her, the powerful chief editor for Fact File News.

Frances kept busy on the phone for the remainder of the day, slowly revealing a mysterious and intriguing picture.

Derek Hampton was the sole owner of DIA International, celebrated by peers yet partly a hermit and a painfully shy media personality. Apparently, his business strategy has been to undercut the competition, which helped him flood the market with his three different models of household and support robots.

Over the years, all models had become far more sophisticated than comparable robots from other companies, and prices stayed affordable. Part of his success was achieved by copying the cuteness of Japanese robots. He had learned early on that making robots larger and stronger did not appeal to the market.

People were fearful of more powerful-looking robots. His models stayed cute and half the average human size. He also shied away from making the robots look entirely like humans. As early as 2003, he had successfully created a small human-like robot. The head and upper part resembled a human, but the lower part was machine-like. Market research revealed that a human likeness freaked people out, particularly people over 50, who were lonely or in need of medical care, which was the biggest market for his household robots.

Hampton also owned other companies, the extent of which was still unknown to her.

One of these companies, known to Blake because of his e-car, was a testament to Hampton's diverse business ventures. The common thread among all his products was their superiority due to his software expertise and extensive use of Artificial Intelligence.

As with any super-successful human, there were rumours about Hampton despite his insistence on deep privacy, or maybe because of it.

Frances wasn't sure what to make of it. One rumour, which seemed more than a rumour, was that he was referred to as the 'Zookeeper'. Why was that? Was it about him creating and flooding the market with robots or something more sinister? Was it linked to his mission statement?

'In Service of Humanity – Indefinitely'

It sounded noble enough. However, the rumours pointed to the suspicion that humans could be controlled and influenced. Were humans the creatures the Zookeeper wanted to control?

Was that a rumour or a conspiracy? Frances thought, "Maybe it is always a conspiracy until it isn't."

She spent the rest of that Monday making phone calls. At night, she was happy with the results. She even succeeded in inviting herself and Blake to a high-class charity ball teeming with politicians, highfliers, and actors. It would be a feast for Blake's android identification efforts; she couldn't wait to tell him.

10

L anding safe and sound in Rockhampton, Blake didn't even bother to try to detect an android at that airport. He went straight to the rent-a-car counter, and 10 minutes later, he was on the way to Blackwater, the former coal capital of Queensland. The self-driving DIA e-car gave him time to read up on the DIA International's manufacturing complex. He had arranged a tour of all three manufacturing halls to learn about the various robot models, followed by interviewing the chief operating officer.

He couldn't help but think, *Is the car spying on me?* Jess was also still on his mind. For the first time in his life, one female managed to get deeply into his brain and forever changed him, not because of love, but because of who she was and how she acted.

He wouldn't have minded so much if she had been someone he wanted to be with for the rest of his life, but that was never on his mind. Frances was much more likely to capture his mind and heart for good.

How sad was it that an android had changed his life? Nothing, absolutely nothing, was the same anymore; no amount of trying could recreate his old self. Trust was a verb of the past, while doubt, scepticism, suspicion, and uncertainty were verbs of his future.

"Thank you, Mister Newcome, for travelling with DIA. We will arrive at your destination in three minutes. I hope you had a pleasant journey. You will be welcomed by Jerry, your tour guide. There will be no need to park the car; it will be available once you have completed your visit to bring you back to your Rockhampton Hotel."

Why does one talk to a machine? "Thank you," Blake said. The car replied politely, "You are welcome."

The car stopped, and Blake saw a uniformed man waiting. That must be Jerry. How did he know I would arrive this very minute?

The car door opened like magic. Blake stepped out. "Welcome, Mr. Newcome," said a polite Jerry, a 6-foot perfect-looking male specimen with not a hair out of place.

"Thank you, Jerry; call me Blake."

"Can I offer you something before we commence the tour, a drink or a snack? Do you have to visit the bathroom?"

"No, thank you; very considerate of you. I am fine and eager to start the tour, but may I ask a question?" Blake had engaged his journalistic brain.

"Yes, sure; how can I be of help?"

"When was this complex of factories established?"

"The company started construction in 2002 and manufactured the first robot model in 2003. At that time, there was one basic model called Bengo and one lonely factory hall. At this complex, we now have four halls, three for our present three robot models, and one dedicated to research and custom-built models."

They had reached the entry door to "Hall 1." It opened automatically, revealing an area as large as a football field and contained more robotic machinery than Blake had ever seen.

"I can't believe what I see. It's like a scene from a science fiction movie. It's imposing," Blake commented when they entered the hall. "I understand why some people worry that robots will take over our world; it looks like they already have. Those assembly robots look a bit scary, but then, I have never been into a manufacturing hall of any kind."

Jerry explained, "It looks this way because every part is made in this hall, manufacturing the parts on one end and assembling and turning out the completed robot on the far end."

"Impressive," Blake commented.

"There are three main sections, and we only have human interaction and monitoring in those sections; the rest is robotic," Jerry further explained.

"The basic model is what most people require, especially those who need help with household chores or desire a companion. All our robots have basic emergency capabilities. The robot will call an ambulance if its owner has a medical episode. For more advanced functions, customers will need model two."

Jerry guided Blake through the labyrinth of fast-moving robotic arms and exited Hall 1 at the other end. A brand-new completed robot in testing mode approached Blake and said, "Goodbye, sir, and thank you for coming."

"Nice party trick," Blake said, smiling at Jerry.

They didn't stay long in Hall 2; it looked the same to Blake.

Jerry clarified, "You will not see much difference between models 1 and 2. The advanced functions are revealed when you see the robots in action. Model 2 is called Denko; it has an advanced AI program and is fitted with health monitoring systems. It can measure blood pressure, oxygen saturation, and blood sugar, but it has no function in treating its host. If readings are out of the normal range, it will alert a medico or an ambulance."

"Why do those robots have those strange names?" Blake asked.

"The names are chosen because they are not gender specific. The new owner can rename the robot with their preferred name and gender."

"I like that; now I wonder what is happening in hall 3?"

Hall 3 was a revelation. When Blake thought that Halls 1 and 2 looked like science fiction, Hall 3 was science fiction, a step further into the future, and there were aspects in which Blake was most interested.

For starters, there were no robotic machines with long-moving arms that looked like they were trying to get you. Hall 3 looked more like a hospital ward, with people in white overalls attending to human-like body parts. This was definitely Frankenstein revisited and provided Blake with the evidence he was looking for. The upper parts of the Model 3 robots were human-like. They were not as sophisticated as Jess the android, but human-looking, if smaller.

"As you can see, the model 3 is far advanced. You can't compare them to the others. For the last few years, we have experimented with new materials and have succeeded in using synthetic muscles, tendons, bones and joints instead of aluminium and motorized joints to achieve movement."

"I don't understand," interrupted Blake. How do those robots move if they have no motors or levers?"

"The material and the natural way the robot moves is under strict security, and giving information is prohibited. However, I can explain the principle of functions easily without revealing secrets. It has come about from one of our founder's inventions, an artificial nervous system controlled by AI. Have a closer look at the bone structure on the arm. Can you see the netlike structure encasing the bone?" Jerry asked.

"Yes, I can; it's very fine and of a fishnet structure, little knots connecting individual strands; what does it do?"

"It mimics a nervous system; each knot of the net is a trigger point for the overlying muscle. The robot's AI and computing system is far superior to even the fastest desktop computer, allowing it to move and control its limbs through nerve commands. It means the moves are fluid and simulate real human movements."

"That's incredible; I can't believe what I am hearing. Does it mean you could create a robot or android looking and acting like a human?"

"Not yet, and the model 3 has only the upper part looking similar to a human, but it's still smaller and non-threatening. The lower part, however, has mechanical limbs for specific reasons. This model has the ability to be much more attentive to a human host in an emergency. It can lift a body and reach nearly double its height because it has telescopic legs. The robot is still child-sized, but because of the telescopic legs, it can reach high shelves, stack items or retrieve items from great heights, and lift a human up to 150kg onto a bed or into an ambulance."

"All I can say is, wow, you have blown my mind; thanks, Jerry, for showing and explaining."

"You are welcome. You can see the CEO, Ms. Porter, now. She is waiting for you. I'll show you to her office."

Walking along to the next building, Jerry pointed out a glass door. "Walk through. Ms. Porter's secretary will welcome you, and I will pick you up when you are ready to leave."

"Thank you," Blake said, walking into a spacious, well-decorated room with abstract paintings on every wall. It looked more like a gallery than an office reception area.

"Good morning, Mr. Newcome. Ms. Porter is expecting you." The secretary showed Blake to a heavy-looking, precious timber door and opened it for him.

As Blake stepped into the room, a wave of disbelief and fear washed over him. No, it couldn't be. He turned to look back at the secretary, but she had already closed the door. Taking a deep breath, he approached the desk. Ms. Porter rose, a smile on her face, and extended her hand in welcome. Blake hesitated, his mind still reeling. It couldn't be Jess, could it? What was happening? Was he dreaming? Did he have a post-traumatic stress response?

11

Oliver and Mona sat in their combined private office in the late afternoon over a cup of coffee and discussed their progress.

They had delegated their cases and work to their junior solicitors, enabling them to concentrate on Blake's research, which was far more interesting and intriguing than their routine cases. Where else would one get the opportunity to research the possibility of androids' existence, a key element in their ongoing investigation?

"I have contacted George. Remember, we used him for forensic accounting work during the McCracken fiasco," Oliver said.

"What does he think? Will he be able to track down what Blake calls nano-skimming bank accounts?" Mona asked.

"Yes, I could provide him with cases where we suspected foul play. I also received the OK from three clients who are willing to allow George full account and bookwork access. He will have the results by the end of next week."

"Anything else?" Mona asked.

"Yes, he had valuable information about DIA International. A couple of years ago, he had met the owner of DIA at a charity function. Apparently, he's a nice guy but extremely private. George thinks that charity ball was the last time he was ever seen in public. By the way, his name is Derek Hampton, but what is more interesting is his nickname, the Zookeeper, which is spoken in a hushed voice. What do you think about that?" Oliver asked, raising his eyebrows.

"Could it be because of him having a zoo of thousands of robots?" Mona offered.

"I don't know; it sounds more sinister than that; maybe there is more to it," Oliver answered, changing the topic.

"I guess you haven't tried to use your mobile apps and ultrasound scanner to find those elusive androids?"

Mona shook her head, "I thought about it but didn't meet anyone suitable. I also worried if it was revealed that I took ultrasounds of unsuspecting people, it may constitute a breach of privacy, and we could be sued. What about you?"

"That's why I asked you first. I hesitated too, but couldn't resist. It felt like when I was a kid and played detective, following people around for no particular reason other than we liked the exhilaration of the chase. It was kind of exciting; this morning, I checked out three people. My secretary was the first one I tested. She didn't notice anything and proved to be a real human.

At court, I talked to Judge Conner, patted him on the shoulder and said 'good on you' when he told me about winning his club's golf competition over the weekend. I can certify he is human; thank God for that. I need him with my next case. My next target was nerve-wracking: I noticed Sir Koblinski, our crown prosecutor, rushing out of the building."

Mona butted in, "You didn't, did you?"

"I did. It was easier than I thought; I stopped him. He seemed annoyed, but someone called his name, and he turned away from me. I held his arm for a moment and said, 'Catch up soon.' He didn't suspect anything, said, 'Yes, see you,' and headed off.

"Spare me the suspense, what's next?" asked Mona.

"My mobile kept beeping a few times. Next time, I will put it on silent mode. Luckily, no one seemed to bother. When Koblinski was gone, I checked the phone, and all apps responded. He was a hotspot for Wi-Fi, sending impulses, and when I checked the ultrasound, it looked like a human, but then I saw a faint net-like structure around the bone under the muscle fibres. It's hard to get your mind around it, but our crown prosecutor is an android. Can't wait to tell Blake, but I am worried about saying anything on the phone," Oliver said, waiting for Mona's response.

"God, that's terrible. I don't know what to think anymore. What do we do? How can we trust anyone?" Mona exclaimed, sounding worried and clasping her hand over her mouth.

"We have to perfect our surveillance testing to ensure that the people we trust are trustworthy beyond doubt," Oliver replied.

"It's awful," Mona said as if to herself. "Imagine the power a crown prosecutor has; he may be able to influence the Attorney General. What does that say about national or public security? I don't know what yet, but we have to do something. Blake will be the key to unravel that whole sorry story."

"He will be back soon, and we can have another meeting with the whole gang," Oliver responded, picking up the coffee cups and reminding Mona they had a late staff meeting.

12

B lake had a hard time even looking at Ms. Porter, a perfect copy of Jess, let alone asking any sensible question.

Luckily, Ms. Porter was oblivious to all of that and started the conversation in a friendly way.

"It's so nice to meet you, Mr. Newcome; I looked forward to talking to you. I have a few requests if you don't mind. I am an avid reader of the Fact File News and enjoy your articles. However, they make us look bad, and I wonder if I may explain our side of the robot equation, bad vs. good, and hopefully convince you to change your message to a more positive scenario."

Blake had composed himself enough to give a sensible answer.

"Yes, please. I do want to hear that." Blake braced himself for what was to come.

"Thank you. We have noticed that most of your articles are fear-associated, feeding into the polarized concept that 'Robots will take over the world'."

"My articles are based on facts and researched evidence, not polarized in any direction. I don't go after fear for the sake of it," Blake interrupted sternly.

Ms Porter didn't react and continued her prepared speech.

"Right from the outset, let me stress that DIA is absolutely committed to serving humanity. Our robots are hard-coded to be servants; they cannot harm humans and cannot change their coding or algorithm. Indeed, our company's motto is: 'In service of humanity'.

Blake took a deep breath, trying to keep calm, but couldn't stop himself from cutting in. "Where is the evidence DIA's robots can't change their coding other than your word?"

Ms Porter looked at Blake emotionless and proceeded without answering Blake's question.

"Jerry has introduced you to our Model 3 robots; let me expand on their capabilities. Even so, they can be customized to fulfil the special needs of a host; the standard model is likely to be already more capable than a nurse or a doctor in taking care of patients. We envisage that, in the future, they will serve in hospitals.

However, for the moment, we have designed them for our ageing population, people who may need support to live in their homes and enjoy constant companionship and medical expertise from one of our robots."

Blake didn't let her finish, his voice noticeably louder, "You don't have to go into your marketing spiel; I need more than that. I need to go now." Blake stood up.

"Sit down, please. You have been granted a tour of our complex, and you will listen to what I have to tell you."

Blake sat down reluctantly, losing his poker face, frowning.

Ms Porter rattled on: "Our robots can do complete medical checkups. They can check blood pressure, blood sugar, heart rate, and oxygen saturation with minimal physical contact. By placing their hand on your chest, they can do an ECG and also an Echocardiogram. The robot can diagnose and administer first aid CPR and has a built-in defibrillator.

Its right index finger hides an injection mechanism, and within the arm of the robot are ampoules of insulin for diabetics and epinephrine for severe allergic reactions and anaphylaxis, among others. All functions aim to preserve and make human life as comfortable as possible." Ms. Porter allowed a short pause for a more significant impact before she continued.

"I hope, with my short speech, I convinced you that we are the good guys, and I can't stress enough that it is time you rethink your bias against robots, AI, and cyber security and report positive facts as well." Ms. Porter leaned back, indicating she had finished speaking and done her job.

Blake wasn't about to leave without a reply; a few things needed to be pointed out to the demanding-sounding Ms Porter.

Blake had overcome his shock being confronted with a Jess look-a-like. He even had considered Ms Porter to be Jess, fixed and reprogrammed. Nothing would come as a surprise anymore. He was done with surprises, felt a strong sense of duty, and was invigorated to put things straight. His face relaxed, showing a hint of a smile with a touch of arrogance. He was a human; she wasn't. Why was he even annoyed by her programmed talk?

"Thank you." Irony flavoured his voice. "This factory tour has been enlightening, and I am truly convinced DIA's robots have 'not a mean artificial bone in their cute little robotic bodies.' I am not worried about robots taking over the world and harming us poor humans. I am concerned about humans manipulating and using robots for fraudulent endeavours." Blake stood up, taking charge, and pressed on with his speech.

"My sentiment is not born out of suspicion about robots; it results from having lived and experienced what humans are capable of. A single corrupted human being is all that is needed to create a chain reaction with catastrophic consequences. I am sure I don't have to mention history's evil, destructive personalities. However, I will report on the mind-boggling positive capabilities of robots and AI, particularly in a medical scenario. Thank you again, and I think my time has come to leave your pleasant company."

Blake gave Ms Porter a nod, turned around and headed for the door.

Ms Porter didn't object and kept silent.

Jerry waited for him on the reception desk. *Smooth operation they have here*, Blake thought and followed Jerry out of the building to the waiting DIA e-car. Could he trust that car? Would he get back safely to his hotel? Doubts crept in.

13

J ake had been a busy boy. He had his own methods for finding and
extracting information from people reluctant to come forward.

A handful of people knew Jake used to be an undercover police officer
before he was pulled out of that scene and promoted to his present position
as detective inspector. Four years undercover is more than enough. When
people pretend to be someone they are not for a long time, they are in
danger of losing the plot and sometimes even their lives.

Even Blake, one of Jake's best friends, had only a limited idea about those
particular hard times Jake had experienced. Did something good come out
of it? Yes, Jake was responsible for unravelling large underground drug
syndicates, and he still used his questionable connections and skills to lay
his hands on vital information. People owed him favours, and he knew how
to cash those in. He had methods to get what he needed, excusing himself
by arguing that sometimes it needs more than the arm of the law to swing
a confession.

Jake had found out the name and address of the morgue technician
present at the autopsy on Jess. All he required was a first-hand description
of what exactly had occurred. Was there an eyewitness who could confirm
the body was an android? He needed that evidence to believe Blake's
version that Jess was indeed an android.

Jake detached himself from his official police duties at 4 pm; no one
questioned his early absence. He drove home to slip into a pair of jeans
and a T-shirt. He left his house, making sure he wasn't seen and walked
a fair distance before catching a driverless taxi, which dropped him off a

5-minute walk from the morgue, where Daniel, the morgue technician, would soon knock off from his duties.

Jake had come to the conclusion that if he was interested in Daniel, someone else might be too. To rule out a surprise confrontation with the opposite party, he ensured that no one but him was following Daniel. Waiting for Daniel at his home, therefore, was out of the question.

Daniel strolled leisurely out of the building at 5 minutes past 5 pm. He looked pleased with himself, rightly so; he probably had planned a pleasant weekend. He was wearing a flower motive bright yellow and green shirt.

Thank you, Daniel. You make it easy for me to spot you a mile away. Jake was grateful; it would be easy to follow him amongst the crowds of pedestrians rushing home.

He stayed a fair distance behind, paying close attention to his fellow footsloggers. He admired Daniel, who, at 40, was not that young anymore. Walking daily to work and home again was most likely his primary exercise, judging from his mildly overweight body. It was a 30-minute hike along Elizabeth Street up to 71 Eagle Street to his unit, which had cost him over $1,300,000 in 2011. *How could he have afforded such a costly unit?* Was another question on Jake's mind.

Daniel made a couple of stops, one at a chemist and the other at a ready-meal self-service depot. He came out with a paperback, likely to store his dinner.

By now, Jake was sure no one else was following Daniel, who reached his building 10 minutes later without further interruptions.

Jake had hurried along, arriving at the building and unit a couple of minutes before Daniel. Jake had no difficulties getting into the unit, which was part of his undercover training. He slipped a beanie over his head, left the mouth free, poured a glass of whisky from Daniel's collection, sat down at the darkest corner of the room and sampled the goods.

The unit door opened. Jake pulled up his right trouser leg, grabbed the handy, fully automatic 9mm Glock 17 pistol as a convincer, took another sip from the excellent whisky, and waited for Daniel to come in and close the door.

The door closed. Daniel unloaded his paperback on the kitchen bench, turned toward the upper cupboards, and pulled out a plate. He felt something cold on his cheek, dropped the plate and froze.

"Hi Daniel, nice to meet you. I like your taste in whisky, but that's not why I am here. I need you to sit over there on your comfy couch, relax and tell me a story I'd like to hear," Jake spoke softly into Daniel's left ear.

"What do you want? I got no valuables or drugs". Sweat developed on his forehead. A sign of guilt?

"I don't want any of your ill-gotten riches; I want you to cast your mind back to the night you were called in to assist in an autopsy on the body of Jess Brindly."

"Oh."

"Yes, oh, you can say that again, but I need more than that."

"I don't know anything. You have to ask my boss, Kayla Osborne, who ordered me out before she started the autopsy."

"That sounds convincing, but no one saw you leaving the building; you left more than 2 hours later. Can you explain that, or do you need some gentle encouragement?"

"I stayed in the building but not for the autopsy; I didn't see anything."

Jake picked up the expensive bottle of whisky, threw it up, caught it on its neck, and smashed it on the stone kitchen bench.

"Is this helping your memory?" he asked politely as if nothing had happened.

"Please, I can't say anything. I can't. I would like to, but I can't." His eyes were wide and terrified.

Jake lifted his Glock, looked at it, and walked over to switch on an old-fashioned but trendy Hi-Fi system. Music played softly, too softly; Jake turned it up, looking dreamingly at his Glock, and stroked it lovingly with his left hand before bending down and retrieving a silencer from under his left trouser leg.

He slowly, deliberately slowly, attached it to the Glock pistol, pointing it at Daniel and then pointing it next to him at a pretty pillow, 'plop'. The pillow didn't survive. The pistol pointed at Daniels's groin now.

"Let's start again; the body was placed on the table; what's next?"

"The usual, my boss talked her way through the first procedures, like undressing the body and looking for marks, to determine if death was by accident or foul play. I entered the data into the computer."

"Good, excellent, we are getting somewhere; please, at your pleasure, continue," pointing the gun at Daniel's groin again; it seemed to help his memory.

"I can't; I don't even know what to say; it's too weird."

"OK, I understand. Try it in your own words. By the way, as soon as I know what I need to know, I will leave you, never to return. I will not ask how you could afford this nice unit."

"Kayla took a dissection scalpel to open up the chest. She looked confused, looked up at me, and raised her brows; something must be wrong; cutting is usually quick. She tried again, but I saw she needed to apply more force. I can't explain, but the open chest looked like something I had never seen before. We saw muscles, bones, weird-looking mesh structures, and boxes with tubes coming out instead of real organs.

We didn't talk. She attempted to open the skull, but the bone structure was like steel. She shaved off all hair and found a soft section at the back of the head. It revealed sealed parts that looked high-tech, I can't describe it; there was also a blinking faint light." Daniel stopped, looking questioningly at Jake.

"What came next?" was Jake's short reply.

Daniel had lost his apprehension about talking, relieved to get it all out in the open.

"Then, the door opened, and the crown prosecutor, Sir Koblinski, arrived with two men in black suits. One of them approached my boss and took the scalpel away from her. The other guy pulled me to the side. The prosecutor told us in no uncertain terms that what we had seen was strictly protected by the national security law. He mentioned that he was under direct order from the Minister of Defence and the Minister of Justice, which would make violating the security order an act of treason."

Daniel stopped, too petrified to go on. Jake opened a new bottle of whisky, handing Daniel a generous serving.

"You are doing well; go on, please." No further encouragement was needed.

Daniel sculled the rest of the whisky and went on, "Koblinski explained it was a government counterintelligence defence project. Two more guys dressed like paramedics took the corpse and her belongings and carried her out on a stretcher. One guy deleted all my computer entries.

Five minutes later, we had no evidence left, and Koblinski cautioned us again that if we didn't keep what we had witnessed a secret, we would be prosecuted with treason, which used to be punishable by death. Now the penalty is mandatory life imprisonment." Daniel finished talking, wiping sweat from his forehead, longing for another shot of whisky.

Jake hadn't finished; he fired off more questions.

Did they say where they took the corpse? Do you know the names of the other guys? Did they mention any other departments or names?" But to no avail, the answers were no, and it was time for Jake to leave.

He used cable ties to tie Daniel's hands and feet.

"Why do you have to tie me up? I told you everything."

"I don't want you to follow me; by the time you have freed yourself, I will be gone, and you can forget the whole episode."

Jake left. He didn't take the lift. A moment later, he was out on the streets, swallowed up by the busy city. No one had noticed him.

14

B lake had arrived home. As he opened the door to his apartment, he felt a sense of serenity and comfort that he had never appreciated more than on this early morning. After worrying about a potential attack from a DIA e-car and spending an uneasy night in a cheap hotel in Rockhampton, he took the first flight back to Brisbane. He dropped his bag and undressed as he walked to the bathroom, where he relaxed under a long, hot shower. It felt wonderful to wash away the unpleasantness of the past few days.

He was more convinced than ever that something significant was going down, not exclusively in Brisbane or Australia but worldwide. As far as he knew, DIA's robots, cars, and other high-tech gadgets were sold and manufactured all over the world. Yes, robots were here to stay; they had revolutionised life and enabled people to do more in less time. But what was the cost and the consequences?

Ms Porter had tried hard with her speech to convince him to see the benefits, but Blake was not likely to get advice from an android programmed to persuade him of DIA's holiness.

He stepped out of the shower, dried himself, wrapped a towel around his midriff, and went to the kitchen. The aroma of his favourite spices filled the air as he prepared a meal, a ritual that always brought him a sense of calm and relaxation.

Have I left the door open? He thought, noticing the unit door was ajar. He closed it, but not before he stuck his head out of the doorway, looking along the hallway. He was sure he heard footsteps running down the emergency staircase. *I am getting paranoid*. He looked around the unit. *Has anything changed?* Yes, the desktop computer was switched on; someone had paid him a visit while he was showering. Blake sat down to check the computer. Whoever tried to extract information didn't get far, and with layered security passwords, even an experienced hacker, Blake knew, would need more time to crack it open.

What do they want from me? He wasn't in the mood to cook anymore; instead, he picked up his mobile and called Jake.

Jake promised to come over within one hour; he had something important to tell Blake.

Blake placed his mobile on the desk and sat before his computer. What if whoever had visited him left a virus on his computer? He powered down and restarted the computer before he did a virus scan. Nothing showed up. He opened the lower desk drawer, which was filled with old magazines. Lifting the magazines revealed what he was looking for: his laptop.

He switched it on and did another virus scan. Nothing. He left it on the desk; it was his working computer. The desktop was a ploy, used mainly for general searches and social media and filled with old articles, Blake's kind of security. It was unlikely that someone had found or tampered with the laptop.

What if the intruder had planted a listening device, would Jake find it?

For the next half hour, Blake was consumed by his quest for answers: why were androids infiltrating human society? He compiled notes and files, his fingers flying over the keyboard, trying to make sense of what he knew so far. It was a lot, but nothing that could be published or used as evidence to accuse someone of wrongdoing.

Did Jake and the other guys have more details to complete the puzzle? So far, he couldn't form a picture of what the whole android affair would come to, but he was determined to find out.

The intercom and his mobile were buzzing, breaking the silence of

Blake's thoughts. *That must be Jake.* A quick look at the screen confirmed Jake's grinning face.

"Come up." Blake activated the old-fashioned espresso coffee machine, using freshly ground coffee beans, and opened the door of his unit.

"Glad you are here. Do I have news for you," Blake said while making coffee.

Jake arrived with a briefcase; Blake calls it a detective set. Jake went to work dusting the unit entry door, the desk and the computer keyboard for fingerprints.

"You never know. We may find an old friend, probably not, but I need to exclude the possibility. Anything else you noticed, nothing missing?"

"No, he, she or it must have gone straight to the computer, but even if they had been able to get in, they wouldn't have found anything. The real stuff is on my laptop. Can you check if they have planted a listening device?"

"Good thinking, will do that next."

For the next hour, Jake went around the unit checking for devices while they shared their news and tried to make sense of it all.

They couldn't find a logical explanation for why a second android looked like Jess. Was it an oversight in manufacturing?

"We have proof now that androids exist, I am convinced of that, but that by itself does not help me to convict anyone. It's not a criminal offence. It needs to be you who has to take the risk and write an article about it," Jake said, still thinking.

"But before you do that, we need something to stop people from panicking. It would help if you wrote about suggestions for how we can assure ourselves that, in the future, humans can be differentiated from androids. Not everyone can go around and test everyone they come in contact with."

"I thought about a solution already," Blake said, nodding in agreement. He wanted to explain, but Jake stopped him.

"Be quiet," Jake said in a soft voice, holding his index finger to his lips and pointing to something between two tilted standing books. He removed one of the books to reveal a listening device. He smiled, took out a pair of pliers from his 'detective case' and cracked the device like a hazelnut.

"That was fun. Someone is targeting you, but it's clear they don't want to harm you, otherwise they would have left an explosive device. OK, what were you going to say?"

Blake looked up, thinking, "Where were we? Yes, about the differentiation between humans and androids. First of all, it has to be a government-initiated security policy and it needs to be free for all citizens. We will need that for the future anyhow, no matter how our enquiries work out."

"Go on, what do you suggest? Jake asked.

"It's controversial, but in the end, it may be the only way."

"Spit it out; what is it?"

Blake still hesitated, pressed his lips, and nodded his head once, "Ok, here it comes, a system that certifies individuals as true human beings. A chip implant, with data showing and confirming that someone is human, and which can't be copied. It will be a blockchain application, showing three ancestry generations, DNA proof and general info, like their names." Blake stopped talking, looked at Jake, and waited for a response.

"No, I don't believe that is going to happen. People would revolt against it. You are talking about the greatest change in protecting human identity ever. It may conflict with our constitution. I can't imagine any politician or party taking up this chip implant idea, particularly if people would be forced to have it. Can you imagine the backlash, demonstrations and citizens' disobedience against a chip implant?" Jake asked, shaking his head.

"I know, of course, we are not there yet, not by a long shot. But it will work better if it's voluntary or if we find direct evidence of illegal action. What do androids do that is illegal? What is DIA International's endgame? It must be more than mere data collection to siphon money fraudulently. I think it is more complex, something we haven't contemplated yet, and even government officials could be involved.

We have evidence of the crown prosecutor being an android; what is that for? Does someone want to influence the courts? I don't want to speculate too much, but maybe someone crazy wants to influence society for his gain. If it is the guy from DIA, he is not called Zookeeper for nothing," Blake concluded.

Jake was not convinced, "Mate, you've come up with some profound ideas, but in the end, it's all speculation. Call another meeting tomorrow with all of us if you'd like. But I can't imagine we'll get anything out of it." Jake said, finishing his coffee and heading towards the door. He called back, "See you tomorrow."

"Hi Dave, everything good with you? Do you have time tomorrow for a meeting at 6 pm? We have lots of news.

"Sounds good, but I am flat out, and you will not believe with what."

"Tell me."

"My firm has taken up the offer to prepare the initial public share offering for DIA International, and yes, you heard me right, DIA is going public, and my firm will be the lead underwriter. This is huge and will take up all my time. For the moment, I need to forget about androids.

Even so, I think Jess may have been checking us out, and you were the accidental casualty that led to her death, or however you want to call it. I'm not sure what to make of it, but for some reason, the owner of DIA International intends to raise more money than he already has. Sorry, mate, this is big business; I have to get cracking."

"Be careful with that guy, Dave. I am off to Sydney on Friday and will call you when I return. I'm sure the others will greet your news with enthusiasm; it shows something weird is going on. Catch up soon." Blake hung up, *thinking: Was Dave too involved with DIA International? Could he still trust his old friend, or was Dave blindsided by the money?*

He called the others, excusing himself for the short notice. Everyone had time, and they were eager to hear more about the android saga.

15

B lake was totally absorbed in finishing his article about the significant influences wielded by billionaires. He tried to convey that they hold a considerable amount of power, if not an excessive amount, and can sway someone's decision. Money corrupts, and more money will corrupt more and potentially tilt politics in a billionaire's favour. It aligns well with a famous quote, 'Power corrupts, and absolute power corrupts absolutely.' How much power do billionaires have, and how can we ensure they use it wisely?

He finished the article in the afternoon and sent it to Frances. Later, he called her to check if she received it, using it as an excuse to talk to her.

"Are you still OK with me coming up on Friday?" he asked tentatively.

"Yes, sure, looking forward to it. I was keen to tell you that I have secured a fundraising gala invitation for Saturday night. It's a black-tie dress code, so make sure you bring your finest attire. There will be politicians, lobbyists, corporate bosses, and celebrities galore. If checking for androids is your main objective, no one will notice whom you touch, but hopefully, you will leave time for dancing.

"Great, looking forward to it. Thank you for organising it. I can't wait to see you in one of your beautiful dresses. On a side note, I also have lots of news, but most importantly, I can't wait to spend time with you. I have to go now; the guys will be here at any moment for another meeting; see you soon." Blake looked at his mobile, daydreaming momentarily before the intercom buzzer snapped him out of it.

Bidi arrived first, looking excited to share her news. Jake, Oliver and

Mona arrived together. The pizza order was delivered a little later, and the meeting could start. Would it bring any answers?

Blake had his notebook in front of him, making sure to write down vital information to give his active mind the opportunity to form new connections.

With his authority as an officer of the law, Jake cleared away any doubts about whether or not androids exist. And the revelation that two independent sources confirmed a crown prosecutor as an android made everyone aware that whatever was going on was way bigger than they could have imagined.

The general consensus was that all government officials, or at least some ministers, could be aware that androids exist. But who pulled the strings? Was it the so-called Zookeeper?

Bidi cleared her throat and addressed Blake. "After you told me about the security officer at the airport, I went there and hung around him at a fair distance, observing his every move. Knowing this guy was an android was fascinating; I had to stay and observe. But, nothing out of the ordinary, except that he didn't drink or go to the toilet for three hours, which sounds like your Jess girl."

Blake chipped in, "Thank you, Bidi, for doing that. Now we know more androids are around, and we also know some of the peculiar behaviours that will help us recognise them."

"Can I go on? Bidi asked. "We know androids are around, but we haven't figured out what they do other than performing normal work. I do understand the prosecutor; he could influence people. That guy commands considerable power. But why has no one asked where the real Sir Koblinski is hiding or whether he has been kidnapped and exchanged for an android?"

Jake butted in, "There is another possibility: the android is a doppelganger, and the real Koblinski is not aware of it."

"How can we find out?" Bidi asked.

"Not sure yet, but any investigation needs to be discreet to protect the real Koblinski."

Bidi hadn't finished; she had an ace up her sleeve, but first, she answered Jake. "I like the doppelganger scenario; it sounds like Oliver and Mona's department; discretion is their middle name."

Mona laughed, "Thank you for that, but before we can approach Koblinski, Blake needs to write an article to let the world know that androids are among us. As long as Koblinski has no idea about androids, he would be seriously offended if we talked to him about it. Let's wait and see how everything develops."

Bidi retook the stage, nodded to Mona and continued with her news scoop. "I snooped in the darknet for Hampton and his dubious title, the Zookeeper. There is some noise, no evidence, but it may help us pin down his motivation. He is known, among other things, to be a data collector. His robots collect a lot of private data.

He is mainly interested in banking details but sells other harvested data on the dark net. He supposedly makes millions, if not billions, of dollars from unspecified bank frauds and selling data. No one knows where the money ends up, but he is obviously using it to capture the world market by selling his robots at a cost price."

"Wow, Bidi, that's great info," Blake clapped towards Bidi. "I am glad we came together tonight. If we can prove his data collection activity, Jake may have what he needs to charge him with bank fraud." Blake lifted his glass of wine. "Cheers, everyone."

Bidi piped up, "Can I go on?"

What, there is more? Sure, you can." Blake gave her the nod.

"OK, there are some mind-blowing revealing factors; he makes no money from selling his robots. He is boasting that he is a "non-profit" business. He links that up with the company's motto, 'In service of humanity'". Bidi took a bite of her cold pizza before continuing.

"There is more vague information, which may or may not shed light on what this is all about and why he is called the Zookeeper.

Nothing is set in concrete; it's all speculation, but his goal of serving humanity has an evil background. He wants to control people with the help of his robots. That is why he is called the Zookeeper; it is people who are supposed to be the inhabitants of his zoo.

Basically, he is a psychopath who, with the help of his androids and by infiltrating the government, wants to rule the world. I know it's a lot of innuendos, conspiracy even, and no evidence, but possible clues of motivation."

Mona shook her head in disbelief, "This is crazy; it may be true, and worse, there's no way of stopping that guy without any evidence because nothing he is doing is illegal," Mona said, with Oliver nodding in agreement.

Jake contributed his two cents: "I can't charge Hampton for wanting to rule the world. Maybe it's like in the past: gangsters were not put in prisons for their violent crimes but because of tax evasion. That's what we may have to do: assemble the evidence to charge Hampton with computer or bank fraud or for creating a monopoly by manipulating the global market against the competition. Whatever we can prosecute him for would take him out of circulation and therefore stop his world domination crazy idea," Jake said.

Oliver stood up, pipe in hand, addressing the gang.

"I had a phone call from George, our forensic accountant. He looked at some of our elderly client's financial affairs with household robots to see if money was missing from their accounts. He followed hundreds of transactions. It's not what someone buys at the supermarket; it's all those small transactions, money-back deals, interest calculations, amounts rounded up and the difference transferred to saving accounts. No one checks if a few cents are missing. Blake had the right idea when he called it, 'nano skimming'; which is precisely what it is.

Every day, cents disappear from accounts in Australia and most likely worldwide. It's not the few cents; it's a few cents a million times over, which makes the fraud so successful. No wonder Hampton can afford to sell his robots at cost. So far, George has only an inkling of the scheme; it will take more time to produce sufficient evidence to take him to court." Oliver sat down again, looking at Blake.

Blake looked at Oliver, "Are you ever going to smoke that old pipe?" He didn't wait for an answer and went on talking.

"I think we are getting closer to the truth, even in the question of androids, which may be instrumental in influencing important people. I will see Frances in a couple of days; she has managed to secure an invitation to a prestigious fundraising gala event where I will have an opportunity to scrutinise high-ranking politicians and corporate figures to see if they are androids. It will provide us with evidence of where androids are active. I think that's it for the moment. Let's keep checking for androids and possible undue influences they have," Blake said and continued,

"As you know, I had an unwanted visitor who didn't take anything but left something, a listening device and tried getting into my computer. Please be aware of the people around you. If they shadow me, they will know about you. I still don't know if I was the target or if Jess was targeting David's office and I was involved accidentally. It could be related to my articles or the share fraud I was investigating," Blake stopped.

Oliver raised his pipe. He had something to say: "I think you were the target, and I have the feeling Hampton was teasing you. I don't think he is violent; nothing he does is violent; he simply lets you know with his little interference that he is watching you. He's the chess master, and you're his most valuable pawn."

"Thank you, Oliver; I feel much better knowing I'm a pawn, and Jess falling off the balcony can't be called teasing," Blake objected, lifting his eyebrows.

"No, it's unlikely he planned that, but my instincts tell me there is more behind the other encounters. Make sure he is not playing you," Oliver said.

"How would he do that?"

"By calculating your reaction through your articles," Oliver replied.

Blake looked like he had swallowed a bitter pill. "That's an intriguing thought. Not sure what to do with it, but I will keep it in mind."

Blake poured himself another glass of red before continuing.

"Something else: Dave told me that Hampton is floating his DIA company, and Dave is handling the account. We speculated that he wants to raise more money or diversify and have sections of his corporate empire split off, making it harder to pin everything to his name." Blake paused for a moment before asking a final stack of questions.

"Does anyone have questions? No? Good. By the way, it occurred to me that Hampton must live somewhere. Can we find out where he lives? Jake, what do you think? And, maybe we need to buy one of the household robots to check where it sends data? Bidi, is that something you could do?"

"Sure, it will be an interesting exercise." Bidi nodded.

After a sip of red, Blake went on, "I have another theory about what Hampton wants to achieve."

Blake waited, making sure he had everyone's attention before delivering his next statement.

"He wants the public to use his robots and become complacent. He is actively breeding complacency. And I think it's happening already. If I compare the frantic activities and protests against everything between 2010 and 2025 and what's happening now, I can see that everything has calmed down, even on the political front.

It coincided with China's colossal popularity stunt when it announced its acceptance of Taiwan as its daughter country. This released Taiwan from its obligation to be a direct part of China, the mother country, resulting in China and Taiwan being best friends and trading partners. That political move changed China's status to that of a responsible world power. One result was that no one in Australia worried about China anymore.

Finally, can we check if the possession of robots has correlated with society's becoming more complacent? I am leaving for Sydney tomorrow and will be back the following week; we can meet up and discuss these topics further."

16

What is it with airports that made them so attractive to have androids in service positions? The same security officer Blake encountered at Brisbane's domestic airport on his way to Rockhampton was again on duty. No problem with that if that is the shift for a security officer.

It was curious to see that there was now a second security guard at the arrival gate; Blake couldn't restrain himself from testing that guy, either. And sure enough, it was another android. Who controlled those androids? It wasn't that someone liked airports.

The flight was uneventful, but unfortunately, Blake had to put his mobile into flight mode and couldn't use it to test anyone. Based on how people dressed, most passengers were business people heading to Sydney. The same couldn't be said of Blake, even though journalism is a serious profession. Blake had not adopted a business dress code; he looked like he was heading for Bondi Beach, sneakers, shorts and a T-shirt he had designed and printed. He was tempting fate and living dangerously; his T-shirt showed an image of a robot and the text, 'Kiss an Android'.

"Don't you think that is too provocative?" Bidi had asked him when she saw it. She worried that Blake was monitored and could piss off the Zookeeper. But the T-shirt was designed for the purpose of mildly aggravating whoever was in charge and causing a reaction. *If they haven't got rid of me yet, they are not going to kill me now*, was Blake's thinking.

Blake wondered how Sydney Airport's security staff would compare to those in Brisbane. He had activated all his mobile monitors, and there was something else he would attempt whenever he talked to an android test subject: he planned to record their voice.

Not far from Blake's Brisbane unit, a few streets down, was the Alchemike Recording Studio, and Blake knew the owner. They could check if there was a difference between a human and an android voice. The idea was that, most likely, the human had a full spectral voice readout, and the android wouldn't, and a spectral analysis reading could prove it.

Blake looked around to locate a security officer. It took a while; the airport was too busy. Eventually, he spotted one and did his old trick, asking where the toilet was. When he thanked the officer, he touched his arm, and, unsurprisingly, it was another android. Enough of this testing at airports; he couldn't wait to test people at the gala function and was determined to record all speeches. He hoped that no politician would be revealed as an android; the implications of such a discovery would be nothing short of catastrophic.

Blake arrived at Frances's doorstep in time for morning coffee. He looked forward to staying at her apartment, which was a short walk from Bronte Park and Tamarama Beach. The unit was surrounded by trees and had an ocean view, and he imagined how the sunrise would look.

"I missed you," Blake said, greeting her.

"That's a new one," she laughed. "I have missed you too. Maybe it is true: absence makes the heart grow fonder."

"That's why I came a day earlier; I thought we could spend some 'us' time instead of always discussing work topics. Can I stay till Monday?" Blake asked.

"That's another new one, what happened? But yes, I love you spending time here with me. I've always loved it, but you've always hurried back to Brissie."

"Yes, I know, it's so hard living far apart; I didn't want to turn our friendship into something complicated," Blake said.

"I am certain we both sensed our connection was more than friendship.

Was it your recent, peculiar experience that altered your perspective?" Frances inquired, her voice tinged with a mix of curiosity and concern.

"It has made me vulnerable, I think. I'm probably less assured about the world; everything seems fake, only our relationship appears more real than ever. I don't know. What I know is that I missed you and want to spend more time with you." Blake answered, his face taking on the appearance of a guilty-looking dog.

Frances was touched, holding Blake's face between her hands and kissed him tenderly.

"Let's make it a little holiday, with a grand gala ball in the middle, "she laughed. "Can't wait to see you in a tux."

Saturday arrived way too fast, but spending all Thursday and Friday had brought Frances and Blake closer together, the invisible barrier gone for good.

Friday night's dinner was an eye-opener for them both. It was the first time they had let their guard down. They opened up about their similarities and differences and about how they felt about each other.

Trust was the cornerstone of that evening's dinner, which unexpectedly turned into a romantic affair. Despite their different personalities, they shared a deep trust and respect for each other, cherishing the other's opinions and achievements.

"A toast," Blake said, "To us."

"To us," Frances replied, fully aware that those few words held more weight than an entire novel. Amidst the pressures of work and concerns about the influence of androids and AI, they had discovered a renewed, deeper meaning in their relationship. But so far, neither had the nerve to mention that little word, love.

They watched the sunrise on Saturday morning while sitting on Frances's balcony, having breakfast and continuing the closeness they had built the night before. Slowly but surely, their topics returned to the matter at hand.

"What does Jake, the ever-sceptical detective, think of the whole affair," Frances asked.

"He didn't believe the body was an android; he reminded me of having no evidence, which is true. I started to doubt myself for a moment, but Inspector Moorhead had seen it, and he knew. I don't think I told you he took his long leave the next day and can't be contacted any more. How strange is that? Anyhow, after Jake talked to the morgue technician, he was sure Jess was an android. His objective is to find evidence to convict someone, which is fair enough; he is a policeman.

I have different concerns. I'm worried that some psychopath wants to influence or even rule the world. I know that sounds far-fetched, but why is someone called the Zookeeper producing androids identical to humans and wanting to breed complacency in our citizens by pampering them with household service robots, virtual reality glasses and other gadgets."

Blake stopped and listened, "Was that the doorbell?" He asked.

"Yes, I think so; let me check." Frances turned down the radio and went to the door. A moment later, she returned with a parcel addressed to Blake.

"For you, did you tell anyone you are at my place?"

"The boys from the last meeting know. Let me see. Do we need a sniffer dog or take the risk?" Blake laughed and carefully opened the parcel. He looked at Frances with a stunned facial expression and showed her the contents: a toy robot and nothing else.

"What?"

Blake answered, "That is a message. I have been put on notice; someone is watching us. That is what Oliver told me; the Zookeeper is playing with me."

"That is a sick game. What do we do?"

"Nothing yet. It's not all bad news. Oliver also mentioned that being played is better than being eliminated." Blake smiled.

"How can you smile? It's not funny."

"Yes, but don't you see, it has become a game, and I intend to win it."

Frances wasn't happy, but Blake carried on: "Tonight, we could find evidence that politicians are directly involved in one way or another. I am sure we will meet some professional lobbyists as well. It is their business to influence legislation, regulation, policies, or other government decisions, and maybe they do that on behalf of Hampton." Blake held Frances's hands and softly pleaded:

"Think about it: corrupt governments work hand in hand with corporations and banks to profit through human exploitation while their citizens become complacent, being served by robots, without realizing what is going on. I know it sounds like a conspiracy theory, but I never thought I'd meet an android either," Blake mused, his voice tinged with a hint of mystery, becoming more light-hearted. Frances nodded in partial agreement before confiding her worries to him.

"I don't understand the whole thing. It's no wonder Jake needed evidence. What will you do if you can't prove misdeeds and Jake can't lay charges?"

"Not sure yet, but if it is about androids infiltrating human society, I hope to convince the government to implement a 'Certified Human' program. If we can differentiate between androids and humans, androids will not be a direct threat," Blake clarified.

"Don't we have the same problem with artificial intelligence? We don't know if what we hear or read is real or written by AI."

"Yes, same principle, and still no solution on hand."

"And didn't you say Hampton stripped millions of dollars of bank accounts in small amounts and that androids may not even be involved?" Frances asked.

"Yes, that's all correct. We're tackling these issues from different angles. Jake follows the money trail with the assistance of Oliver, Mona and George. Bidi is also on the case."

Blake stopped talking and looked at Frances, a half-smile playing around his lips. It was time to shift the focus, and he reached out to gather her into his arms. "What about we relax now and enjoy the rest of the day?"

17

T he venue was packed. Blake was glad they had booked a limousine and arrived in style, not that anyone paid attention. Maybe that was a good thing.

It was and looked like Sydney's premier event space, the newly refurbished 'The Venue'. *It's not very creative to call a venue The Venue*, thought Blake, walking slowly towards the entry, trying to dodge the celebrities. He was happy that he had the most beautiful lady on his arm. Frances looked stunning in a long red evening dress. They looked at each other as if to say, *Let's do it.*

Blake held their entry tickets, which read, 'You are cordially invited to the annual Sydney Fundraising Gala'.

As they stepped through the entry doors, Blake was awestruck by the spectacle before him. The lobby was crowded with a sea of guests, celebrities, and VIPs, all united by a common hope that their presence and contributions would trigger positive change. As in previous years, the funds raised would be directed towards aiding the underprivileged and homeless. As a devoted activist against poverty, it was a cause close to Blake's heart.

How come they can't fix those problems? Blake thought. That night the goal was to raise $5 million towards the supply of housing, employment, education, dignity and a new start for hundreds of families across Australia. That amount of money showed the calibre of people present. It wasn't unheard of that one of the rich celebrities handed over a check for $500,000.

They arrived at their table. It wasn't the best spot, but they didn't expect that. After all, they didn't pay for their $450 tickets because of Frances's helpful connections. Even better, the tickets included a three-course meal and sparkling wine.

Blake looked at the program for the night. It was full-on, with one attraction after another; it felt like a variety show interrupted by speeches. To top it off, there was an orchestra and dancing—something for everyone.

The MC was a retired judge of the ACT Supreme Court. Other speakers included distinguished guests, such as the Ministers for Public Service and Finance. They had to show their faces to impress the audience for the upcoming election in late October. Other big shots were CEOs, solicitors, and lobbyists.

At any other fundraising extravaganza, Blake would be bored stiff, but not this night. He was energized to the max and overflowing with nervous energy.

He had to figure out how to get close to the ministers and their faithful followers, the lobbyists, and anyone else wielding enough power to influence the government.

The MC approached the podium, flicking his finger on the microphone several times, signalling the crowd to quieten down.

Blake started recording. Would it work or were they sitting too far away? Never mind. It was only a short introduction speech before the MC gestured to the orchestra and invited the guests to dance.

Luckily, the ministers and their wives approached the dance floor first. It was a matter of skilful manoeuvring for Frances and Blake to dance next to them, allowing Blake to get a possible Wi-Fi frequency reading.

"Was that your mobile vibrating?" Frances asked.

"Yes, I think so, but it didn't react when we were close to the ministers; it must have been the couple behind us."

"I know him from one of our articles; he owns a well-known professional lobbyist firm and is a lobbyist himself. I saw him talking to the Finance Minister when we came in," Frances said.

"If he is an android, we know what he is talking to the minister about. I will try to recheck him to make sure. Do you know his name?"

"Yes, it's Michael Norton."

"I wonder if money is also a factor in influencing a minister. Maybe Jake can do a bank check-up on the minister; even so, I can't imagine that, if a minister is bribed, he would use his private bank account."

"Hold tight," Blake said, swinging Frances around to the rhythm of the music from one corner of the dance floor to the other.

"There was something. Get ready for a sharp turn," Blake swirled Frances around, heading closer to a well-known and liked business tycoon.

"Nothing; must have been someone else."

"Try the couple next to them; I have seen her before; she is his personal secretary," Frances said.

Two more turns, one dip, and Blake had positioned himself right next to the secretary; his phone came alive, vibrating.

"I can't believe it, another android; we must find a way to warn him about his secretary. I'm sure she acts like a spy without influencing him directly." Blake said.

"That is terrible; I don't think I can trust anyone ever again." Frances lamented.

"I know I feel the same. We must install the apps on your phone; at least you will know who you can trust," Blake said.

The dancing stopped, the orchestra needed a break, and the MC announced the first act, performing poodles.

"Did he say, performing poodles? Where are we?" Blake raised his eyebrows while the poodles appeared on the stage, silently commanded by their fearless tamer. Blake's eyebrows wouldn't go down; his eyes were rolling. He couldn't believe it - finally, the big attraction: a tiny toy poodle jumping through a hoop of fire.

"Wow, a wonder it didn't catch fire. It must have been terrifying, but I guess the treat at the end was more important," Blake said.

"It's probably an android," Frances said, laughing.

"I would say yes, but can you imagine what a poodle android of that quality would cost?"

"Look over to the bar." Blake pointed out by nodding his head in that direction. The bar wasn't long enough to cater to all the men who had escaped the poodle act.

"You stay here and guard our champagne. I will go over to the bar and check out a few more people. Can you take the pics? Whenever I nod, take a picture to help us identify the people later."

Blake mingled between the big shots occupying the twenty-metre bar front; his scanners switched on. Standing next to the lobbyist, Michael Norten, he grabbed his arm. "Excuse me," he said, still holding the arm with his ultrasound-scanning pad in his palm. "A scotch on the rocks, please," Blake called out to the bartender.

"Aren't you Michael Norten? I am Blake Newcome from Fact File News; we have written an article about you before. Is there any chance for another interview concerning what you lobby the finance minister about? Blake asked, having completed his scan.

"Sure, you can put that in one of your articles, which, by the way, I often read. It's right up your alley. I lobby on behalf of DIA International. It's a pretty straightforward request to the government to make it easier for older or health-compromised people to stay in their homes but still get all the help they need. We propose to make personal robots a subsidised service item through Medicare."

"Why do you lobby the Finance Minister? Blake asked.

"I have access to him from former projects, and in the end, the buck or the money stops with him. That's all I have for you." Michael Norten excused himself and went to talk to some other people.

Blake checked his mobile scan. Michael Norten's arm revealed a net-like structure around his bones, exposing him as a certified android.

Blake held his whisky high up, moving through the crowd of thirsty people waiting in front of the bar. He went slowly, stopping and going from one end of the bar to the other. His mobile vibrated twice, and he gave a nod to Frances, who took a photo each time. *How many bloody androids are there?* he thought while walking back to Frances. He knew one of the guys, an independent senator named Greg Hillier. If he was an android, what was he planning to do for the Zookeeper? At least, as it appeared, androids could not fill in the top office or ministerial jobs.

Frances pointed out she knew the other guy; he worked with Greg Hillier.

"What did you talk to Michael about?" Frances asked. Blake filled her in.

"I still have no clue what DIA is trying to achieve, other than having a successful business. At the moment, it seems like normal big business. Like any other business, they work on ensuring they get bigger, cutting out the competition and, in DIA's case, dominating the personal robot market." Blake looked at Frances, wishing for a new answer.

"I got nothing, but maybe you are complicating the issue. As you said before, there may be two things: controlling the market and making lots of money and harvesting private information for the sake of power and control over people. If he is a psychopath, he wants the power. If his lobbyist is successful, the government will subsidise his robots to make them even more affordable, giving Hampton ultimate power over his competition."

"I still have nothing I can use for an article other than congratulating DIA on their service to lessen the burden of old age and health care, and probably a caveat note that we must protect our personal information. I can't write anything about androids yet, and because it's not illegal to create an android, the police can't do anything either unless I can prove that the android is doing something illegal. In a way, it still sounds more like a conspiracy theory than of shrewd business undertakings, but I still believe there is more to it." Blake leant back in his chair, raised his glass towards Frances, and stood up again.

"Let's dance."

The momentous social event had ended. The crowds had dispersed, and only a few dedicated drinking buddies stopped the bartender to call it a night. The money raised had outperformed all expectations.

Frances and Blake stepped outside into the mild summer night.

"I feel like a late-night swim, but we better not do that again." In a moment of melancholy, Blake remembered that tragic night when Mark drowned because of young foolishness.

They moved a few more steps on the footpath away from the entry when they noticed a police car.

"What are they doing here? The ministers are gone already," Blake said.

He didn't have to wait long for an answer. The police car door opened, and an officer climbed out and walked over to Blake and Frances.

"Are you Blake Newcome?" The officer addressed Blake.

"Yes, I am; what can I do for you?" Blake said, not disguising his surprise.

"We have received a request to take you to a police station for questioning," the officer replied sternly.

"You have what? Why?"

"Regarding a threatening phone call you allegedly have made tonight. It would help if you came with us to clear the matter up."

"I haven't made any phone calls tonight; I have been here at the Gala function all night."

"Please, sir, you are not charged for anything; we need you for questioning."

"I have heard that before," Blake turned to a worried-looking Frances.

"Don't worry. You head home, and I will come later." He kissed Frances goodbye, but it didn't settle her worries.

A short time later, Blake was once again sitting in one of those small rooms with a suspicious-looking glass wall, a table and two chairs. *I have to stop making a habit out of this*, Blake thought, when a plain-clothed man entered the room, followed by a lady officer in uniform.

"I am Detective Jennings; sorry to bother you this late. I have to ask you some questions. Did you call Inspector James Moorhead tonight on his private number?"

"Inspector Moorhead? No, I haven't talked to him since an unfortunate situation I had in Brisbane two weeks ago, and I never had his private number. I wished I had; I tried getting hold of him but was told he was on long leave. Why?"

"He claimed you called him and threatened him with his early demise. He recognised your voice and phone number and traced it to the location of the gala where we apprehended you. Is there anything you can say to the contrary?"

"Absolutely, I haven't made any phone calls. I don't know his number, and I can prove it." Blake confidently took out his mobile phone and opened it to show the absence of recent calls.

"See, no calls made. The last call was in the afternoon to Jake, who, by the way, is another police officer. I have nothing to hide, and you may know that I am a journalist for the Fact File News."

"You may have made the phone call from another phone. Moorhead was absolutely certain he recognised your voice." The detective countered, his suspicion palpable in the air.

"Please, you mentioned that Moorhead had my mobile number, which is this phone. Someone must have pretended to be me."

"Can I have your phone to check it, please?"

Blake handed over his phone, and the detective left the room, leaving Blake alone with the female officer, who looked concerned. Blake couldn't stop himself.

"Don't worry. I'm not going to kill you." It wasn't the right thing to say, but it made Blake feel better.

A quarter of an hour must have gone by before the detective reappeared.

"Yes, your phone is cleared. We can't trace any calls after the one you made to your mate Jake, the detective inspector."

"How do you know that Jake is a mate?" Blake asked.

"We have made a few more enquiries on your behalf and are satisfied you had nothing to do with what we now call a prank call."

"I think it was more than a prank call; someone tried to frame me; maybe that is what you need to investigate. I know a thing or two about these things. It must have been a deep fake; someone has obtained my voice file and used it to my detriment. If Inspector Moorhead has a recording of that call, it can be checked with a spectrometer to determine whether it is machine-made or a real voice." Blake stood up, "Can I go now?"

"Yes, you can; we will take you to your destination."

"No, thank you. I had enough police for one night; I'll take a taxi. Before I go, I have a question: Are you certain it was Inspector Moorhead you talked to? He has been uncontactable for the last couple of weeks, and no one knows his whereabouts." Blake observed Detective Jennings's facial expression, which had changed from confident to doubtful. Blake served him another curve ball.

"I am sure the caller wasn't even Moorhead." With that statement, Blake left the interrogation room.

18

It was Sunday, and Blake wasn't up to anything other than Sunday activities: eating, resting, a little walk in the park, and, if he couldn't stop, thinking, summarising, and contemplating.

He looked at Frances, still asleep and lying next to him. She looked happy and carried a slight smile, which must have been leftover from last night's happy outcome of Blake's release from police questioning. They had talked briefly; it was 2 am when he came home, and they were drained and ready for bed.

They had come to the conclusion that someone was out to stop Blake from doing what he did best: researching, alerting, and reporting facts. It couldn't have been a coincidence that they had deep-faked his voice when Blake started recording voices from possible androids, not to forget the parcel with the toy robot he had received.

It didn't take a clairvoyant to see the future of where DIA was going; the physical evidence was clear. Even if it sounded grandiose, he, she or whoever represented the Zookeeper was going for global dominance in everything robotic. Already, they had undercut every other personal, household, and health robot on the market through their aggressive marketing campaign of selling their robots at cost.

Apparently not satisfied with that, they aimed to have their robots subsidised by the government with the help of an android lobbyist. As if that wasn't enough, another android, the independent senator Greg Hillier, also played a role. A quick search on Google led Blake to discover the good senator had formed a new party, the Democratic Enter Equality

Party – DEEP, no doubt to push his or DIA International and Zookeeper's agenda. The search revealed that Greg Hillier had used his influence to drive robotic health care into the medical system. The new party had a few more political goals, but Blake couldn't see any connection to the Zookeeper's possible grand plan yet.

Blake understood the business strategy, of course, and he certainly knew the money had come from nano-skimming.

At this point, nano-skimming and violating privacy were the possible charges if Jake could prove them.

Despite understanding more of the puzzle, Blake found himself grappling with the next steps. In his own words, he was at a loss, but he knew himself well. His best ideas came from not thinking about a problem. He had to let it go and trust himself, and the truth would reveal itself. At least, that's what he hoped for. As for now, he was hungry; it was time for breakfast.

He woke Frances and went to the kitchen to make breakfast. Even with all those problems, he hadn't lost his love for cooking. He brewed coffee the old-fashioned way, filtered, percolated, and cooked scrambled eggs with mushrooms, garlic chives, and spinach on top of Camembert and sourdough bread.

"Breakfast is ready," he called out.

"Coming," Frances yelled back. Sunday could start.

It was a picture book Sunday for Frances and Blake. At least it started that way. The breakfast was delicious, and so was the view from the balcony. They restrained themselves and didn't talk about androids, but staying relaxed with something pleasant on their minds can only last while it lasts.

Their conversation topics concentrated on what to do with that beautiful Sunday. The sun shone, the temperature was perfect, and the beach looked inviting. Maybe a walk along the shore and finding an ideal place for lunch, seafood and Champagne would suit this Sunday. And how about a movie in the afternoon followed by a dinner at one of the trendy restaurants around 'The Rocks', in one of the historic laneways.

Yes, they agreed that sounded like a perfect Sunday, but they couldn't help it; after Sunday comes Monday, Blake would have to head back to Brisbane. Their topic changed, and they hadn't even finished breakfast yet; an old problem raised its ugly head: how long could they sustain their rekindled relationship living 1,000km apart?

"Is there any way you could move to Brisbane and work from there?" Blake asked. A question he had asked before, usually followed by Frances asking, "Why don't you move to Sydney?"

Even on that morning, this eternal question was unlikely to be answered. They left the question hanging in the air, deciding to take the walk they had promised themselves.

Walking barefoot on the wet beach sand, shoes in hand, wasn't enough to keep a relaxed mindset. Their minds had been rattled, and once that happened, one thing led to another, until they were back discussing androids.

"I am sick of those bloody androids, and you are not yourself. I understand the shock you must have had, but you are not getting anywhere with your enquiries; you are not doing what you do best: interviewing people. Get on with it, be a journalist, not a victim of some stupid android. Request an interview with Hampton; as far as I could determine, he lives on the Gold Coast in one of those multimillion-dollar villas on a canal.

You had an interview with the manager in the DIA Rockhampton facility; they know about you, they are threatening you, and they had you arrested last night. What more do you want? Turn it around, take the initiative, and show them you are not backing down. After the interview, get the help of your mates to kidnap an android. Find one like that security guy from the airport, but closer to West End, to make it easier to take him to your place and lock him into your spare room." Frances had finished speaking her mind, not giving Blake a chance to cut in.

"Wow, where is that coming from? You sound annoyed," Blake said.

"You bet I am; you are moping around, going over the same facts again and again; what the fuck is holding you back? You know those androids are real; Jake knows as well; now get one and drag that son of a bitch to a radiology place and get proof you can show someone higher up the rank. Don't you have the CCC in Brisbane?"

"OK, OK, I didn't want to stir the pot too much without better evidence; who knows how dangerous those androids can get? Whoever is in charge will not take it lying down. But you are right; I will talk to Jake and get the CCC involved. I'm not sure if Jake will go along with capturing an android; it even sounds strange, like capturing a wild beast.

Oliver and Mona can help with legal stuff. And yes, as soon as I am back in Brisbane, I will track down Hampton's home address and request an interview. Now, please, let's not spoil the rest of the day; I still fancy a movie." Blake attempted a smile.

19

B lake was back in his beloved kitchen, cooking, the best way for him to relax and plan the next steps. Frances, of course, had been right, but he had to take care of some lateral issues first.

Someone had copied his voice. How was that even possible, when did it happen, and what could be done about it? He knew the one person to help with deep fake cybercrime: Bidi.

He had called her before he approached his pots and pans. She knew how to deep-fake a voice to trick people into believing it was someone they knew but, even better, she knew how to prevent it.

She assured him that deep, fake, synthesized speech could be misused to deceive humans and machines for evil purposes. She also had a novel defence mechanism designed to thwart unauthorized speech synthesis before it happened. All Blake had to do was install an anti-fake app onto his phone and on any other device he used for speech, even the speech control of his DIA e-car, which, incidentally, he discovered could exclusively be modified by DIA itself.

He wanted to know how it worked, and Bidi explained it without being too technical.

"The app will mess up the recorded audio signal, distort it enough that it sounds normal to the human ear, but it's completely different to AI."

"Thanks, Bidi, you better come over here and install that thing; I don't want to be taken in by police for questioning again."

She promised to come soon; he didn't mind how fast she would be. He was in bliss cooking up a storm.

Blake was happy with his cooking efforts and had some time free for phone calls while the casserole was in the oven. He poured himself a drink. It was at most 4 pm, and he had promised himself not to drink before 5 pm, his personal happy hour, but there is always an exception to every rule.

He needed a drink to call Jake. Blake wasn't sure how Jake would react to his android kidnapping idea, which was, of course, France's idea.

Jake answered his phone, a good sign that he had time on his hands.

"Hi Jake, I'm back in town. Is there anything new with your investigation?"

"Not sure yet; the forensic pathologist, Kayla Osborne, is missing. She performed the pathology on Jess; not sure if you have met her. She didn't turn up for work on Friday and not today either; she is not answering her phone. An investigation will start tomorrow. I called her on Thursday to get her in for questioning, and the next day, she was gone; maybe her phone was bugged.

Her assistant, Daniel, the one I had investigated last week, called our station to let police know she hadn't arrived for work. He is currently doing the autopsy pathology as long as nothing too complicated shows up. How did you go in Sydney?"

Blake reported what was relevant to Jake, including his stint in police custody, the deep fake voice recording, and Bidi having an app to prevent it from happening again. Next, he prepared to ask Jake his controversial question.

"It sounds like someone wants to stop us from finding evidence that androids exist. I wanted to ask you a question about the evidence we still need. Could we get away with kidnapping, capturing an android? Someone like the airport security guy? I have the ultrasound image of part of his arm that proves he is an android. Is it deemed legal to kidnap an android, or is that considered robbery, like stealing a suitcase?"

"Not sure if you are allowed to ask me a question like that. What do you want to do when you have kidnapped an android? You can't slice them open?"

"I want to get them into a CT scanner. If they have nothing to hide, they may not resist. I am asking you because we may not have to kidnap him literally. I thought you could apprehend him for questioning and charge him with drug possession, and the CT scan is a precaution to make sure they haven't swallowed a condom filled with an illicit drug?" Blake hastily voiced his plan, looking at the image of Jake on his mobile as if to say, come on, let's do it.

Jake took his time.

"Jake? Are you still there?"

"Yeah, thinking. You have read too many crime novels, but it isn't a bad idea; it could work. It's plausible that a security guy working at the airport was planted there by a drug cartel to make it easier to smuggle drugs. Yes, that is possible. I think I like it. It gives us all the evidence to proceed and notify the authorities," Jake said.

Blake looked pleased and took another gulp of his drink.

"I made more enquiries into what further steps to take. I came across the CCC. At first, I didn't even know what CCC stood for; I called it the Counter Culture Club. But I quickly learned it stands for 'Crime and Corruption Commission', which sounds like the body we need for a deeper investigation. They have a cybercrime department. I wonder if you might know someone from within the CCC?"

"Yes, you are on the right track because they are not the body to convict anyone. The public is not aware of their deep investigation. After they have completed it and established the facts, they express opinions about misconduct and make recommendations for action. Perfect for what you have in mind." Jake agreed.

"Great, that's what I hoped, but before we act on it, we need to know if the other guys have anything new, particularly George, the forensic accountant; I think Bidi has teamed up with him. I'm not sure what Oliver and Mona are up to. I will call them next and report to you tomorrow at the latest. Before I go, I have another question: Can you get me Hampton's address and contact details? I heard from Frances that he lives on the Gold Coast. I want to interview him."

"Yes, we tracked down his address. It will be on his file, but I can't imagine he wants to talk to you," Jake replied.

"I am sure he will, even if it is out of curiosity. I will tell him something to make sure he can't resist my request. Flattery usually opens doors. I will congratulate him on his push to make his robots cheap enough for the elderly through Medicare on a doctor's prescription," Blake said.

"That could work; go for it. I will text you his details later. I have to go now; talk later." Jake hung up.

"That went better than I thought," Blake murmured.

His oven timer rang out: the casserole was ready. He carefully opened the oven door, well aware of the cloud of heat escaping. The heat wasn't all that was escaping; the aroma that came with it made his mouth water. He settled on the bench, poured a glass of medium-strength beer, took out a plate and dished up a generous amount of slow-cook, scrumptious paprika chicken and lentil casserole. It was a winter dish, but he loved it; it beat any of those mass-market-ready meals.

He dug into it, notebook on his side. A good meal stimulated new connections between events and facts, which he usually overlooked when sidetracked by too much mental activity.

Half an hour later, he had finished. If anyone had been watching him, they would have noticed his movements had slowed, even the way he put his cutlery into the proper position on his plate before he lifted it and carried it towards the sink; it was evident his mind had trapped him in deep mental effort.

He stopped, nearly froze, motionless, a 7-second pause. He dropped the plate into the sink, "Fuck, totally forgot." Blake looked for his phone; it was at the other end of his formidable kitchen. He quickly walked over, picked it up, and speed-dialled Frances. She answered.

"Frances, the other guy, did you find out his name?"

"And, hello to you, too. What are you on about? Whose name?"

"Sorry. You know the other guy I tested at the Gala event, who turned out to be an android, and you mentioned you have heard about him and wanted to check him out?"

"Yes, now I know who you mean. Yes, I have his name, and also know what he is lobbying for. I don't think he has anything to do with what you are after. He lobbies for one of your pet likes, a 'Universal Basic Income'; that's why we saw him talking to the Minister for Social Services. I think you can forget about him."

"No, that blows my mind; it fits perfectly into my idea of what this is all about, but it is too hard to believe. What is his name?"

"It's Carl Feldon; he is relatively new to this lobbying game and is working and supporting Greg Hillier, who will take up the 'Universal Basic Income' policy for his new party, and Carl is a part of that as well.

"Are you still focused on the idea of world domination?" Frances asked.

"Yes, I am thinking in terms of Dostoyevsky, who said, 'The best way to keep a prisoner from escaping is to make sure he never knows he's in prison'.

"Sure, I get that, but what is the connection with world domination, androids and the Zookeeper?"

"Still too early to speculate openly, but between you and me, the connection is what we have briefly discussed: breeding complacency."

"Still don't get the connection."

"If you want to control people, you make them feel content and pleased with themselves, which makes them complacent, and a Universal Income is part of that. They will go along with anything, even though situations may be dangerous and call for action. I call it the complacency trick, people becoming unaware of potential dangers or threats."

"And you believe the so-called Zookeeper initiates a scenario like this? Then yes, it does sound like a conspiracy theory."

"I know, that's why I haven't written anything about it, but I will as soon as I have the interview with Hampton," Blake said.

"I can't imagine that guy would admit to any of your suspicions."

"Probably not, but I need to feel him out and get a sense of what kind of person he is before we publish that androids are around us, and we have the right to know who they are and how to tell them apart from humans." Blake explained.

"Do you have his address?" Frances asked.

"Yes, Jake will text it to me today. Something else: when will you come to Brisbane? You haven't seen my unit. West End is superb. There are many restaurants and cafes, and it's a quality place to hang out and relax," Blake said.

"I would love to. I will try for the following week. I will be able to stay for a few days. I can do most of my work away from the office these days," Frances said.

"Yes, I am sure you can; that's why I want you to move here and stay with me," Blake said, his voice filled with a hint of hope.

"Back to that, are we? I love Sydney; why don't you move to Sydney?" Frances countered.

"Ok, yes, I know. Somehow, we have to make it work and enjoy the best of both worlds. Anyhow, talk soon. I have to get going; the intercom is buzzing. See you soon," Blake said and walked to the door.

It was Bidi; she stormed into the kitchen and grabbed a glass of water. "Sorry, I haven't got much time. Let me fix your phone."

"Thanks for coming. Here you go, do your tricks," Blake handed her his mobile to install the voice app.

A couple of minutes later, Bidi passed over the mobile.

"All done, no need to do anything; use your phone like always; the app will do its magic, stopping your voice from being recorded."

"Thank you. How did you go? Do you have time for a progress report?" Blake asked.

"A quick one, yes, I didn't do check-ups to find androids; I was way too busy tracking down possible nano-skimming and money laundering channels with George. We didn't find any compromising details to nail down the Zookeeper.

One thing is sure: his DIA conglomerate has a clever, intricate web of hundreds of companies and divisions scattered across the globe, posing a formidable challenge. The nano-skimmed money is transferred and dispersed to such an extent that tracing a path was impossible," Bidi explained.

"Sounds like bad news. Sorry you guys spent that much time for nothing," Blake looked disappointed; he had hoped for a more tangible result.

"I have some good news as well. I tracked down the robot's signal pathways to harvest and transmit the data. First, the robots install a surprisingly simple algorithm into their host's devices to collect bank details and passwords. Even two-way security is no help.

The robot harvests the security code and applies it when accessing the bank to skim off a few cents before transferring the money to another account. I now know how to install a code into a host computer to stop harvesting bank details, but only for individual clients." Bidi said.

"That sounds promising, and what is George up to?" Blake asked.

"That is a different story altogether. I didn't know George before. He is a hard-to-read guy. He worked incredibly hard; I think he believed in his capabilities to outsmart Hampton and get him arrested. He followed the money trail across different companies and countries from one obscure finance institution to another. He discovered that the harvested money was divided even more and transferred in a never-ending fashion, dissolving into nothingness.

In the end, he got depressed. He had no tricks up his sleeve to expose Hampton, and at no point during the money-transferring journey was there a connection to DIA International. He left my office without even saying goodbye," Bidi pointed out.

"Thanks, Bidi. I'm sorry to hear George felt distressed. If you see him again, thank him from me and ask if he wants to stay involved. But I think this avenue of investigation is closed. We have to find something better to nail the Zookeeper. Thanks again; I know how busy you are with your work." Blake said.

"Hang on; I found something else. I followed up on some of DIA's companies. I am as convinced as you are that something big is happening right under our eyes. I'm not sure if you know, but one of DIA's sub-companies is the premium manufacturer and supplier of virtual reality headsets. They also supply games, movies, and virtual reality content, replacing the real physical world with their content. It's all legal; I don't think you can pin any wrongdoings on Hampton. People love that virtual stuff; it's like a drug, and people can't get enough of it," Bidi said.

"There is more, but I'm not sure if it interests you. Yet another one of DIA's companies is developing AI software to treat mental illnesses, such as depression and anxiety. I am sure the Zookeeper has dubious aims. He could use those programs to cause anxiety and depression and brainwash people," Bidi said, her voice tinged with disgust.

"It doesn't stop. That guy has his tentacles everywhere, and all in the name of making life better. People don't recognise they are sucked in and become complacent. Most people couldn't care less if they found out their next-door neighbour was an android. They are too busy being content with their own life. I will have to find a strategy to make people aware of what is happening to ward off being controlled by AI and androids. I haven't told you yet, but I think the Zookeeper's ultimate goal is to make people complacent and go along with everything. Regrettably, I will have to write an article causing fear to shock people into action," Blake said.

"I can't help you with that, but you will find a way. Complacency as a goal to control people, you could be right; very sneaky. I will continue devising programs to stop unsolicited data retrieval and anti-deep fake apps. I better be off; I am late already; I have more work to do." Bidi hurried out.

Blake walked around his kitchen island; he could think better when walking. This time, circulating for a few minutes made the situation more painful. In his mind, everything was clear as water. Life was changing, and someone was controlling that change and the outcome. It wasn't something Blake aspired to do; it was what he considered the worst horror story ever conceived by a sick mind.

Blake imagined a bleak future ahead. The human race had been manipulated for the super-rich to survive, and the poor and manual working class were slowly dying out, replaced by androids.

He had the whole scenario in his head but wasn't ready to spell it out in one of his articles. It would read like a fictitious horror story.

He picked up his mobile and rang Oliver and Mona, updating them and including what he had found out from Bidi. He further asked them if they had heard from George, but they hadn't.

They had been busy throwing themselves into an android testing spree and were shocked to learn that many legal staff, solicitors and barristers were androids. They couldn't get close enough to judges, but the two they tested were humans.

So far, the trend has been that top-ranking people have not been replaced with androids. It was logical; top-positioned people have a history that could be traced back. To replace them would mean killing them and substituting them with androids.

Blake had agreed with them and added, "I don't know what else you could do other than keep on testing and documenting the androids you find, and if possible and your time permits, establish a file on each of them, including pictures." Blake paused, thinking about the android kidnapping before he asked.

Mona jumped in, "Yes, sure, we will keep on with it; I wish there was more we could do."

"Maybe you can; I talked to Jake about kidnapping an android. We have someone in mind. Can you think of negative legal implications? Can we get into trouble kidnapping an android, even if it is under false pretences?" Blake asked.

"That's a loaded question, it depends on how you would do it, but it could lead to serious implications. Is it kidnapping or stealing? Either way, the owner of the android may take you to court." Mona's voice carried an urgency.

Blake was less concerned, he smiled, but voiced other complications.

"What are the legal implications of 'raping an android' or injuring one? Leave the ruling of the world scenario alone for the moment and think about the new ethical frontier and legal importance of androids within our society..."

Mona interrupted, her voice sharp. "Yes, human rights, moral and legal entitlements. How is civilized society protected?"

"Exactly," Blake acknowledged, "Will we have to extend human rights to androids? Is that too far-fetched? I don't think so. Maybe you guys can work through those issues because they will arise soon. But don't worry, before we kidnap an android, I will try to get an interview with Hampton, and I am sure I will get one."

Oliver cleared his throat, "You made some good points, and yes, we will have answers for you soon. It's a new topic for us, too. The AI technologies are moving at warp speed: they're way ahead of our existing laws, and we're playing catch up. Will let you know more soon."

"Thanks guys," Blake switched off his mobile; he needed quiet and time to think.

He continued his 'walking around and thinking inspiration routine'. This time it worked. After two rounds, he remembered that he hadn't told any of his friends about Carl Feldon, the guy lobbying for Universal Basic Income. In the past, as Frances pointed out rightly, it was one of his favourite possible policies.

Twenty or thirty years ago, it may have inspired people to do more with their lives because they had a basic income and didn't need to worry about security, taking a greater risk to create their own unique lifestyle income.

Blake had changed his mind over the last couple of weeks. At a time when complacency had already set in, the Universal Basic Income, he argued to himself, could be used to enhance complacency rather than inspire action. Like the virtual reality headsets, he considered the Universal Basic Income yet another tool to breed complacency.

20

On Wednesday, Blake called Hampton's office number and asked for an interview. The secretary sounded nice enough and promised to call him back, which she did a day later. The message was clear, loud, and positive. Mr Hampton looked forward to seeing him; his busy schedule allowed for a 30-minute timeslot.

Blake was granted an interview with Hampton for Friday at 11 am at the Gold Coast Office and Home complex, a space large enough to erect a football stadium, occupying 5 acres on Intrepid Drive. Was it the name of the street that attracted Hampton to move there? Intrepid, he thought: extremely brave and showing no fear of dangerous situations? It is a tricky term, neutral in nature, and used in positive or negative scenarios.

Blake planned carefully; he didn't trust the guy. He called Jake about the upcoming interview and stressed that if Jake had not heard from Blake by 1 pm, he had better arrive with the SWAT team, emphasizing the potential threat.

It was supposed to sound light-hearted, but Jake didn't take it as such; he promised to be on alert.

Being turned into an android was not one of Blake's worries; he was more worried about becoming a 'missing person'. Surely, Hampton knew everything there was to know about Blake. Would he try to bribe him with heaps of money and drag him down to the dark side?

Blake ran around in circles again, planning every step of the upcoming interview, knowing all the right questions and how to deal with interruptions, like changing a topic and preventing him from becoming the object of the interview.

How could Blake out-trick Hampton? He considered recording the interview even if Hampton would not allow it.

Blake picked up his mobile; he knew who could help him and made the call.

"Hi Bidi, I have a favour to ask. Is there an app I can use to record my interview without being detected?" Blake asked and told her what it was for.

"Yes, I will send you a link. It's an app that is not available to the public, but you can get it from the dark web. It works like your normal mobile phone recording function, with the difference that it does not switch on any other function on your phone while at the same time blocking incoming calls, Wi-Fi detection apps, and keeping the mobile dead silent."

"Fantastic. I will use it when I interview Hampton. I have a few more things occupying my mind. If you had a service robot, could you hack into them to find out what they are capable of or where the data is transferred?"

"Sure, that would help. Will you buy one?"

"I am thinking about it," Blake said before continuing. "One more thing: we need an easy-to-use android testing device, something everyone could have on their phone. Can you come up with something like that? It has the potential to be a business as well. Once people know androids are roaming around, they will want to buy that app to know if androids live or work around them. That's all I have for the moment." Blake laughed, "That's enough, isn't it?"

"Yes, thanks, more than enough; challenging, exciting, and as you said, having a patent on a detection device could become a huge business. Thanks for the idea; I may take time off work and concentrate my mental resources on android detection. See you soon." Bidi sounded upbeat.

"Good on you; I will not bother you for a few days unless something more exciting happens." Blake put his phone down and picked up his notebook.

What else did Blake have to think of? Are there any legal implications to interviewing a highflyer? He decided to call Oliver or Mona once more.

Oliver's mobile was on message, but Mona's phone answered.

"Hi Mona, sorry to bother you again, and thanks for your good work. By the way, Bidi will work on an easier detection device to track down androids. I am sure it will be handy for you guys to have, especially since you are confronted at court with hundreds of people to test on a daily basis. I have a question. I will interview Hampton tomorrow. Is there anything I need to be careful about legally, so that he doesn't turn the table and get me into trouble?"

"Yes, definitely, but I am sure you already know not to make any accusations he could use to sue you for defamation. Tread carefully. That guy is a billionaire who can hold you up in court for years out of spite or to nail you down and rob you of your power. Ask open, harmless questions about where he wants to go with his company and whether he has any personal ambition or intentions. Does he have a mission statement?

And most importantly, never insinuate anything. Don't give him the opportunity to become defensive, or in other words, don't attack him. The other approach is asking for his opinion; what do you think about the fear that robots are taking over?"

"Ok, thank you. I will control my tongue even if it is hard for me to do so. Wish me luck."

Blake's day began and ended with a singular focus on androids. He jotted down more queries, installed the app from Bidi's message, and sought comfort in his kitchen. It was time to create a culinary masterpiece, a desperate attempt to divert his mind from the conspiracy theory that was inching closer to reality. As the saying goes, it's a conspiracy until it isn't".

Sydney - Thursday 20. October 2033 - Frances

After talking to Blake, Frances spent some time deep in thought. She kept looking at her mobile. The last few days had turned her world around. She had been in love with Blake since when she first met him. Everything was going so well till it didn't, and all because she moved to

Sydney to accept the fantastic promotion to become the 'Fact File News editor-in-chief.'

The excitement and joy of the first few weeks of living and working in Sydney overshadowed everything. She had to confess that she didn't dwell on her relationship with Blake; life in Sydney was too exciting. She was the boss now; she decided how the Fact File publication would look and feel and which policies would prevail.

Thinking back to that time, she still could feel the excitement. The exhilarating joy of managing her team of writers and editors for the Fact File newspaper and magazine, one of the foremost news providers in the country, she had it all.

Did the power go to her head? Perhaps, but it was also a lot of work. And as the initial excitement waned, reality set in. Maintaining a long-distance relationship was a challenge. They met only a few times a year and had slipped into a friendship mode. That was until the last long weekend when everything changed. The shock of Jess falling from his balcony was one thing, but the revelation that she was a machine, a human look-alike robot, was a whole new level of disbelief.

Frances was initially sceptical of the whole story, suspecting there was more to it than Blake had revealed. But her focus wasn't on uncovering the truth; it was on the change in him. He was more attentive, and she sensed his longing for her. And despite everything, she still needed him.

It was after hearing that Blake's friend Jake had evidence that the woman who fell was an android that she believed it fully and started to worry about the possible consequences.

How could she deal with it? Having uncovered a dark secret, was Blake in danger? Still, the idea of androids roaming about undetected made her hair stand up. The potential consequences were too much to handle.

Frances thought she could publish little hints to make people aware, because she knew Blake was most likely right in his suspicion that someone had set out to pacify humans, or as Blake called it, breeding complacency.

There was something Blake had no idea about, and she never told him, but as part of her job as editor-in-chief, she had to take care of statistics.

The Fact File News was much more factual and in-depth than your run-of-the-mill newspapers, online or otherwise.

When the Fact File News first hit the market in 2015, it quickly established itself as the leading serious online newspaper. After one year of publication, subscriptions and stats soared, keeping it at the top position over all other papers for a solid ten years. However, a shift occurred around 2024. A slow, unsettling trend emerged, and the Fact File readership and subscriptions declined.

Simultaneously, cheaper news outlets peddling gossip and trivia gained traction. This trend persisted, a fact known to everyone in the head office except for Blake. Working from his unit in Brisbane, he remained oblivious to the dwindling statistics, which confirmed France's suspicion that people had become complacent and hooked on social media trivia.

Frances was troubled; perhaps she was the only one of his friends who was convinced Blake's thoughts were on the mark. Blake had a suspicion, a theory that intrigued and scared her in equal measure.

Unbeknownst to anyone other than Blake's small group of friends, the Zookeeper was orchestrating the population with service robots and androids, all for the sinister goal of world domination.

In Frances's mind, Blake's article about billionaires had to be more direct to catch the readers. As it was, it started with a question-and-answer scenario:

Should we be concerned about billionaires and their ever-growing power and influence? The answer is a resounding yes. They wield unlimited power. It's not the wealth itself that's the issue, but how it's used. Once the appetite for power takes hold, it's ravenous. Governments, the supposed barrier to billionaires' power, are just as influenced by power. In other words, no one is in control, and governments willingly align with influential power shifters to stay in power.

It sounded dramatic already, but when it came to talking about billionaires and robots, that's where Frances wanted to add the idea of androids.

Frances, with her understanding of what drives readership, had already made a significant impact on the Fact File News. She introduced a new section on media gossip, a touch of sensationalism that always piques readers' interest. Her editorial prowess was evident in her edit of Blake's article on 'Power and Billionaires', where she briefly mentioned the rising trend of household robots.

Her role wasn't to add something to that article, particularly not without checking with Blake. On the other hand, if she could dramatize the headline, people would be more inclined to read that important article, even though many readers barely skimmed the headlines. Her statistics showed total readership and which pages people read or not, and Blake's articles were down in the dumps.

Frances couldn't help but wonder how Blake would react to her proposed changes. Would he be furious? Would their newfound fondness be at risk?

The next edition of the Fact File will be out on Monday, so there was still enough time for her to change her mind.

She went ahead and made sure she had two versions of the article, Blake's and hers.

Her version would read: "Is your Neighbour an Android?"

She also would add a straightforward line to Blake's text: *In conjunction with the dramatic development of household service robots, do we have androids walking among us? Has a generation of androids been developed yet? Ask your friendly billionaire - they have the power.*

Would Blake agree to text like that if she tells him about the statistics and declining readership?

There was one way to find out: call him. He may even know if he has been granted an appointment with one of the most influential billionaires, the one they call the Zookeeper.

Brisbane - Thursday Night – 20. October 2033 - Blake
Blake sat down for dinner, opened a can of beer, and tucked into

his latest culinary masterpiece: lobster with organic baby caramelised carrots. This dish could have been a centrepiece for royalty, so he thought, especially how he had arranged it.

He wasn't a big eater. He believed his granddad's motto: "Stop eating before you are full; you will live long and never gain weight." It has worked for Blake so far and led to a greater appreciation of quality food.

He was in the middle of his culinary experience when his mobile phone interrupted his pleasure. He took a sip of beer to clean his mouth and throat before cheerfully answering, seeing it was Frances.

"Hi, Darling, nice of you to call. Are you missing me already?" Blake asked.

"Yes, I miss you, but that's not why I called. It's about your article and something crucial about the Fact Files and its readership." Frances' voice conveyed a hint of concern as she explained the paper's history and statistics, and she concluded that complacency had set in, at least when it came to reading quality informative articles.

"I had no idea. You could have told me earlier, and I would have adjusted my articles accordingly."

"That's exactly what I wanted to talk to you about. Could we change the headline and add some text for dramatic effect? I want to mention androids, or the suspicion of androids without pinpointing to anyone in particular, other than mention DIA International's efforts to popularise service robots even more with government support. I'll send you what I am suggesting, and you can take it from there?" Frances was happy to have that off her mind.

"Yes, sure, I'd love to. No problems, but let's wait; I will write something more sensational after my interview tomorrow morning with Hampton."

They talked for a while, Blake longingly looking at his dinner, which was getting cold, but Frances was more important.

Was Blake absent-minded? Did he use that little word accidentally?

"See you soon, Frances; love you."

There was a pause before Frances replied, "I love you too."

21

F riday morning, Blake was ready to go. *Interview, here I come*, he thought.

He had meticulously familiarized himself with the new recording app, practising its activation without raising suspicion. As any seasoned journalist would, he planned to ask for permission to record the interview, activating the standard recording function on his mobile. If the answer was 'no', he would discreetly switch to the undetectable one, slipping his phone back into his pocket to put his host at ease.

He would also take an old-fashioned notebook and ballpoint pen, again hoping the host would be satisfied and not suspect underhanded behaviour.

Blake couldn't help but chuckle at the irony. In his youth, he had devoured every Sherlock Holmes book, and now he saw the Zookeeper as his Moriarty, the criminal mastermind and formidable evil enemy of Sherlock. If his deductions were correct, he would soon come face to face with the world's enemy number one.

Blake was no Sherlock, but the question was: is the Zookeeper a Moriarty? *I will soon find out*, Blake thought.

He checked his time while driving out of his building's lower car deck. It was 9 am sharp, a perfect time, even if there would be heavy traffic. He was glad the traffic had diminished over the years when electric cars overtook the driving scene much earlier than expected.

Speeding was hardly heard of anymore, and the same was true of accidents; cars were driving at 100km in an orderly row, keeping a safe distance commanded by the cars' robotic systems. The highway had become a safe, train-like track. Blake had suggested increasing the speed limit to 130km in various articles.

Blake had one hour of driving time to kill. He flicked through his car's online TV stations and settled for the news. As luck would have it, an interview with independent senator Greg Hillier being grilled about integrating robotic health care into the medical system and his plan to form a new party, the Democratic Enter Equality Party - DEEP.

The public needed to know that he was an android, Blake thought.

He took notes. Maybe he could ask the Zookeeper if he is the one who uses Greg Hillier to push DIA's robots into the medical system.

His car smoothly navigated him along the highway to Hampton's residence. Blake had never been there before. Even from the outside, it was an impressive complex of buildings, not that he could see much except the rooflines. The rest of the property was hidden behind a wall, made less intrusive by being planted out with whatever nature had on offer.

"Pretty," Blake remarked. He was way too early, so he drove on to check out the neighbourhood.

He returned at precisely 10:55 am, opened his driver's side window and pressed the intercom button. A voice greeted him.

"Good Morning, Mr. Newcome. Mr. Hampton is awaiting you. Please drive in and park at the designated visitor parking spot opposite the entry door."

"Thank you," Blake replied, but the voice had disappeared, and the gate had opened. Blake drove to the front door on a long, curved driveway that was at least 200 meters long. He spotted the car park; he couldn't have missed it if he had tried; it was marked 'VISITORS'.

He took his notebook, pen, and mobile and walked to the entry door. It opened by what he had not expected but might have guessed: a well-dressed customised butler service robot, complete with a black suit and bowtie. "Welcome, sir, to Hampton Estate; please follow me."

They could have at least sent the secretary to fetch me, Blake thought and followed the robot along the hallway to a lift. The lift door opened, and

Blake cleverly deducted to walk in. No deduction needed, the butler robot told him, "Please take the lift."

Blake stepped into the lift, ready to press a button, but again, it was unnecessary; there were no buttons. Not a good feeling. The lift ascended, or did it descend? It felt ascending, and it was. A short ride: no time to relax. The lift door opened, and who greeted him this time? Was it the same butler robot?

"Please follow me," it said, not a robot of many words.

The robot stopped in front of a door and knocked. "Yes, please," sounded the voice behind the door.

"Mr Newcome has arrived," replied the robot.

"Please show him in," the voice said.

Lots of effort for a visit, thought Blake while he walked into the gigantic room, his eyes fixed on an impressive-looking individual behind a desk on which one could land a helicopter. Blake had shifted into his amused personality trait.

The door closed behind him; the polite butler robot had vanished. Who was standing to the left of the big desk but another robot with a tray at hand, waiting patiently for a command from his keeper to fetch some drinks.

Blake had a hard time suppressing his smile. That many robots turned the whole scene into a comic strip, with the big evil guy hiding behind the enormous desk. Blake was a professional; he was capable of not laughing in a grotesque situation. He didn't laugh; he kept a straight face and his stand-by emotion: amusement. He knew it was an arrogant emotion, but he needed it in this confronting, stressful encounter.

The whole situation was hideous and tinged with conspiracy. How could he not be amused, sitting opposite the possible ultimate villain who wants to rule the world? It can't be real, can it?

It was undisputable that the guy looked the part: chiselled chin, strong nose, firm, determined lips, and short hair styled with a touch of grey. He was wearing a dark-looking suit, complete with tie and stiff collar shirt. As the saying goes, he was 'dressed to impress'.

"Can I offer you something to drink, tea maybe?"

Tea? Blake thought, *at 11 am, what will be next, cucumber sandwiches?*

"I could do with a coffee if it is not too much trouble." He answered.

"Milk, sugar?

"Black, please, long black."

Hampton turned to his robot, "One long black and an Earl Gray with milk for me, please."

"Yes, sir." The robot answered, speeding out of the room through a side door Blake hadn't noticed before.

To Blake, it felt like he was in one of those chess tournaments he competed in back in high school. Who will take the first move? Blake was sure it would be him; he was the journalist questioning his subject.

It's not a good idea in a chess game to be too sure; it may backfire.

"I heard you enjoyed the tour at the DIA International robot research and manufacturing plant," Hampton said, opening the game with a surprise move.

Blake recovered quickly, but not quickly enough.

"I am glad you agreed with the CEO's message to cease writing alarmist articles about robots." Hampton continued.

Who is interviewing whom? That guy is not mucking around, Blake thought and considered his next move. He decided to let Hampton's attack dissolve into nothingness, leaning back, not reacting, and waiting for the next question without answering. It didn't come. The robot serving tea and coffee interrupted the game.

The scene was set. The opening game had taken place; Blake's move next. He pulled his mobile from his left trouser pocket, pressed the recording button, and placed it in front of him.

"It's OK to record the interview, isn't it?"

"NO, it isn't," Hampton replied firmly.

"That's fine," Blake said. He picked up his mobile, showed it to Hampton, and pressed the icon to stop the recording. He placed the mobile in his front left shirt pocket while pressing the smart recording device button with his thumb. Happy with himself, he smiled, took out his note block and a pen from his right side trouser pocket, and showed them to Hampton. "OK?" Blake asked. Hampton nodded.

"I wanted to congratulate you on your success in attracting a government subsidy for your service robots. Who was the lobbyist who made that happen for you, and why was it important?"

"I have good connections at a political level, and my efforts to help humanity have been well received.

"Why is it important for me? OK, let me tell you. My mission in life is to support humanity to the best of my abilities. Having a background in engineering and computer science, I specialise in artificial intelligence, human-computer interaction, software engineering, and, obviously, robots.

"I became fascinated with what could be achieved for humanity with robots, which resulted in my first generation of household robots. My great love, however, is reserved for medical help robots to enable people to stay in their homes into ripe old age even if their health is compromised.

"You have seen my different categories of robots and surely appreciate the enormous support they can achieve. It was an obvious logical conclusion that they must be accessible to everyone, even if someone could not afford one. It is the government that can give support like that. That's why I reached out to have medical robots included in Medicare, and Doctors can prescribe a medical robot to a patient. Does that answer your question?" Mr Hampton asked.

"That sounds like a worthwhile endeavour, and I must congratulate you on your efforts. Now, do you think it is also possible that the robots could harm their host or humanity?" Blake asked.

"Why do you journalists always concentrate on the negative? But to answer your question, anything can be compromised, altered, hacked into or whatever. You know as well as I do terrible people are around us. However, as of this moment, none of my robots have been hacked or altered for someone else's devious benefits."

"I drive one of your e-cars and know it is updated occasionally, similar to a mobile phone or computer. Are your robots also remotely updated without the owner's consent or awareness?" Blake asked.

"Here we go again, suspecting more negativity. Yes, of course, the robots are connected and updated with new applications or functions whenever new research has developed enhancements."

Blake sensed that Hampton was becoming frustrated by his line of questioning, but he wasn't finished yet.

"Does that mean that your robots could be updated with functions that are not beneficial to their owners, such as collecting data from the owners' computers? I am not suggesting your company would do such a thing; I am more concerned about a third party hacking into your network undetected and using your robots for data collection," Blake asked.

"You are coming very close to insinuating wrongdoing. As I have expressed before, and as history has proven, there is always a criminal element to reap gain by unlawfully obtaining money or data and a constant effort to hack into systems. We aim to prevent this; if it happens, we respond accordingly with an appropriate security update. Are you finished with this line of questioning?" Hampton asked.

Blake didn't respond and instead continued with a more harmless-sounding question.

"I have learned in your Rockhampton facility that you have invented a new system in hall three to customise robots and make them more natural in their movements and looks. Does that mean we will be confronted with androids in the future?"

"If there is a call for more human-look-alike robots, called androids, we may further our development in that direction. People may feel more confident in being medically supported by robots that look friendly and confident with human features and behaviours."

"In your estimation, how long will it take before we see a full human-robot and android indistinguishable from a human being?" Blake asked.

"That is a loaded question; knowing you, I can see where you want to go. If there is a call for such an android, it could be achieved within a few years, but even then, the android would always be recognisable as an android.

"I think I have answered enough of your questions. Let me make one more important point: robots, or indeed androids, are designed and hard-coded to serve humankind and never to harm a human. I suggest you leave your paranoia at home. The fear factor that robots are harmful to humans is a pure negative fantasy developed by the media to grab attention. I think we are done here," Hampton finished.

"I had hoped to ask a few more personal questions for the reader to get to know you better. No one knows anything about you. Are you married? Do you have any kids or hobbies? What books do you read? Do you like art or the opera, things like that?"

"I am a private person and intend to stay that way. But to satisfy your curiosity, I love the arts, philosophy, and supporting human life on this planet. My whole motivation is the betterment of humans and their living conditions, and to clarify some of your misconceptions, everything my companies do is legal. Here is a metaphor for you: ask people what they want more: to sleep on a concrete floor or in a cosy soft bed. 95% of people choose the bed and feel content. 5% will ask, what is the catch? I am happy with my 95% because I can provide better living conditions and contentment, while your 5% provides scepticism and resentment. Guess who is more appreciated and valued in our society?"

Mr. Hampton stood up. It was clear the interview was at an end.

"Thank you. My butler will show you out."

Blake also stood.

"One more quick question: are you in favour of the Universal Basic Income, as Senator Greg Hillier and lobbyist Carl Feldon promoted, and do you support their push to form a new political party?

Mr Hampton looked at Blake in a slightly amused fashion and said, "No comment."

"Thank you for your time and the coffee. Goodbye, Mr Hampton."

On the way back, sitting in his car, Blake reflected on what he had learned.

Did he know anything new besides the guy was slick at spinning his answers to make himself seem like the world's greatest benefactor?

Blake had not expected anything more; his main objective was to get to know the man. Now he had, and he was sure that Hampton was a devious threat to society.

Blake also knew that he would do everything he could to derail Hampton's goals.

It was intriguing that Hampton had no smooth comeback on Blake's last question about Universal Basic Income, which seemed to indicate his involvement. Blake was clear about that anyway because he knew Greg Hillier was an android, the first new 'would-be politician' to emerge as an android. He was supported by Carl Feldon, another android. Both promoted a Universal Basic Income, a policy where every adult receives regular payments from the government without a means test.

But Hampton was right for the moment; with his strategy, he was sitting comfortably at 95% popularity. Blake had an uphill battle before him; how he would write articles to increase his percentage would be as crucial as preventing androids from taking over.

Blake thought there was a distinguishing difference between Hampton and all the other monsters of past centuries, who had the distorted view in their psychotic brains that they knew how to rule the world.

Past dictators used fear and ruled by aggression, suppression and violence.

Hampton was a hundred times more dangerous and cunning by pretending to be the good guy, doing everything possible to support humanity and leading humankind into his version of utopia. The most dangerous part of that plan was its perceived legality.

Blake reflected on his youth when he read about the 'Antichrist' and the predictions people made about it. Although Blake didn't believe in the Antichrist, he thought it was a befitting metaphor for Hampton.

If Blake couldn't prove that Hampton was doing something illegal, like money skimming, there was no avenue that he could pursue to stop Hampton other than to foster awareness in the population and outing androids. As sad as it was for him to be a fearmonger, it had to be done to spread awareness of an android invasion and worse to come.

The longer Blake thought about it, the more pessimistic he became. He let himself drift into a downhill negative spin and concluded that Hampton was planning the destruction of surplus humans, replacing them with androids to supply the workforce. Wealthy people would virtually live forever, thanks to the innovation of artificial organ replacements or becoming androids themselves; they would be left to enjoy a rejuvenated planet Earth.

"Stop this," he said out loud. He had allowed himself to dive head-over into conspiracy theory. His excuse - this or something even more ghastly - was probably in the mindset of the Zookeeper. Blake firmly believed in the adage that you must think like your enemy to understand your enemy.

More than before, Blake was keen to kidnap an android to get the ball rolling, gather the needed evidence, and expose it to the public.

He snapped out of his deep, destructive contemplation. His DIA e-car had arrived at his home and parked in the designated spot. It was time to concentrate on reality and matters at hand.

Gold Coast - Friday 21. October 2033 - Derek Hampton

Derek Hampton leaned back in his comfy arm swivel chair and looked at the ceiling. Would he find the answer he was looking for there?

He pressed a hidden button under his desk. Moments later, his companion stepped into his room. She was as beautiful as Jess Brindly, her android lookalike, with one difference: She was the real deal.

"How was it, as expected?" Jess asked.

"Pretty much, but I'm sure he knows more than I assumed. He suspects our robots collect data from the owner's computers, harvesting bank login details."

"I can't imagine he would suspect anything like your money-skimming strategy, could he?" Jess asked.

"Not sure; we have used it for a few years, and no one ever suspected anything or complained of missing money. After all, it is always only a few cents."

"Any indication at all he suspects your 'complacency' master plan?" Jess asked.

"No, nothing, not a hint; no one would suspect that ever, even you didn't. I had to explain it a few times until you recognized it as a workable philosophy.

"And you think he has no idea we will use him to facilitate part of the plan, waiting for him to expose our androids, cause panic for a couple of days, and then explain our motivation?" Jess asked, but not receiving an answer other than an encouraging nod from Derek.

Jess continued painting a beautiful picture of Derek's master plan: "The panic will go down, complacency will take over, and no one will worry about androids ever again. Even better, everyone will love your security androids, and no one will ever detect our pacifier androids."

Derek was visibly pleased with himself. If it was possible, his chest expanded while he waited for Jess to applaud.

"Do we wait for Blake to do his thing? Is there nothing else to do, no need to push him in the right direction?" Jess asked.

"No, all good. Be patient." His short reply and turning away in his chair, gripping a thin screen, said it all. The conversation was over, and Jess was expected to retreat, having played her role. The left sidewall's sliding door opened to tell her, "Disappear."

22

B lake needed the weekend to empty his mind onto sheets of paper. It was another one of his peculiar habits. Whenever his brain was overwhelmed, he switched away from his computer to pen and paper. Maybe it was the hand-brain coordination that set his creative mind free.

It didn't matter; whatever it was, it worked for Blake. He settled right down, and between writing, cooking, and leaving his unit to visit coffee houses in his neighbourhood, he made it into a joyful weekend.

At the end of those two days, he had reclaimed his equilibrium. For the first time since Jess tipped over the balcony balustrade, he felt he had regained control over his life. From now on, his goals and motivation were streamlined towards preventing the harmful influence of his now-declared personal enemy number one, the Zookeeper.

Actually, there was no need to number his enemies; he wasn't aware of any others; he was surrounded only by friends.

One of his friends, David, had called him with another snippet of information demonstrating Hampton's influence. The finance minister's wife had been allocated shares even before they had come onto the market for DIA-International Robotics; too many shares to have been given accidentally. Based on that news, Blake was sure the minister would ratify the law allowing healthcare robots to be included in Medicare.

The consequence was also predictable: DIA-International Robotics' shares would go through the roof. Who else in the government had Hampton 'donated' shares to?

Another thought had come into his mind: Are conspiracy theories just theories? Who comes up with that stuff? And considering everything else crazy we see on this planet, are those theories really so outlandish? Does one have to have a mindset or tendency to see the world in black or white or right or wrong?

Blake blamed the limited polarized view of black or white on most argumentative worldviews. He preferred a complete colour palette. We live in a colourful world, and as a journalist, he stuck to rigorous fact-checking, not leaning to one or the other side. There is always more than meets the eye.

He relied on recognizing personality traits as a skilled technique for identifying potential believers in conspiracies. In his opinion, anyone who tends to be righteous and insists on one view also tends to believe in conspiracy. Insecurity, paranoia, emotional volatility, manipulation, and egocentricity also play into it.

Blake thought those traits were not in his personality. What he knew about Hampton was real and not a conspiracy.

I better write my next article on that topic.

Something else had occurred to Blake: Conspiracies usually have a dramatic, negative, and aggressive message. Has there ever been a conspiracy theory involving peace and a comfortable lifestyle?

He wasn't aware of any; he was aware, however, of past conspiracies that have come true. He had written about that in one of his articles, "A conspiracy is a conspiracy till it isn't."

Adding all that together in his overworked brain, he admitted he needed another weekend to relax. Anxiety rose from the pit of his stomach: the android conspiracy was not a conspiracy; it was real and dangerous. Most people would not recognise the imminent danger of Hampton's plan. No conspiracy theorist will notice that something evil is brewing because of one extraordinary fact: everything Hampton has planned looks positive, peaceful, and supportive. One could even say, 'Utopia is coming'.

That was one part of the danger. There was another danger: everyone who talked against Hampton's supportive plans would be labelled a "Conspiracy Theorist".

Blake could see it coming. If he writes about the dangers of robots and androids, he will be labelled as an alarmist and conspiracy theorist, and no one will take him as a serious writer. That is why, Blake thought, Hampton is so sure of himself.

He will need all the help he can get from Jake's police reports and other government bodies.

Time to call Jake and get the android kidnapping underway.

When Blake eventually called Jake, it was past 3 pm, most likely not a good time.

"Yes?" Jake answered.

"Sorry, mate. I am touching base. When can we talk?"

"Let's have dinner at 7 pm at Southbank, the Turkish restaurant at the far south end." Jake was gone before Blake could respond.

Blake had four hours to kill, enough time to finish at least one of his articles so Frances could check if it was cutting-edge enough to attract more readers and better statistics. It was depressing that social media influences one to write targeted catchlines for better statistics.

Blake left his unit by 6:30 pm, enough time for a leisurely walk to the restaurant. Jake had already arrived, relaxing with a glass of wine.

"How long have you been here?" Blake asked.

"10 minutes; I needed a drink to unwind."

"Sounds good; I could do with a pre-dinner drink as well."

He gestured to the waitress, pointing at Jake's glass of wine.

"Why did you want to meet here to brief me on our little project?" Blake asked.

"I don't trust our mobile phone connections. I don't believe in coincidences. Kayla, the pathologist, disappeared after I talked to her. It reeks of foul play. I don't want you to disappear as well. I also don't want you to get involved directly. Here is the plan: I will be at the airport tomorrow morning with two officers in uniform and take the security guard back to the station for further questioning on suspected drug charges and a scan to make sure he hasn't hidden drugs internally."

Blake agreed, "Perfect. Do we have to notify the airport administration?"

"I talked to the airport manager; I knew him from a former drug case in the airport packing department. I asked him if the security guard, Duncan Bates, had any references. He sure had; guess what, he worked for the DIA International Office in Melbourne."

"No surprise there," Blake nodded.

Jake continued, "The operation has been well planned and will go down without a hitch. After that, we will have to let him go unless I get different legal advice, and we can hold a person suspected to be a robot or android. Obviously, it is something new, and no one has written the rulebook for androids yet.

I will pass on all findings to the CCC, and we will await their report. By the way, as your name will be mentioned in connection with Jess and her disappearance, they may contact you for questioning. That's basically it. It's time to order," Jake smiled.

"OK, it sounds like you have it all worked out, and I will be waiting on the sidelines. I would have preferred to be present when you apprehended the android to see his reaction. Will the uniforms have their body cameras activated?" Blake asked.

"Yes, of course. I may be able to show you the videos. It will be interesting to see how an android reacts. Does the android know it does something potentially wrong when it poses as a human? Will he do a runner? How fast can those things run? No wonder you want to be present; anything could happen; maybe he, or it, deactivates itself. Let's eat now; no point writing a science fiction plot now."

"Make sure you call me as soon as you get the scan."

"Will do, no worries. By the way, a lady behind you to your right, a few tables away, has been looking at you for a while. Maybe you know her?" Jake said.

Blake took a sip from his glass of wine and peered over to the right. He froze and nearly dropped his glass.

"Hey man, what's up, an old flame? Jake asked.

Blake took a deep breath and looked at Jake. "It's Jess or someone or something that looks like her, or the same person or android I saw in Rockhampton, the manager of that DIA company. How many are there, and what is she doing here? Is it another of Hampton's surveillance tricks?"

"Why don't you go and ask her?"

"I will," Blake walked over to the Jess lookalike.

"Excuse me for interrupting your meal, but you look familiar. Have we met before?"

"I thought the same, but now, when you stand in front of me, no, I don't think so, but thanks for clearing that up."

"I'm a journalist; I get around. You may have seen my profile image in my articles if you read the "Fact File News."

"Yes, I do. That's what it is. Nice articles, by the way."

"Thank you, and enjoy your meal."

"Thanks, you too."

Blake turned to walk back to his table when that lady continued, "And don't let the androids bite you."

Blake froze the second time that night. He turned slowly back, "What?"

"The ones which may come, as you mentioned in your last article," she laughed.

"I'll be careful, and you watch out too."

Blake returned to his table, looking like he needed a cold shower or a stiff drink.

"What was that all about? Did you know her?" Jake asked.

"Not sure what that was, maybe a warning? It was another Jess look-alike. As you said, you don't believe in coincidence. Was this interaction coincidental? I don't think so; I think we are being monitored. Please be careful tomorrow. Now, let's try to enjoy the rest of our meal, and I want some desserts later."

There was no further interruption; they didn't even notice when that Jess-like lady left the restaurant. They had relaxed enough to enjoy their desserts, coffee, and another couple of glasses of wine, which rounded up the night beautifully.

"Mr Jake, dear detective inspector, are you fit enough to drive?"

"Sure, we had a good meal and coffee; I am good."

"OK, drive slowly, not that you'd get a ticket."

Blake arrived at his unit half an hour later. He let himself into the lobby, took the lift up, stepped out of the lift, and froze for the third time that night.

In front of his unit door stood a 'butler robot' of similar appearance to the one he encountered at Hampton's place.

Blake composed himself once again; he was learning and getting better at it. But when he wanted to ask, 'What the heck are you doing here?' the robot beat him to it and greeted him.

"Good evening, Mr. Newcome; how can I be of service?"

"For starters, can you tell me how you got into this building?"

"My system worked out the code, and I applied it," the robot answered.

"You are one clever robot. Do you have a name?"

"Yes, I am clever, and yes, my name is James."

"Of course it is, and where do you come from, James?"

"I am coming from the outside."

"OK, can you be more specific about who delivered you here and who your owner is?"

"I have no pre-arrival memory."

"I see; this could take all night; you better come in."

Blake opened his door, which had double security: an electronic lock and an old-fashioned key lock. Not that it had helped the previous person who had violated Blake's privacy.

"Is there a way to deactivate you? Do you have an on-off switch somewhere?

"No sir, I deactivate myself to preserve power when needed."

"As you may suspect, I am worried you will hack into my computers."

"I don't suspect, but I will have to connect to your Wi-Fi to help you order supplies and tasks you want me to do."

"That was important information. Have you got a port where I can add code to your algorithm?"

"I have no information about that."

"I will bring you down and store you in my garage. I am not letting you close to my computers. You can deactivate yourself until I require your service."

"I am here to support you in any way you require," were the robot's last words for a while.

"Good, please follow me," said Blake, proceeding to walk to the lift. Sure enough, the robot followed, and they ended up in Blake's garage, where Blake locked him in.

"Good night," said Blake. *I am too polite.*

"Good night, sir," said the robot.

It didn't think anything; robots don't think, don't feel and don't care.

Blake thinks, feels and cares, and at that moment, he feels upset. *When will this ever end? I have to call Bidi tomorrow; maybe she can hack into that thing. At least I don't have to buy a robot.*

23

Blake woke up at 6 am, restless. Today was the big day; it had hardly started, and he felt tense already. He dismissed his inclination to call Bidi about the butler robot. That had to wait until he heard from Jake.

He cooked his breakfast and settled down with a new book about the harmful influences of social media and what the owners of those services are up to. It sounded like another conspiracy theory, but it was worth looking into to keep his mind from wandering into negative territory.

Brisbane - Tuesday 25. October 2033 – Jake

Jake had no restless feelings at all. He concentrated on the task at hand.

His team arrived at the domestic airport at 10.15 am.

The airport manager was aware that Jake would arrest the security officer on the grounds of drug trafficking but not the real reason behind the bust. To be on the safe side, the manager ordered the second security guard to work at the International Airport so as not to interfere.

Everything was set. The domestic airport was as busy as ever. Jake and his team waited in the background to observe the security guard's actions and behaviour. There wasn't anything to go on; the guard slowly walked up and down in his designated stretch between gates.

Time to make a move.

Jake and two uniformed officers approached the guard, who watched them approach him without raising an eyebrow.

"Are you Duncan Bates?" Jake warmed up the conversation.

"Yes, I am; what can I do for you?"

Jake presented his ID card and stated his name, rank and station. "It has come to our attention that drugs have been distributed from this domestic airport. I need you to come with us to the station for further questioning. I have notified your superior; he is aware that you have to leave your post for the day."

"Am I a suspect or only wanted for questioning?"

"At this point of our investigation, we only need you to answer some questions."

"If the manager knows, I have no objection. I need to use the toilet, if you don't mind."

"One of the officers will take you."

"That won't be necessary; I know where the toilets are."

"Good, one of the officers will escort you," Jake said.

Jake's team walked Duncan to the toilet. Duncan headed for the far corner cubicle. The officer checked; it was clear, no escape was possible.

Jake knew that androids don't need a toilet. There was a locked door at the far end. Did Duncan plan to escape?

Duncan emerged from his cubicle, still with no visible expression of worry or emotion on his face. What had he been doing, transferring data?

"What about my car? If I am not back in time, I have to pay extra, or it may be towed away," Duncan said.

"Not to worry, your boss knows about your car; time to go," Jake answered.

"And my backpack with my lunch, can I get it?" Duncan asked.

"Lunch? You seem to be avoiding coming with us to the police station. If you don't want to come, I must arrest you for hindering our police enquiry. Can we go now?" Jake asked.

Duncan nodded, and Jake guided him out of the airport to the waiting police car.

Not much later, they arrived at the police station, and Duncan was shown to the interrogation room.

As the investigating officer, Jake waited ten minutes before entering the room with a second police officer in attendance.

He followed basic procedures for commencing an electronically recorded interview, stating the time, date, and place of the interview and introducing himself again. The other officer followed suit. He also obtained a statement from Duncan that no other officer was present.

Jake had planned everything to the last detail, asking open and direct questions about the possibility that Duncan was directly involved in drug distribution or aiding the process through his authority as a security guard and officer.

Jake had also planned when to stop the interview, at which time the off-the-record interrogation would commence.

"Thank you for helping us with our enquiry," Jake said, turning off the recording device.

"We are worried you may have swallowed evidence when you insisted on visiting the toilet at the airport. If you have swallowed a condom with drugs, it may break and cause you harm. To check on your health, we have decided to do a CT scan. to ensure your health. I am sure you would like to agree to our request; if not, we must assume you are guilty of drug possession." Jake declared with a stern facial expression.

Duncan did not object, and he still showed no emotions. Had his algorithm and AI system no data on how to respond in such a situation?

Jake had arranged an open appointment at a radiology clinic. Ten minutes later, Jake, his two officers and Duncan arrived at West End Medical Imaging Services.

Duncan proved to be surprisingly serene. Didn't he know that the scan would expose him as an android?

It didn't take long. The radiologist looked pale; he handed Jake the scans and report. Jake made sure the radiologist had signed a non-disclosure document.

"It's impossible, I can't believe it," the radiologist muttered.

"Keep it that way," Jake replied, "and you better forget about it, even forget that we have been here."

Now what? Jake pondered, his mind racing with the sudden change of plans. *What do I do with him?* The original plan was to release him, but a new idea emerged. He decided to lock him up.

"We have to keep you here in a special room for your security till we know what to do with you," Jake told Duncan.

No visible reaction from Duncan.

"Do you need anything? Can you deactivate yourself or power down?" Jake asked.

"If my special room has no power source, my system will hibernate after 72 hours," Duncan answered.

The police record showed the following entry: Brisbane - Tuesday - 25. October 2033 – 14:30. The android named Duncan Bates, a security officer at the Brisbane Domestic Airport, was detained at 11:30 for the public's safety until further notice.

Jake had issued a strict order for the android's constant surveillance, a measure designed to detect any potential changes and any electronic or Wi-Fi transmissions from the android or directed towards it.

The android's present state has been recorded as:

State of being: Motionless

Submitting/receiving data: Positive - Source can't be traced.

Additional Notes: No nourishment or fluid needed.

Jake glanced at his watch. It was 15:30 pm already; Blake must be on edge. He shut his office door, sinking into his chair. Retrieving a bottle of scotch from the left lower desk drawer and a glass, he poured himself a double. He took a long, deep sip, exhaling with a sigh. He sat in silence for a few moments, trying to calm his thoughts. He hadn't felt this emotionally drained in a long time. It was official now; even though he had known about the existence of these androids for the past few days, the stark reality was like a sudden blow to his senses.

From now on, life on this planet will be different, even more different than when artificial intelligence first had an impact.

What would happen now? There were too many unknowns to make predictions. Earth had become a new planet with new rules.

The whiskey helped; Jake was ready to let Blake know and picked up his mobile.

"Hi Blake, sorry for calling late. It was the strangest investigation I have ever done, and yes, we have 100% evidence that the security guard is an android, and therefore, androids exist. I'll tell you the whole story later. For now, we have put the android on ice. All the gang should meet. I am sure Oliver and Mona can enlighten us about legal implications. They already mentioned that once we know someone is an android, it could be legally treated like a 'computer on legs'. It becomes an object. We have taken Duncan, but we can't keep him or it; we must find the owner. If we can't find the owner and no one comes forward after one year, the android becomes ours. We have to take all reasonable steps to locate the owner." Jake stopped to take another sip of his whiskey.

Blake had a question, "Did you ask him if he knows other androids or where he comes from?

"No, I didn't; I asked questions related to drug charges, but we detected Wi-Fi transmission. Maybe Bidi can work her magic and decode the transmitted data. Our cyber security guys are still working on it. Anyhow, let's get the guys together as soon as possible, preferably at a neutral place, maybe even out in the open. We don't want to get confronted by more androids."

"Good idea; which day is best to schedule the next meeting, and what will you do next?" Blake asked

"I will pass on my report to the CCC. It needs to be processed quickly, and maybe we can even get an appointment with our prime minister before the election at the end of the month. Can you call everyone and organise the meeting for Friday the 28th?"

"Yes, sure. I wonder what will happen and what the other guys think about the new android paradigm. It's like the full realisation of androids hits you more and more. Since the Jess incident, I feel as if I am in suspended animation. Nothing seems real anymore, even though it is more real than ever. OK, Jake, you do your thing. I don't want to hold you up with deep philosophical questions. Catch up soon." Blake put down his mobile. It was his time for a Scotch.

Nothing new had occurred other than the final undeniable fact: Androids do exist, and not only in the domain of science fiction.

What else was in Hampton's mind? Blake wondered. How far has Hampton's mind expanded? Is he aiming to become an android himself and live forever?

24

B lake arranged the meeting for 4:30 pm at Musgrave Park. He had brought blankets, beer, and his signature homemade bread and dips. Nothing looked more harmless than a few people relaxing in the park late afternoon after work.

Blake arrived first, 15 minutes early, to set the scene, making sure to pick a spot away from any possible Wi-Fi connection.

As Bidi arrived, Blake couldn't help but feel a surge of anticipation. "Is it ready?" he asked, his voice barely concealing his excitement.

"Yes, it's all set up, "Bidi confirmed. "It's a simple concept. I re-coded and combined a few existing apps into a new, single app. And the best part? It comes with a surprisingly low price tag. If it takes off, it could potentially bring in a substantial amount of money. I've decided to donate 50% of the profits to our group as a fighting fund."

Before Blake could answer, Jake arrived with Oliver and Mona. Dave parked his car at Russell Street and walked over to the cosy picnic setting.

Blake welcomed everyone, handed out the beers, and summarised what had happened in the last few days before asking Jake to give them the newest information.

"I still feel weird about having an android at the police station locked up. It's too alien. One day after I gave all the information to the CCC, they contacted me to let me know the government machinery had taken over, indicating that the new security threat of androids had become the internal security issue number one."

Bidi interrupted, "I don't know much about the CCC, but why haven't they taken the android for further investigation?"

Jake answered, "I was coming to that point; yes, the android has left the building, but the CCC is not responsible for taking that action; ASIS security officers picked him up in a black limousine. Do you want to hear something funny? I felt sorry for dear old Duncan Bates. How can one possibly feel sorry for an android, I ask myself?"

Mona nodded and gave her two cents worth: "It's easy. Whatever you give your attention to creates feelings, leading to emotions and attachments. Lots of people are more attached to their cars than their partners."

"Sure, Mona, it still surprised me, and I think it was the android's humanity and resignation that got me," Jake said. But let me continue. Blake and I are invited or requested to be present at 1 William Street on Monday, the 31st of October, at 11 am at the reception desk. We will be led to a meeting room to talk to the prime minister and other related officials. It's not called the 'Tower of Power' for nothing.

I probably don't have to mention it; you know about the upcoming election and the prime minister's shaky re-election status. The android issue, and how it will be handled, could be the deciding factor for the prime minister's party to be re-elected." Jake paused and looked at Blake, "By the way, the prime minister knows about your idea for citizens to become 'Certified Humans' using a chip implant. I had to let them know." Jake raised his hands in apology.

"Thanks, Jake. I'm not sure I want to be that deeply involved, but it's too late to run away from it. Bidi, you are next," Blake said.

Bidi didn't take long to explain her app and showed them where and how to pay to download it onto their mobiles.

"Thanks, guys. You are the first to buy the app; I feel rich already. Imagine a million people buying it at five bucks a pop. The potential for that to happen is real. To say I'm excited is an understatement. I guess it depends on what we and the government do to inform the public about the androids."

Blake took over, "For that to happen, we need to wait for the government. I've prepared an article that will hit the news tomorrow morning. I have mentioned the app and recommended downloading it for people to be sure who they are dealing with.

The app download count will indicate how many people take the message on board," Blake said before addressing Oliver and Mona.

"OK, so far so good. Are there any legal implications to what we are doing?"

Mona, speaking for Oliver and herself, answered, "No, everything we mentioned to Jake is still relevant and true. Now that we know for a fact that androids are among us, we can deal with them as we deal with our mobiles or computers. Androids are just computers on legs. If it comes to legal interpretation, they have no special rights as yet. However, that could change in the future, and it probably will. If androids become part of daily life, they will need basic rights. One thing is certain: life will change for all of us."

"Thanks, Mona. Dave, what do you have for us? You are the one dealing directly with DIA," Blake asked.

"I wish I could contribute more, but I have nothing on androids. However, it's a strong possibility that wherever DIA International has factories, whether for robots or e-cars, they may also create their androids. Maybe that is something we have to check?" Dave said.

"Thanks, Dave. Yes, we will soon know to what extent androids are distributed. I am sure that after my article hits the news and spreads over the Internet, people will download Bidi's app, and surely, if anyone detects an android, they will post it on their social media accounts.

By the end of next week, I guess the Internet will be awash with android discovery stories, Bidi's bank account will be bursting with money, and she will be a self-made millionaire. And something else," Blake said, looking over to Mona.

"I wanted to suggest inviting George, the forensic accountant, to our meetings. I am sure the androids have more functions than simply hanging around, working, and looking pretty. If basic household robots can log into home computers, androids can do that as well. Maybe they are capable of getting into your mobile phones by being in close proximity to you to access your bank details. Are we all in favour of inviting George?" Blake asked.

Mona interrupted, "George has not been in contact. I don't think we can count on him anymore. He indicated the android business was too much for him to handle."

"I completely understand. The invitation was just a way to include him," Blake said. "OK, are we all good? No more questions? Then let's have another beer."

The official part of the meeting had ended, but they stayed on to enjoy the newfound relaxation of a simple picnic in a park. They even talked about Mark and how he would feel about the androids.

It was past 8 pm and dark when everyone made their way home. Bidi left with Blake; he wanted to show her the butler robot he had in his garage. He hoped that Bidi could hack into the robot and learn more about its capabilities, particularly its function to log into someone's computer and extract vital data like accounts and passwords. He needed more strong-hitting info for his article when it came out tomorrow.

"Here he is," Blake said, opening the door to his garage and storage lockup.

"Let's wake him up. Hi James, are you awake?"

Apparently, he was. He came out of hibernation, and his first question was, "Yes, sir, what can I do for you?"

"You can give us access to your database," Blake said, wondering what that instruction would do. It didn't do anything.

"Sorry, sir, I have no capability to grant you access."

Blake turned to Bidi, "What do you think? Can you do anything? I don't want to bring him into my unit for obvious reasons.

Would you mind trying to get access down here? I have to get up and finish my article; Frances will be waiting for it."

"Yes, sure, go up," Bidi took her laptop from her backpack. "Will you still be working in a couple of hours?" she asked Blake.

"Yes, probably much longer; if you are not up by 1 am, I will get you."

Blake left, taking the lift to his unit.

After a quick drink, Blake sat at his desk, fired up his laptop, and continued his hopefully hard-hitting story. Most of it was already written, but it needed the information he had gathered from the meeting and a few rewrites.

He looked at his headline. Was it punchy enough? It needed to be clear, factual, and a call for action.

'*Androids Confirmed Working and Walking Among Us!*'

Will androids take over our workforce? Find out if your neighbour, co-worker or lover is an android. Learn how you can tell the difference between a human and an android.'

Blake wasn't proud of what he had written, but he didn't write it to win a literary award; he wrote it to scare the public into action. The rest of the article went into details and possible future scenarios.

At the end of the article, he stressed that everyone needs to help expose androids and demand that the government formulate laws and policies to keep citizens safe.

He further stressed that the government was aware of this and that the prime minister had established a task force to deal with it; undoubtedly, it would become an important election issue.

In between, and voicing it carefully, he added a section about the availability of apps that can indicate if a person is an android.

He had Bidi's details. Her apps were easy to find and download, with names like Android Detect, Android Wi-Fi, and Find Android.

Bidi had her android app duplicated and uploaded under different names to ensure it could withstand a rush of downloads without crashing. By duplicating under various names, traffic would be dispersed over numerous platforms.

Blake spent another hour carefully revising the article before he emailed it to Frances. He had talked to her before the afternoon meeting. She was expecting his email, but probably not that late. It was 1:00 am, time to rescue Bidi from her garage workstation.

Blake was on the way out of his unit when he heard a ping. He knew it could be only one thing: Frances was still awake and had replied to his email. He quickly checked. Yes, she thought it would work. Blake responded to her email, 'Thank you,' and left his unit.

Bidi was immersed in her world and had lost track of time.

"How did you go?" Blake asked.

Bidi jumped. "Oh, you scared me; I didn't hear you coming. Yes, it went well, up to a certain degree. I could hack in, connect my laptop, and access and download the data already collected by the robot, such as your address, name, and code, to open the door to the ground-floor lobby.

It also had the code to open your unit door but could not unlock your old-fashioned key lock. Haha, it didn't have a key or something to pick a lock. It's funny; if you think about it, your liking for vintage gadgets and lifestyle has protected you."

"Anything else?" Blake asked.

"We know your butler is capable of hacking into whatever, storing the data, and transmitting it. So far, I have been unable to add codes to stop the robot from accessing your computer data. But I could add codes for movements and navigation. If your robot moves or tries to run away, we can track him down. Anyhow, you better leave the robot down here, out of harm's way."

Bidi closed her laptop, gave a long sigh and stood up, stretching her weary limbs.

"You look tired," Blake said. "Better come up, have a drink, and crash on my couch. I have sent off the article already. Frances has replied and is working on it. It will be good to have you here in the morning once the 'shit hits the fan'. The hardcopy newspaper will be delayed and on the streets by 9 am. The worldwide online version will be out by 5 am. Let's get some sleep."

25

Blake had set the alarm for 5 am. He dragged himself out of bed into the bathroom and bravely had a cold shower. Halfway revived, he dried off, smartened himself up, and prepared breakfast. Bidi was still flat out on the couch, not moving.

Blake, with a mix of excitement and nervousness, calculated the first reaction to his article could surface on social media by 5:30 am, with downloads of the app likely to start around 6 am. Would there be a buzz on the news already? He switched on the TV, eager to see the world's response, and woke up Bidi.

"Wake up, sleepy head, let the fun begin."

Bidi took a moment to collect her thoughts and fumbled for her mobile. She looked up to Blake in disbelief.

"It has started," she said. "There have been a few hundred downloads already, and I haven't even checked all the apps yet."

"Get yourself ready for breakfast. There's no point checking downloads every few minutes. You will be a millionaire by tonight. Can those apps crash, or did you do something to prevent that?

"That's why I duplicated the apps, all with different names. In addition, I added a code to add downloads to a queue. That queue automatically stops before it crashes and issues a message to try again in 10 min."

"All good then."

The 6 am news came on. Sure enough, it briefly mentioned the android article and that they had tried to contact the author. Blake checked his email and messages; yes, he had several interview requests. He would call them back later when he better understood the public's reaction.

Next, he checked his social media accounts. He wondered who would look at their mobiles that early. Apparently, a lot of people do, certainly more than he had expected.

"Hurry up, Bidi," Blake called out. "It has started big time. The first conspiracy theories have emerged. Some claim it is the government itself that has created the androids to control its citizens. They are calling for a demonstration."

Posts, calling him a vulture, a cash-grabbing bastard, and a scammer, also confronted Blake. People didn't believe his article and claimed he wanted to scam people out of their money. Other posts called to boycott the app.

So far, negative comments received more traction.

Bidi came out of the bathroom and sat down at the kitchen island. She looked at her mobile, checking her apps, not just the downloads, but from where those downloads were made.

"People have downloaded from the USA, most European countries, Russia, Hong Kong, China, everywhere; your article post has gone viral," Bidi said.

"Look at these posts; people have exposed androids already. Some posted images to name and shame. Let's hope it will not get out of hand. I'm feeling worried for the androids," Blake said.

Blake's mobile rang; it was Mona, and she sounded worried.

"Someone smashed up an android. Can the 'Fact File News' post a follow-up? People need guidelines on what to do if they have detected an android. Smashing up private property, and that's what an android is under the law, will lead to major legal consequences. Someone will sue for serious money," Mona explained.

"I will get onto that straight away. If you like, come over and follow the action from my place. I will call Frances now."

Blake's social accounts were inundated with android response posts. He quickly posted basic instructions and pinned them to the top of his account.

* Identifying an android is all you need to be aware of; don't do anything

else.

* Do not, under any circumstances, act aggressively.

* Attacking or harming an android will have serious legal consequences. The android's owner may sue for hundreds of thousands of dollars in damages.

* NOTE: Androids have artificial intelligence, and as the name suggests, the intelligence is artificial and based on data. Humans think, but androids sort data and calculate without emotion and consequences. Therefore, they may sometimes react differently than you expected. Don't aggravate them.

After a couple of minutes, the first responses to Blake's post came in. He felt better already and called Frances.

Frances had seen his post, copied it, and pinned it on the Fact File News social media outlets.

The hardcopy newspaper appeared on Sydney's newsstands at 9:30 am; by then, it had not triggered any specific reactions.

That's all Blake and Frances could do now: monitor and answer questions.

The onslaught of heated discussion on social media continued. So far, they were aware of two severe cases where androids had been attacked.

Blake scanned all of DIA's media outlets, but they didn't mention the android article. They either hadn't seen it or decided not to comment. Blake wondered how long it would take before someone would ask a probing question on DIA's news feed.

By lunchtime, the whole crew had assembled at Blake's place. The mood was upbeat; the slight stress of the first reaction had diminished and was replaced by a more positive mood aided by Blake's decision to cook for all.

There was something else: everyone kept an eye on Bidi, who sat in utter disbelief in front of her mobile phone, trying to keep track of the downloads that had reached the millions.

Blake handed out beers; "Let's toast Bidi for being the newest millionaire. Here's to Bidi!"

Being the level-headed solicitor, Oliver turned the discussion back to possible consequences.

"We must be aware that other news outlets will likely figure it out that someone made a ton of money from Blake's articles and the Fact File News. Like some of the social media posts, they might accuse you of setting all this up as a ploy to sell the app."

"We may not have to worry about that too much. The prime minister will do his speech about androids, including devising new laws and, of course, claiming that only he and his party can handle this issue. It may well be the issue that gets him re-elected. He will use fear as a motivator, pass laws aiding his party and recommend Bidi's app." Blake said.

"One thing is sure: now that we have androids among us that we can't easily tell apart from humans, new laws need to protect us and the androids. For example, what happens if an android is raped? Can androids be switched off? There are probably hundreds of scenarios we don't know yet, but they will need to be addressed by lawmakers in the future." Blake looked around before continuing.

"We found out a few days ago that Sir Koblinski, the crown prosecutor, has a double as an android. Is the Koblinski android used to infiltrate the law system in this country? How do we deal with that, and how many androids will we come across in higher positions? So far, it seems they haven't worked their way up into high political positions. So, the question for our politicians is: What kind of position are androids allowed to have?"

"Hopefully none," Dave cut in before Blake continued.

"I will write my next article about those real and hypothetical questions and their answers. I also think the prime minister loves all this. There is nothing better for a party to keep power by concentrating on a new problem, causing fear, and offering their party's policy solutions. Anyhow, lunch is ready, let's eat." Blake said.

26

T wenty-five days to go, the election was looming, and the prime minister had the time of his life. It was now or never. He could make the android crisis his saving grace.

Blake wasn't sure if it was an honour to meet the prime minister or not. He hadn't done anything special to deserve that privilege, if it could be called that. He had a relatively low opinion of politicians, the political system and the process. He didn't display his dislike much to other people. Still, deep in his mind, he despised political discourse and media appearances where ministers attack and usually denounce the opposing party's policies to look right or better themselves.

That morning, Blake left his unit and walked to 1 William Street; there was no point in taking a car and finding a parking space.

As always, he arrived early and took a moment to absorb the surroundings, having never been in the tower of power before. Yes, it smelt, felt and looked like power.

He approached the reception desk.

"Good Morning. My name is Blake Newcome. I am supposed to be here at 11 am and wait at reception for someone to meet me."

"Someone will come to collect you in a moment. Please take a seat." The receptionist pressed some buttons and spoke a few words into the receiver.

A few minutes later, a professional-looking young lady dressed in a dark suit approached him from the elevators.

"Good morning, Mr. Newcome. My name is Gloria. Will you please follow me to the conference room?"

Blake followed Gloria to the lift, unable to resist the urge to activate the android detection app. He was relieved to find she was human. It reminded him of his visit to Hampton, where he was guided by a butler robot. He couldn't help but prefer the human touch, even though Gloria's behaviour mimicked that of a robot, too formal for his liking. He understood, of course, that this was a crucial meeting with the prime minister and other high-ranking officials.

Gloria opened an oversized door without knocking. Blake stepped into a high-class space with elegant furniture, expensive-looking abstract paintings decorating the walls, and strategically placed pot plants.

At a large conference table, Blake counted 17 people, all in dark business suits, including the women. One chair was unoccupied; it was next to Jake's spot on that intimidating table. Jake nodded his head towards the chair. Conversations had stopped while Blake sat down. He had thought he was too early. Why was everyone here already, including the prime minister and other ministers? Was there a reason they started without him?

Blake leaned over to Jake, "How come everyone is here already?" Jake nodded and stood up.

"Please, let me introduce Blake Newcome. Most of you will know Blake from his column in the Fact File News. Let me state the obvious: we wouldn't be here without Blake. It was his encounter with an android, his incredible personal experience, and his investigative journalistic abilities that opened up a new paradigm of life in this country and probably for the entire planet.

"His latest article, which came out on Friday, has introduced the concept that we live with androids and how to detect them. The feedback worldwide has been phenomenal and has thrown up more questions than answers.

"Today, we are here to urge the prime minister and his government to develop new policies regarding security and other implications for our country's future.

"The main laws we can apply to androids in their present state are property laws, seeing an android like a computer with legs. However, whereas computers usually can be tracked down to their owners, so far, no one has come forward to claim the androids that walk among us. This leaves us facing a dilemma with no existing guidelines for how to react when encountering an android. Recently, I had an android in captivity, if it can be said that way. The android had done nothing wrong. Its captivity was purely to obtain evidence that androids exist. A CT scan proved it was an android without a doubt.

"The question arises, what do we do with that android? Send it back to work at the airport, which it fulfilled without a fault? No, we couldn't; in that particular case, ASIS collected the android, and I have no further details about it." One of the ministers raised his hand, "I wondered, did the android show any aggression towards you?"

Jake shook his head, "No, not at all. In human terms, I would have described him as a perfectly behaved prisoner, calm and obliging. There is one more confusing issue linked to my department. The Queensland Crown prosecutor, Sir Koblinski, or a look-alike, has tested as an android.

Sir Koblinski, or his double, was also instrumental in collecting Jessica Brindly from the morgue. Does Sir Koblinski know he has an android double? Does he have information about who manufactured and owns the androids? How did he or the android know to collect an android from the morgue?"

The prime minister interrupted Jake's questions.

"Can we arrange to have Sir Koblinski present himself here within the next 30 minutes?"

One of the seated participants answered, "We will collect him now," he said and walked out of the room.

Must be someone from security or federal police, Blake thought.

Jake continued, "I will now hand you over to Mr Newcome, who will give you more insight and address questions that need to be answered, as well as possible solutions to differentiate humans from androids.

Blake stood up and waited to get everyone's attention before addressing the table.

"The most urgent policies that need to be released are ones to inform our human population how to deal with androids.

Consider questions such as: Is it an offence to damage an android? What rights do androids have? Various companies already employ androids; how did that happen? Did those androids look actively for work, or does someone want them to work in a specific company or position? I have detected that a few lobbyists are androids. One android has successfully lobbied to make household robots a Medicare item, which can be prescribed by a general practitioner. Once again, the company behind it is DIA International."

The prime minister objected, frowning at Blake, "At no time were we aware that androids have been used for lobbying."

"That's right, no one knew. And I am not accusing anyone, but pointing out the facts about how we have been infiltrated by androids already.

We know the person pulling the strings but have no hard evidence. So far, whatever that person and his business conglomerate do is legal. That person is Derek Hampton, and he claims to be in service to humanity. We can't prove any wrongdoings by him; he seems above board."

Blake addressed the prime minister directly: "Prime Minister, your government may have more information about Hampton than we have. After all, he has won huge contracts regarding household robots and generous tax concessions for building his manufacturing facilities in Australia, including for the DIA E-cars. My research has proven he is behind the manufacturing and distribution of androids. It's up to the government to control what he or his company is planning or doing to influence our daily lives."

The prime minister answered, "That's why we are here."

"Thank you, Prime Minister. Back to the androids. One way to detect an android is through an app a friend of ours has created. Other options, like scans, are possible but much too involved. To permanently tell androids apart from humans, I recommend considering a device, like an implanted chip, certifying someone as a human being.

I am aware of the privacy implications and, under normal circumstances, would warn against such a device. But the government could roll that out like voluntary vaccination. People who want to be certified humans will get injected with a chip. Information on that chip is protected by blockchain technology, which stores personal data, like names, plus DNA and a family history of two or three generations.

An android doesn't have a family or DNA. However, it has to be ensured that those chips and information can't be copied and implanted into an android. I am not a technician; the government must procure the technology to make that possible."

Blake had finished his long speech when the door opened, and two security guards entered the room, with Sir Koblinski between them.

The prime minister addressed him, "Sir Koblinski, thank you for coming and assisting with our enquiries. I am sure you are well aware of the content that has hit news outlets and social media about the discovery of androids. We are here to discuss the implications.

Please don't be offended, but a couple of highly regarded people have used their android detection app and confirmed that you or a double is an android. Can you say ...." The prime minister couldn't finish his sentence; Sir Koblinski was outraged and interrupted.

"That is preposterous; how is that even possible? I demand an apology. I am as human as hopefully you all are. I want to be tested now."

"Mr Newcome," the prime minister looked at Blake, "do you have a testing device?."

Blake stood up and walked around the large conference table towards Sir Koblinski. Everyone turned in that direction.

"Yes, I can do a test now. Excuse me, Sir Koblinski. I have an ultrasound pad connected to a mobile app here. May I please hold your upper arm for a few seconds?"

Koblinski, with a stern but annoyed facial expression, held out his arm.

"Thank you, sir," Blake touched Sir Koblinski's arm with the scan pad and activated the detection app. "OK, all done; I can assure everyone that Sir Koblinski is human."

Koblinski pulled back his arm and stormed towards the door, calling, "That's not the end of it; you will hear from me."

The prime minister became active. He stood up, calling, "Please, sir, stay with us. This android problem concerns everyone, including you. You have been a victim of it, something we are working on policies and laws to avoid in the future. Please take a seat." The prime minister sat down, looking over to Blake, who stood up.

"We have witnessed another problem with androids. Whoever is behind that, and I think we all know who that is, has intentionally created an android with the likeness of a real human being to take advantage of a specific situation. We can all agree that it is of the utmost importance to certify humans and be able to detect androids.

I cannot add anything else; it is now up to the government to take appropriate action. Prime Minister, the election is coming up in three weeks. I don't have to tell you that having policies in place would be to the government's advantage. Thank you for allowing me to speak today." Blake sat down, looking at Jake, who nodded his approval. A moment later, Blake stood up again.

"Sorry, one last issue. Our team has done research into what we call nano-skimming. Hampton's household robots hack into their owners' computers and bank accounts, skimming small amounts of money off the accounts. Small enough that no one will notice, a few cents at a time. We have been unable to follow the money trail or link the fraudulent behaviour to Hampton. This could be something for the appropriate government departments.

If the government or police can prove illegal behaviour by those service robots, it will be one way to take Hampton to court. Our team has another theory that may sound like a conspiracy: Hampton's ultimate aim is to foster complacency in society and infiltrate the government. This is a serious threat that we cannot afford to ignore." Blake concluded, his words resonating in the room.

The prime minister acknowledged Blake's speech with a thank you. Did some of the guys roll their eyes? The discussion continued, but not in the manner Blake expected.

The social minister, in an earnest tone, cautioned the rest of the political audience about the opposition's potential claims of fraudulent activities. He emphasized it was a significant issue, as someone had profited from selling the app. To underscore his point, he directed a critical gaze towards Blake and added, "The apps should have been free to download."

Blake answered, "I will discuss that with Bianca, our cyberspace expert who developed those apps in her own time. Free apps are often not valued as important enough to download. Now, where the android issue has been discussed, a free app will be feasible."

The discussions became more heated about the 'Certified Human' topic. Inserting people with a chip was highly controversial. No one around the table thought it was possible to get the opposition or Senate to agree to a law like that, and no one suggested possible solutions.

Blake and Jake stayed on for a bit longer, but the discussion became tedious. No one made any constructive suggestions about how to deal with this brand-new phenomenon.

The prime minister, firm and decisive, took charge and ended the unruly discussion. He announced, "We will establish three working groups: one to set up rules and regulations of permission to employ androids, the second to investigate all avenues to track down ownership, and the third one to establish policies of ethics and behaviours towards androids, as well as working out the 'Certified Human' chip dilemma." He looked around the table as to check if everyone understood that he was deadly serious.

"I will engage with the public tonight in a TV interview, simply outlining that androids do not harm; they are here to support humans and can be employed for a range of services. I will also outline that harming an android in any way will be a criminal offence; the perpetrator will be charged with property destruction." He stopped and turned to Jake and Blake.

"Mr. Newcome and Mr. Benson, thank you for coming forward and informing the appropriate departments. Please be assured that we deeply appreciate your commitment. However, we would like to remind you that the topic of android investigation is now in the hands of the government. You can leave the meeting now. Thank you again. Mr. Newcome, my private secretary, will speak with you in another room. Please follow him."

That was it. Blake and Jake had been politely dismissed with a hint of a warning not to interfere by carrying out further investigation. Did the prime minister forget that Blake was an investigative journalist? And what about Jake? Any day now, he could be confronted with further android offences, by them or against them.

Blake went with the private secretary into an empty room.

"Please close the door behind you," the secretary said. "The prime minister is a good man. He is doing more than his fair share. He has a few private consultants who have a particular skill or know-how and are not bound by party political rules. He wants you to become his consultant in your specialty. He has followed your articles for years and appreciates your writing style of not dramatizing an issue but bringing awareness in an unbiased way to new technologies and, lately, to your cautious approach to the android issue.

He will consider your proposal for the implant to be certified as human. Here is the prime minister's private mobile number; he will answer with his first name, Dean. The calls will be encrypted. Only call him if you have new important information; otherwise, he will call you if he has a question. This is top secret and needs to stay top secret, so don't tell anyone. Don't tell Mr Jake Benson." The secretary opened the door for Blake to leave.

Jake and Blake left the building, which was easier than entering it.

"What did they want to discuss?" Jake asked.

"A caution of what not to write about, not to interfere with the election," Blake said.

They said goodbye and fixed 6 pm to have a beer after work.

Blake walked home and, for the first time, bought a newspaper from the competition. The headline was not something he could walk past.

The competition news wasted no time rubbishing the Fact File News and Blake in particular.

'Blake Newcome, the renowned journalist of Fact File News, known for his pursuit of truth, is now accused of spouting panic-inspiring conspiracy theories.'

Blake looked forward to having a late lunch to read what else they had to say.

As expected, the article was full of fear and innuendoes, not because of androids but because of what they called the unscrupulous reporting of misinformation and conspiracy. They also had a different take, claiming that androids and robots have been around for a long time; why the sudden hype, they asked?

Were they claiming they knew about androids? That is a new one, Blake thought. Could they be a part of Hampton's scheme? They didn't address the app to detect androids, as if to dismiss that possibility altogether. All the reporting were negative assumptions about Blake's articles and motivation.

There was no need to write a counter article. Blake would wait for the prime minister's announcement before considering his next move. Instead, he concentrated his article writing efforts on data collection by internet-connected devices, such as e-cars, not primary DIA e-cars, but any e-car brands. All those devices collect data, something most people don't expect or know.

He sketched out some notes of what he wanted to write. The e-car data collection function cannot be disabled. In other words, people must be selective about what they communicate in their cars. The e-car knows everything, starting with the car location, where you drive every day, your routine, where you park, and where you shop. Making any mobile calls? Guess what? All phone numbers dialled from within the car are collected, even email addresses. The mobile is connected to the car, and that clever e-car collects everything on the mobile.

Blake had fallen into writing mode. He felt like continuing but needed to get back to his unit. A thought flashed through his mind. His DIA e-car was parked where he had stored the robot. Could it be possible for them to talk to each other, exchange data, and maybe plan an escape? Was he going bonkers? Did he take his speculation too far?

There is but a tiny step from reality to conspiracy. Blake couldn't help himself and rushed home to relocate the robot. Maybe Bidi was interested in studying it more.

He called her, "Hi Bidi, are you interested in having my robot at your place for further study?"

"No thanks, mate, I don't want that thing anywhere near me."

Blake laughed, "OK, fair enough. Do you have any idea what I should do with it?"

"Sure, store it somewhere without power devices nearby to force the robot to stay in hibernation."

"OK, I will do that. Is there any news on your apps?"

"They are still being downloaded; I don't even know what to do with all the money. Maybe we can meet and create ideas on how to use it for something ethical, supporting a valuable charity or similar," Bidi said.

"At the meeting this morning with the prime minister, that topic came up. One minister suggested that it be made available for free download. Would you consider that?

"I have to think about it. It's not about the money. There are functional aspects as well. I prefer to leave it as it is, and use the money for a good cause. Maybe you can mention that in one of your articles. I don't want to be classified as a greedy bitch."

"You are right; the money is more valuable if it goes to a good cause, and people don't mind paying a couple of dollars for something valuable. Maybe add a note about that to your apps? OK, have to rush, immobilizing my robot."

Unable to offload his robot to Bidi, Blake went straight to his underground garage. Nothing had changed; his car and the robot were well-behaved. Had they talked to each other? He wished he would know. Does he need to get another car? Was he getting paranoid? What to do with this bloody robot? He was tempted to chuck it into the Brisbane River.

He rang Jake and discussed possible storage options. Jake thought it could be helpful to have a robot on standby. They had some storage rooms at the Police headquarters at Roma Street. He promised to send someone to collect it.

Blake reminded Jake not to forget to watch the prime minister's address on any news channel, probably between 6 and 8 pm.

Up in his unit, he switched on the telly, made himself a cup of coffee and settled down with one of his homemade cookies.

Flicking around the channels, he noticed that the prime minister's media department had been busy. Every channel had a message ticker: 'Special Prime Minister's public address at 7:00 pm'.

Blake didn't feel like working on his next article anymore; he wanted it to be 7:00 pm.

He pulled out his pots and pans, knives, and every ingredient for a delectable meal, using cooking to distract himself from the impending address. "OK, stop now, start cooking," he called out, trying to silence his racing thoughts.

Twenty minutes into his cooking, a sudden thought struck Blake. Did the prime minister's gov.au media website have more information on the PM's speech? He hurriedly checked on his computer. There it was: Monday 31. October 2033 – 7:00 pm – Prime Minister's response to the public! Androids among us: consequences, task forces, rules and regulations.

That was it; no further information; back to cooking.

Another 10 minutes of frantic food preparations. He wasn't entirely focused; his mind didn't stop chatting away. He put down his knife, carrots half chopped. Frances, that's right, he had to call Frances.

"Frances, darling, have you seen the news? The PM's address is coming soon at 7."

"Yes, seen it, you sound worried, what's bothering you?"

"Not sure; I am having these foreboding thoughts; the PM may screw up the whole issue and create even more fear. Are you prepared for a quick response on your channels?"

"No worries, I am sitting here in my office with our political team of four. Whatever will come up, we can address it quickly. We are not worried at all; we think it's fun. Everyone wants to see what spin the PM dishes out to save his ass for the upcoming election."

"I'm too deeply involved; I wish I could be with you."

"Why don't you cook something?"

"Haha, that's very funny. I am cooking, but it's not working today. Anyhow, I feel better now. Thanks, love you, and hope to see you soon." Blake put down his mobile and picked up his knife, smiling. He managed to get his meal cooked in time before 7:00 pm. He tucked in Chicken Francese with his usual addition of lots of veggies cooked in the same sauce.

With a few minutes to go, Blake fetched a glass of red. He was settled now, all worries gone. He knew he could respond to whatever the PM's message was.

He flicked around social media channels; the PM's upcoming message was everywhere. Blake had never experienced anything like that, such as a PM on all channels, TV, and social media. It was unheard of. Everyone would notice the seriousness of this announcement. He had to credit the PM's media department for pulling that off in a limited time frame.

7:00 pm

Here we go; there he is. That is new. He is not hiding behind a big desk; he is standing next to it, coming across as a strong, competent and forceful leader addressing his citizens.

"Good evening to you too," Blake answered the PM's initial greeting.

The PM opted for a positive spin on his latest policies:

"For the last two decades, we have accepted and become accustomed to household robots supporting our senior citizens. Robots have been a blessing for the elderly to such an extent that we have taken the unusual step to add care robots to the Pharmaceutical Benefits Scheme (PBS), making them available through Medicare and a Doctor's prescription."

The PM allowed a short dramatic pause before putting on a solemn statesman's face and delivering the message everyone wanted to hear.

"Androids can be a possible further advance to help humans navigate our journey to old age. Androids can also have a meaningful role in services and support in work situations we may find challenging." He allowed a small pause, looking meaningful into the camera.

"As much as we are supporting technical advances to the benefit of humanity, we have to draw the line at androids infiltrating society pretending to be humans. At this point in time, no identity or company has come forward claiming the manufacturing of androids and their distribution. Therefore, we as a government take the infiltration of androids into our society extremely seriously and have commenced investigations." The camera switched to an info-board while the PM kept talking.

"The government has formed several task forces.

One: Investigation into the ownership of androids.

Two: Detection of androids and marking androids.

Three: Establishing policies of ethics and behaviours towards androids, as well as rules, regulations, and permits to employ androids."

The camera went back, focusing on the prime minister, a close-up.

"At present, androids work as security guards at airports. In the future, they will wear a uniform, which sets them up as visible androids. We call those androids security androids. A new rule regarding androids specifies they cannot leave the airport unless they keep wearing their uniform." The PM hesitated for a bit before coming out with his most controversial message.

"To further safeguard our citizens, we are working on a system to 'Certify Humans'. After all, if you meet someone, you would like to know if that person is a human. To be certified as a human would avoid this dilemma. We are happy to inform you that some of the rules and regulations will be passed as policies before the upcoming election, assuring you, as a citizen of this great country, will be safe and can rely on your government. Thank you, and good night, Australia."

The PM was done, and regular programs continued.

Blake wasn't sure what to think. Maybe the last few weeks had turned him over to the negative side. He felt the PM would launch and go all out for a fear campaign. Instead, the speech was nicely turned down, with a hint of fear, which could be considered reasonable. He covered all the essential points but never mentioned the app. *The private secretary was right, the prime minister is a good man,* Blake thought.

Blake switched off the TV; he had had enough for one day. A last look at social media confirmed his suspicion: the hype about androids had calmed down.

He will contact Bidi tomorrow to see if downloads of the app have slowed down, too.

Why weren't people more alarmed about the androids? Blake thought. *Surely, their concern would be more significant if they had experienced what he had. After all, it's not every day that a naked android plummets from a balcony.*

Blake decided to observe media responses over the next few days before considering his next steps.

27

Blake was still in bed when the doorbell rang. A few seconds later, there was a knock on his unit door. *Jake must have sent someone to pick up the robot. 8 am - did it have to be that early?* He hadn't planned it. He wanted to sleep in and have a well-deserved rest for a change. He rose, put on a pair of shorts and a T-shirt, and went to the door.

"Yes, who is it?"

"I am here to collect the robot." the voice said.

Blake opened the door. He expected a uniform, but the guy wore jeans and a shirt. "Hi, thanks for coming. I'll be back in a sec, just getting my shoes."

They took the lift to the basement and walked towards Blake's garage and storage section.

"Here we are," Blake said and opened the door. "We may have to carry him if he doesn't come out of hibernation."

"Is it a he? The guy looked puzzled.

"It must be. He told me his name is James, but then, it is a robot; it can be whatever you want it to be," Blake answered.

They shook it and tried to lift it but couldn't get a good grip.

"I can grab a trolley from the car," the guy suggested.

At that moment, James, the robot, woke up.

"Good Morning, sir. Can I be of assistance?"

"Yes, you can; follow us to the car park; you are going for a ride," Blake answered.

It worked. They took the lift to the ground floor and continued towards a small but proper removal truck; it even had a lift at the back.

"Now what?" Blake said," The robot is not designed for travelling in a truck?"

The guy let down the hydraulic lift platform and asked the robot to stand on it. The platform lifted, and the robot rolled into the truck. Two belts from the side of the truck cabin helped squeeze the robot securely against the cabin wall.

"That works well; you have done that before, right?" Blake asked harmlessly enough.

The guy grinned, "That's it, thanks for helping."

"Bye, James. Have a good trip." In a funny mood, Blake waved the robot goodbye and returned to his unit - time for breakfast.

A couple of hours later, Blake's mobile rang; it was Jake.

"Hi Blake, are you OK this morning? Can I come with an officer to pick up the robot?"

"What - are you kidding? Someone arrived early this morning and picked it up already."

"Can't be, I can't believe it. I'll come now. There is something fishy going on. Make sure you switch on encryption on your mobile. That guy must have touched something; maybe his prints will tell us more. Remember, we talked a few days ago about Kayla Osborne, the pathologist. The next morning, she was missing and hadn't been seen since. Someone is listening, and as I told you before, I don't believe in coincidences. It's the same thing with picking up the robot; yesterday, we discussed that on mobile; this morning, someone else picked it up. It's more likely that your phone is bugged." Jake said.

"OK, I'll switch on encryption. See you soon."

Blake enabled encryption and called Bidi, "Didn't you say you installed something into the robot to check his movements?" Blake asked.

"Good morning to you, too; what is the urgency?"

"My robot was picked up this morning. I thought Jake had arranged it; we had discussed it yesterday, but it was picked up by someone else. If we can track the robot, we may find out who is behind all this. I have enabled encryption on my mobile; make sure you do the same," Blake explained.

"It's done already. I'll call you back when I have the tracking results," Bidi said and hung up.

Blake heard a knock on his door and checked that it was Jake.

"That was fast, and how did you get into the lobby?"

"There is always someone who walks in or out."

"That's how the guy must have been able to get in unless he swiped the code from my robot," Blake said.

Jake took prints from surfaces the guy could have touched, including a clear print from the buzzer next to Blake's unit door. He didn't have much hope of finding out something.

Blake told Jake about Bidi's navigation app and promised to call soon with the results. A short time later, she rang.

"I have the location. It seems all normal; it's a huge storage and possible manufacturing complex at the Airport Industrial Park, located at the southern end of the Brisbane Airport. It looks like they have leased or even own a few hectares of warehouses. You guys need to check that out; it looks huge."

"Does it give you any names?"

"Yes, an abbreviation, DID. Who knows, it could be associated with DIA. I will dig around, but I am sure you can drive there and ask the receptionist. It looks legit, lots of trucks visible on satellite view," Bidi said.

"OK, thanks. I'll see what Jake wants to do. I'll call you tonight." Blake looked at Jake, "Are we going?"

Jake nodded; they took his car. They didn't have much hope of finding anything new within the robot distribution warehouse to bring Hampton to justice.

It didn't take them long to arrive at the colossal complex. At least 20 trucks were standing with their rear towards the opened factory roller doors.

They parked at the visitor's car park and walked over to a door labelled RECEPTION.

What question can they ask without being offensive? Blake took over. It wasn't a criminal case yet, and it was more suited to a journalist's questions.

"Good day," Blake opened the conversation. "My name is Blake Newcome, a journalist for the Fact File News. Could I ask you a few questions?" The receptionist, a middle-aged woman wearing huge glasses and a kind smile, was agreeable.

"Is there any connection between your company, DID, and DIA International?"

"Yes, this company is called Digital Inversion Distribution, and as the name suggests, we are a subsidiary company of DIA that distributes robots, maintains, repairs, and conducts research. Was there something specific you wanted to know?" the receptionist said.

"I do; that is why we are here. I had a robot stored in my garage, which was picked up this morning and brought here. Can you find out why that happened?"

"Give me a moment," she turned towards a screen and typed quickly. Yes, here it is, Blake Newcome. A robot that had been gifted to you was picked up because it had been in a state of hibernation for more than 48 hours. That triggers a message, and retrieval of the robot seemed the best option. Is there anything else I can help you with?"

Very professional, Blake thought.

"It occurred to me that I received no document about the pickup. Could you arrange a receipt so that I am not charged for something I had no influence over?"

"We can do that, no problem; let me contact accounting," she said.

A few minutes later, they walked out. Blake had his receipt stating that the robot had been returned and that no charge would be applied.

Once again, Hampton had outsmarted him. The legality of his operation made it impossible to charge him with anything, not even stealing his own robot.

Jake was thinking loud, "We still got absolutely nothing; even if we find androids in one of his warehouses, we can't pin anything criminal on him. If we accuse him of planning to manipulate humans to become complacent and be happy to go along with life as represented by governments, leading humans into submission, he would laugh in our faces.

The only possible crime he could be accused of is money skimming, or as you call it, nano-skimming. We have no other choice; we have to work on that. "Jake looked exhausted and fed up.

"Time is on our side, don't worry," Blake said, "let's go for lunch."

The week went by; every day, the stream of downloads from Bidi's app diminished along with the influx of money into her bank account. Social media comments became less hectic and frequent. The exception was some weird people who had formed groups to hunt down androids to 'out them'.

The outing of androids and what to do with them was something Blake and his dream team had not considered well. They should have provided instructions on how to deal with them instead of leaving it up to the public or anyone else.

Nonetheless, the androids that were outed behaved well, the same couldn't be said from those people who outed them. But even those groups had mostly stopped their misguided actions.

Blake and the others had the impression something else had happened; there was no direct explanation for why android fever had subsided that quickly. Bidi reported that hardly anyone had downloaded any of her apps. Not that she minded; she was still in shock and hadn't decided what to do with all the money. She didn't even know how much it was yet.

Blake, without a specific lead to follow, needed his friends to talk to. He knew something would come up that would lead to further action. By the end of the day, he decided to arrange yet another meeting in the park, if not for problem-solving, then for having a good time.

The meeting was set for Friday afternoon, 5 pm, again at Musgrave Park, with a side note: bring a blanket, food and beer.

28

Derek was in a high mood. Everything had gone according to his ingenious plan. This morning's action to implement the next step of his master plan needed an appropriate wardrobe.

He didn't see himself as a king; otherwise, he would have dressed like one. He saw himself as a conductor, despite people calling him the Zookeeper, which he did not like at all. He also didn't like the term 'puppet master', even if, secretly, he was flattered by those nicknames. Part of his plan was to eliminate the 'Zookeeper' meme and replace it with 'The Conductor', a proper and respectful term. He believed he directed the world and its inhabitants towards a better life.

That morning, he was dressed in a top hat and tailcoat. He inspected his reflection in the wardrobe mirror and agreed with himself; he looked impressive. He had modelled himself on Fred Astaire. Derek's contemporaries may not even know who that was, but that was of no importance to him. He knew, and that was all that mattered. The stiff shirt's upright collar felt tight, so he loosened the white bow tie a touch, cleared his throat, and mumbled, "Ready."

He stepped behind his desk, his conductor's desk, ready to conduct the following action with the wave of his conductor baton, and not just any baton; we are talking white-painted maple with a silver handle.

He waved his baton around for a test. It worked, and he liked the feel of it.

He was ready. There were a few seconds left to go before it would be 10 am sharp. An alarm sounded. He raised his arms, paused, and waved his baton in precise patterns in front of his computer screen. The hologram screens came alive. Buttons, links, and functions were clicked and activated seemingly at the stroke of his baton.

The master conductor at his work: directing to control human reaction to align with his master plan.

A few minutes later, the master conductor's invention, the android defence shield, was activated. The by-now-accepted security androids were not affected by this activation; they had no defence against android detection apps, and they didn't need defence as they were already accepted by the public.

The shield was designed to protect Hampton's pacifier androids. No one knew that an increasing number of pacifier androids were populating cities, taking jobs, and generally spreading a calming influence to everyone with whom they came in contact simply by their positive, reassuring way of talking and personal vocabulary.

Derek once again looked pleased with himself. His chest would have expanded, but his tight shirt and tailcoat didn't allow that to happen. He made a mental note to move one size up in his wardrobe choice; he must have put on weight. It is surprising what psychopathic masterminds think about.

Time to call Jess, and with a flick of his baton, the sliding door opened, and Jess appeared, a smile lighting up her face.

"You look fantastic; maybe wear that more often," she said.

"No, it has to be for special occasions, like today," he answered.

"Will you wear your signet ring all the time? It's great for hiding your Smart Ring. If anyone saw you conducting with your baton, they would think it was real," Jess laughed.

"Yes, I'll keep wearing the ring. I based the design on the papal ring and used it several times as a seal under my signature." Derek proudly stated.

"What will be your next steps in fulfilling your master plan? Jess asked.

"I'll take a wait-and-see approach. Then, I will link the data-collecting functions of the androids with those of the household robots and the e-cars to get a complete picture of our society. At the same time, I will use some of my pacifier androids and those who function as lobbyists to ensure ministers understand my message and introduce the 'universal income' principle. My generous contribution of DIA shares to the minister's wife will enhance that message.

There is no need for me to influence politics directly as long as the present government stays in power and understands my policies to remain in power.

DEEP, the new political party formed under my direction will support the present government.

I will roll out the same masterplan in Europe, the USA, and even Hong Kong." Derek finished his oration and waved his baton; the sliding door opened, inviting Jess to disappear.

"I wonder how you will sort the huge amount of data you will receive?" Jess asked.

"My Guro Android's artificial intelligence will sort the data, and by probing my needs into its algorithm, it delivers what I need in mere seconds." His tone of speech indicated it was enough talking, and Jess disappeared into her section of the vast property complex.

In addition to being his love interest, Jess was Derek's personal approval soundboard. But she was more; she was his connection with the outside of his property. The reason he hadn't been seen for many years was simple: he never left the building, never. He had her and three personal androids similar in appearance to him but not totally like him.

Through them, he interacted with the world around him. Each android was designed for a different demographic. In addition, his vast computer network could directly contact any of his robots and androids, see and hear what they do, and harvest their data.

He hadn't made it a habit to tune into his robots and androids; he only used that capability to collect essential data.

Blake was one of the only people he had focused on. One could say he was present when Jess the android visited Blake on that fatal day. When Jess fell off the balcony, she was what could be called dead, but some functions of her systems were still working and accessible for Hampton. No wonder it didn't take much time, and he could arrange the retrieval of Jess.

His next step to gift Blake a butler robot had backfired. He had underestimated Blake, but he would continue with his plan, nonetheless.

It would not take long for him to reveal who had distributed the androids to the community and his reason for keeping it a secret: to test prototypes without bias influence; only then could one see a genuine reaction from the public. Yes, he thought, that was a masterstroke.

29

Blake picked up Frances from the airport. It meant an early start for him but even earlier for Frances. He was sure she hadn't had breakfast, and neither had he. He looked forward to having a relaxed breakfast with her at his favourite cafe restaurant, a few steps away from his unit.

It was 8:20 am when he saw her entering the arrival lounge.

He kissed and hugged her, "So good to see you. Are you hungry? Let's go for breakfast.

They made their way through the morning traffic, catching up on the news. Arriving at West End, Blake parked the car in his garage, and they walked over to the café and relaxed in West End's cosmopolitan atmosphere. At that moment, there were no worries in the world; the weather was perfect, with the hot summer days still weeks away.

It was one of the mornings when one thought, *why can't it always be this way?*

"This is nice," Frances said, "I could get used to it. Sometimes, I'm fed up with my job, and living in Sydney is too hectic," Frances said.

Blake's eyes lit up, "Does that mean you might come to live here with me – please?"

"I have been thinking about it, believe it or not. I could work from here, even with fewer hours. Some of my work has been taken over by AI, which is fine with me. I have been editing for way too long; I crave writing my own stuff. I have an idea for a novel; I just need to kick myself to start writing."

"Start today. We can hang out most of the time in my unit, only coming down for lunch or coffee, and you could write nearly all day." Blake said.

"What, you want me to work on my holiday?" Frances laughed.

"It could be the perfect start, and as I know you, once you start, you can't stop."

"I am tempted; I have my laptop in my luggage."

"Sure you do, let's go, finish your coffee."

Blake finished off his coffee and stood up.

"Slave driver," Frances said, getting up.

"By the way, we will meet with the other guys in the late afternoon. Guess where? It's in a park not far from here, a picnic meeting," Blake said.

They left the café, returned to Blake's garage, picked up Frances's luggage, and went upstairs.

Frances unpacked; some of her stuff went into the bathroom, and her clothes found space in the large sliding-door wardrobe in Blake's bedroom.

Blake helped hang up her clothes, and then helped her get undressed. After that, it took a while before they emerged from his bedroom and started their other creative activities,

"I can't believe I will start writing," she said.

"Stop talking. I won't disturb you. I am busy enough with my next article," he said.

Blake went into the bedroom to write so as not to disturb Frances. Not feeling settled enough for writing, he fetched himself a beer. His mobile rang as soon as he had finished the first couple of paragraphs. It was the Prime Minister.

"It's Dean here. Thanks for taking the call; please listen. In the coming days, I will introduce the 'Certify Human' initiative on all media channels, along with my general policy announcements. It would help if you wrote about it as well. It must come across as bringing security to our society and protecting our way of life. Is that agreeable to you?"

"Yes .... Dean, that's how I thought it should be presented."

"Thank you. That's all. Looking forward to reading your article." Dean hung up.

Blake went back to his writing. He found it hard to concentrate on his present article; his thoughts went too far ahead to the question of what he could write about the 'Certified Human' topic.

He looked at his watch. It was time for lunch. He dragged Frances away from her writing. At the restaurant, he told her about the phone call in a roundabout way. He didn't want to lie to Frances but knew he couldn't expose the Prime Minister. He mentioned he received a phone call and that someone leaked information. The government wanted to implement the Certify Human project, and he could write about it.

When they were back at Blake's unit, Frances couldn't wait to return her novel writing project.

"I am getting curious. Give me a hint," Blake said. "What topic are you writing about?"

"What I know best. A story about people within the newspaper industry," Frances replied.

"Figures." Blake laughed, thinking about his own writing. His creativity was waning. The follow-up android story was giving him a headache. There was nothing profound he could write at that moment, especially now he knew about the article the Prime Minister wanted him to write. His mind was scattered, worried about how the public's excitement about detecting androids had faded.

He suspected Hampton had remotely updated the androids, protecting them and stopping the apps from discovering androids. But there was no point in writing about that. Instead, he turned his attention to the security androids.

It was getting late; the dream team meeting was imminent. He walked back to the living room. He had no choice; he had to disturb Frances.

"I think we better get going; it's already 5 pm," Blake said.

Frances was possessed and could hardly stop. The words flowed out of her; they had waited to be released for too long.

"I've made a good start; continuing will be much easier," Frances remarked.

They strolled leisurely, a picnic basket and a blanket in hand, down Russell Street towards Musgrave Park. Mona and Oliver came from the other end of the park, passing a group of people. Jake, Bidi, and Dave were already sitting on their blankets.

After the usual greetings and chit-chat, Blake came straight to the point.

"A few new developments: Android detection activity has more or less stopped. I am sure Hampton has managed to fix android detection and installed protection for his precious androids, except for the security guards. The security guards already wear identification; the latest trend is that other institutions and businesses are looking to employ them. Apparently, those androids come out of the woodwork and offer their services."

Bidi said something.

"Yes Bidi, what did you want to say?" Blake asked.

"Nothing; I just wondered how he could bypass the detection app. That guy is a bit of a genius. What is he up to?"

"Whatever he is up to, it will become clearer soon," Blake answered and kept on going with his speech.

"The government will table its latest election updates this weekend, including a host of measures to regulate androids and protect citizens from possible harm. One policy will be about certifying people as humans. I am sure Hampton will confess ownership of the androids with some cock and bull story before new policies prevent the distribution of androids by making it unlawful.

"I am also sure the Prime Minister will be re-elected. He seems to be a better kind of politician than I expected. Even so, it's always about winning. Does anyone else have new info? Dave?"

"Not much. I checked mainly for the DIA share distribution. At this point, four different ministers' wives are now the proud owners of DIA international shares. And let me add, they didn't buy them; they were allocated. There was one more allocation: for Jessica Brindly, obviously the real one."

Mona took the cue: "Oliver and I have carried out more testing. Staff members of the court who had previously tested positive for androids are still around but have tested negative now. We have seven of those androids on our list. I'm not sure yet what to do about those. It's hard to believe, but we do have one security guard android. If androids can harvest data from surrounding computers or smartphones, we could be in trouble."

Jake spoke up and pointed to a group of people, "Look at those guys over there. They are standing around, and it looks like they are not even talking."

Blake butted in, "I have watched them for a while. They are looking and behaving weirdly. They seem to be of similar weight, height, and looks; they are too perfect. If they are androids, those features could be another way to identify them."

"Do your thing," Oliver said, nodding at Blake.

"I will," Blake walked over to the group. They showed no reaction, not even looking in Blake's direction, even though he was heading straight for them. He approached one guy.

"Good afternoon. Sorry, I couldn't help but notice you guys gathering here. My name is Blake Newcome. I am a journalist for the Fact File News. May I ask what your gathering is for?"

The person answered without changing facial expressions or turning towards Blake: "We are security guards, waiting for our assignments. Do you need a security guard for your business? We come with a host of advantages. We are highly cost-effective. Instead of employing a regular human security guard, you can lease us. We work anytime, any day, and have no downtime. We can stay at your premises 24/7."

"Are you an android?" Blake asked the straightforward question and took out his mobile, triggering an android test. The result was positive.

"Yes, we are androids waiting for assignments. We are expecting an influx of requests. Are you requesting?"

"No, I am not. Thank you for your information. Are there more android gatherings around the city?" Blake asked.

"Yes, and more androids are provided to fill the new positions," the android answered. None of the other androids had joined that short conversation.

Blake had one more question, "Why are you not talking to each other?"

"We don't use verbal communication among us, and we have no communication topics."

Blake looked more closely at the android's face. He had noticed something peculiar about android faces before but couldn't work out what it was. Now he knew, their faces looked too perfect. No human face has totally equal left and right-side facial proportions, but these androids have. It gave them a minimal artificial appearance, hardly noticeable.

Blake walked back, joining the others. As weird as that conversation was, he now had another topic for his next article.

Jake looked at Blake, "And?"

"Security guard androids waiting for jobs, can you believe that?"

Blake repeated the whole conversation and added his observation about the equal facial proportion. He thought a facial recognition app could distinguish between a human and an android. Was that something else they could use to detect an android?

"I don't know about you guys, but to me, it sounds like something big will happen any time now. No one in their right mind would distribute androids and let them hang around in a park. I wonder if Hampton will make an announcement?" Bidi said.

"As Blake said, Hampton has to come forward as the owner, which opens the pathway of security guard employment or lease contracts. The whole thing feels as if it's been planned well ahead." Frances said. "I am sure that guy is not missing a beat."

They lingered for another hour, savouring their drinks and food and chuckling at the android group still hanging around. Bidi, in a moment of fancy, suggested, "Maybe we can invite them to play basketball. I wonder if they'd be any good? Could be a fun experiment, don't you think?"

Her question remained unanswered, but Dave, who was more interested in money than androids, had something on his mind.

"Hey, Bidi," he called out, "Just out of curiosity, how much money have you made from the app?"

"Hang on a sec, I will check; I can tell you exactly." Bidi connected to her bank account. "OK, here it comes." But it didn't.

"No, fuck", Bidi cried out. "The money is gone."

"It can't be," Blake said. Try again. I am sure something went wrong; refresh."

Bidi's distress showed as she logged out, closed her mobile and fired it up again to reload the bank account.

Everyone looked in suspense, "And?" Blake called out.

"Nothing, it's gone, the money is gone." Bidi dropped to her knees, looking at her mobile, crying.

Everyone huddled over her, trying to console her. Blake kept his calm. "You get it back. Can you find out when and where it went? Come on, think. It must have been something you came in close contact with."

Bidi thought for a moment, then jumped up, "Shit, that bloody robot in your garage. I connected my laptop to it. The thing must have pinched my bank logins. Why didn't I think about that – stupid." Bidi folded down again, her head between her legs, crying.

"Anything you can do?" Blake tried again to find a way.

Bidi didn't answer.

She looked at the group of androids and said, "Bloody androids, I am sick of them."

"I wonder if they stay here all night?" Frances remarked, not waiting for an answer but talking to Bidi instead. "Will you be OK on your own? You can stay with us if you like."

"I am OK, just angry at my own stupidity; I can't believe I didn't think about the robot's hacking tricks."

Francis picked up her blanket, grabbed Blake's arm, and called, "Bye, everyone," dragging Blake away.

"Do you think she will be OK? Frances asked as they walked back to West End.

"I think she will be. She hasn't done anything about that money yet. I think it hasn't sunk in; she did not feel it belonged to her. Don't worry, she will be fine. She may be able to trace the transaction and find a way to get it back."

Blake hugged Frances, "Come on, let's have a nightcap and forget about androids and robots for tonight.

30

B ack at the unit after the delightful but strange meeting in the park, they reflected on the bizarre gathering of androids. Blake prepared a light meal while he and Frances continued discussing what the heck Hampton wanted to achieve.

They also talked about the upcoming election. How could they not? They expected the Prime Minister's policy announcements any day now.

Both were mindful of the new political contender, DEEP, an acronym for the Democratic Enter Equality Party. Despite its relatively short time in the public domain and media, it had managed to establish a presence in every major city. The question on their minds was: Could DEEP challenge the two-party system? The answer was uncertain, especially considering Hampton's potential influence.

Equality, even in 2035, was still a big topic. For that particular party, equality stood for equal wages for all genders, equal recognition for all ethnicities, including First Nations people, and for all people a 'Universal Basic Income,' with the motto: No more poverty.

Blake knew of Bob Hawke, a former prime minister who, during an election campaign in 1987, promised that "No Australian child will be living in poverty."

Would that statement ever be repeated? Considering it failed miserably in the first place, even now, in 2034, poverty was still prevalent and visible in all cities. These were good enough reasons for Blake to favour the 'Universal Basic Income' strategy. However, Blake suspected Hampton could use it as a weapon to make people more complacent. But then again, he had his doubts as to whether poverty could ever be eliminated.

The DEEP party leader was no other than the independent senator Greg Hillier, and as Blake and Frances knew, he was an android. Did it mean he would support equality between humans and androids and curb poverty, all to support Hampton's maniac goals?

Blake called out to Frances, "Dinner is ready."

They sat down and started to eat, helped by a glass of red, when the news coverage changed to an interview with the Prime Minister.

They knew what that was about: new policies would be revealed.

They stayed glued to the TV for over 10 minutes. It was a comprehensive policy update, starting with business as usual: money for better education, childcare, sports facilities, roads, and bridges, and then it became captivating.

The government's promise to implement the Universal Basic Income if re-elected was a game-changer. This policy had the potential to lift over 4 million people out of poverty, securing 4 million votes for the government. The implications were profound.

In addition, the PM introduced various policies regarding androids, both ethical and functional. He made it clear that anyone messing with an android in an unethical way would face the consequences of the law. A court will apply the law for damaging property in Australia to a person or group who destroys or damages an android, which would result in imprisonment for up to 12 years.

Several new functional laws also made sense: androids used for security and those with no precise functions were allowed to be employed. The critical point was that instead of employment, they would need to be leased, and for that to happen, the owner, the company that produces the androids, had to come forward or face fines and a possible prison sentence.

One important new policy was to force androids to be registered before they were permitted to work.

He also mentioned that androids were related to national security; therefore, policy development needed to be bipartisan.

Right towards the end, he talked about the introduction of becoming a 'Certified Human' by having a chip implanted voluntarily by injection. Even though it was his idea, Blake was sceptical about whether people would be willing to accept it.

Blake rose and cleared the table, "I think our Prime Minister will be re-elected. The call for a bi-partisan approach will give the opposition less ammunition."

"The DEEP party has a similar approach regarding poverty, so there is a possibility they will join the government. And what about the Greens? Would they agree with the Universal Basic Income? And what about the android policies, there's nothing green about androids?" Frances thought out loud.

"It's like watching a game; now we wait for Hampton's move. It has to come quickly, or his android revolution may become unlawful," Blake said.

Gold Coast - Friday Night 4. November 2033 – Derek Hampton

At the same night and time, Jess and Derek sat down to their dinner, occasionally glancing at the television screen where the prime minister was being interviewed about his election promises.

"I anticipated this response. It's time to initiate phase two of my master plan." Derek murmured as if he had momentarily forgotten about Jess and was lost in his own thoughts.

"Is your response ready?" Jess asked, startling Derek for a second.

His attention diverted from the television back to Jess. "Yes, it will be a nationwide media release of my mission statement, which will explain in a logical way why I kept the androids a secret and didn't come forward earlier," he replied.

"How will you do it?" Jess asked again.

"It's easy; I obtained all the email addresses of media outlets I want to target, as well as government ministers, including the Prime Minister. I also have email addresses from business organizations to ensure my androids will land jobs quickly.

All I have to do is hit one button, and the task of sending out the emails is done. But before I do it, I'd like to finish my dinner. Please relax, have another glass of wine, cheers." He raised his glass to Jess.

"It's fascinating how composed you are in the face of all this commotion," Jess said with a hint of awe.

It wouldn't have been Hampton had he not selected a specific time to initiate phase two of his master plan.

He stood up and went through his usual ritual, putting on his tailcoat and top hat. He picked up his conductor's baton and took his position behind the desk in front of the hologram computer screens, waiting for the alarm bell to ring at 7 pm.

There it was, the bell, and Derek swung into action, conducting elements on the screen with his baton. If Jess hadn't known this was a ploy, she would have believed he was actually conducting, but he simply enjoyed swinging the baton. In reality, he directed elements on the screen with eye movements in combination with a smart ring.

It was done in seconds. He waited a minute, standing motionless before his screens, making sure none of the emails bounced back. None did. He had left contact instructions on his mission statements, and all he had to do was wait for Monday, when he expected the first replies.

The mission statements did not include the number of androids waiting for release. Derek, the conductor and puppet master in charge of the androids, had a whole army on standby at his Digital Inversion Distribution facility at Brisbane Airport Industrial Park.

His mission statement made total sense. In short form, he explained that the perfect way to test his prototype androids within an authentic and natural human environment was to keep the release a secret and evaluate the androids free of bias. He stated that he was happy with the results and that an official, legitimate release could commence.

Interested parties could contact Digital Inversion Distribution in

Brisbane to hire or lease androids for security or secretarial work.

Bespoke android hire was also available.

It was clearly a masterstroke. With one media release, he legalised androids and started a marketing campaign simultaneously.

He also announced he was the preferred household and care robot manufacturer and distributor for the government's Medi Care prescription scheme. That alone, he knew, was all the credentials he needed to be held in high esteem by the public.

Once again, all went his way in a legalised fashion. Everything was well above board, and no one suspected any alternative motives except Blake, of course. Derek was well aware of Blake's findings and had included a paragraph suggesting certain media outlets had dramatized the topic of robots and androids, causing fear bordering on conspiracy.

Derek went back to the living room, happy with himself. He opened a bottle of champagne, handed a glass to Jess, and congratulated himself on his genius.

"Cheers," they toasted his success.

31

E ighteen days to the election, but who was counting?

Blake had no doubt the Prime Minister had the election in the bag. All Blake had left to do was deliver his comments on the PM's policies in his Fact File News column. Of course, with Frances at his side, that was easy. For the first time, they formulated the article together. It worked well; Blake had no ego problems and gladly accepted advice from his lovable editor.

But there was one problem. Hampton's manifesto had already appeared in some news outlets on Saturday morning, and more followed on Monday.

"That guy gives me the creeps," Blake said to Frances. "He is clever, I must say, turning my articles into hype, fear and conspiracy. I didn't see that coming. To come out with his mission statement that fast after the PM's message, he must have planned for it and had it ready. I probably shouldn't, but I will add a few lines to piss him off."

"Be careful; that guy is always one step ahead. We don't have anything we can use against him." Frances said.

"I'm sorry, I can't let it go. I will add a few lines indicating that some androids are already in positions where they have to be out of. We need protection from being deceived. The 'Certify Human' approach is one way. The other way is that all androids need identification marks like the ones that have already been introduced for the security guard androids. I will also recommend that government institutions install facial recognition systems to alert them of possible androids.

"I will not name people, but the Fact File News is aware of influencers in the form of lobbyists who have access to ministers and that at least one senator is an android. All that means is androids have to be outed to protect the public from undue influences." Blake added, "That may get under his skin."

"OK, let's finish the article. It needs to be out tomorrow morning," Frances said. Blake agreed and started typing; he knew what he wanted to write.

32

The week went by without further drama. Frances enjoyed staying with Blake, and he enjoyed having her at his side. They were tempted to forget the whole sorry android debacle but couldn't. Even without drama, Frances was still the chief editor and now worked from Blake's office for the next few days. The daily occurrences resulting from the fallout of the new android paradigm were invitations to write more advanced articles. Organizations and businesses had rushed to sack their security guards and lease androids instead.

To put it mildly, the unions were unhappy and caused an uproar, but that was to be expected, not that it changed anything. However, it led to the discovery that robots and androids were manufactured with hardly any human workers. There were no job opportunities, unlike when computers came on the market. Hampton only employed a handful of human staff members to oversee the production.

Blake was happy; his last article propelled him back to the level of a believable journalist. Once again, social media was active, requesting to know who in the political field is an android and generally demanding more answers.

There was also a slight backlash against the Prime Minister. Did he know that one of the senators was an android, and who else knew about it?

Once again, it bordered on a conspiracy theory. This time, on social media, the conspiracy went around that the PM knew about Senator Greg Hillier, the party leader of the Democratic Enter Equality Party (DEEP). Conspiracy theorists called it corruption and accused the PM of trying to win the election with the help of androids.

The PM wasn't happy; he blamed Blake and called him on their private line to rectify the problem by writing another article clarifying that no one else knew about those politically inspired androids.

Blake interrupted Frances, who was busy writing her novel: "Looks like I have to write a follow-up to my last article. The PM is not happy being linked to an android senator. Do you have any bright ideas from your perspective? And can we get it into the Saturday issue?"

"If you hurry up, Saturday will be fine. It will be a good opportunity for you to highlight the importance of android registration and the 'Certify Human' project."

Blake sat at his desk, "Yep, I thought the same. I better get cracking," and started hammering on his keyboard.

From time to time, they looked at each other, not saying anything, smiling and continuing to type—happy.

That afternoon, Blake's article was ready. Frances put on her editor's hat, made a few changes, and handed it back to Blake, "OK?"

Blake read through it one more time; yes, he liked it. The text flowed nicely, with good arguments, and the prime minister would be happy.

Blake had asked in the article for androids that had integrated into public life to come forward and own up. People may not mind having androids around if they knew who they were.

Regarding Greg Hillier, the independent senator and leader of the DEEP party, he was an android and was, therefore, according to new laws, not eligible to be a party member.

Blake worried that some of his articles may be aiding Hampton instead of exposing him for wrongdoings. How could he prove Hampton's devious goal of breeding complacency among humans? He wished he could find something illegal so that Hampton could be charged, tried and hopefully locked up.

Robot companies could keep going under new management and regulations, making sure no data collection or money skimming takes place. After all, it has become a fact that robots, like computers, are part of human existence, and so are androids.

"I wonder if I write too positively about androids?" Blake asked Frances.

"No, there is nothing wrong with androids, robots, AI or computers; it's always what is done with them or how they are used that makes the difference. As I said before, androids are computers on legs," Frances said.

"Androids are computers on legs, yes, I know, and I like it; great metaphor. I will use it in my next article if you don't mind," Blake said.

33

Brisbane - Saturday 12. November 2033 – Blake

B It had only been a week since Hampton's mission statement was released to the media. According to Blake's information, it achieved what Hampton had expected. Everyone danced to his tune. The Digital Inversion Distribution factory had to activate five more receptionist androids to deal with incoming questions and requests from companies about hiring androids.

The DID's distribution machinery swung into action. Androids voluntarily were assigned a registration number and delivered to whoever could afford to lease them.

More media releases made sure that the world knew androids were registered, even though they were not. They had a number, and within the DID network, androids were recognised by their number for better accounting, but that didn't mean they were registered with the appropriate government department.

The media channels were enthusiastic and congratulated Hampton on his bold and innovative move. Androids were now tolerated and embraced by company bosses. Hampton's apparent genius had won once again.

Blake and Frances sat at their breakfast table, skimming media releases, social posts, and comments. No one seemed to be worried about the androids.

"That is worrying," Blake said.

"What is?" Frances asked.

"That no one worries about the android development. Is that

complacency setting in, or short-sightedness?"

Blake's phone rang, "It's Jake, wonder what he wants."

"Hi Jake, what's up? Do you have an android secretary yet?

"Very funny, and no, something much more curious has happened. Kayla Osborne and James Moorhead have been found."

"That's good, isn't it? What happened? Have you talked to them?" Blake asked.

"Yes, they didn't know anything. They had been kept in different houses at different locations; we are not sure where, and they can't tell us. They could walk around the house freely, had enough to eat and drink, and watch television, but they had no communication whatsoever with anyone. They were dropped off 30 minutes apart at Roma Street.

Both made their way to our headquarters. That's it. I talked to them half an hour ago. As you know, James was aware that Jess was an android, and so was Kayla, obviously, as she had discovered it. I guess now that androids have become the flavour of the month, there was no reason to hold them anymore," Jake explained.

"Have you contacted Hampton at all?"

"I have. He claimed he had no idea what I was talking about, and we can't pin it on him at all. But I received some good news. Our cyber department has tracked down the first connections of nano-skimmed money flowing to his company's bank accounts. It's too early to act on it, but it will come. We may get him on that eventually. Anything on your end?"

Blake thought a moment, "No, nothing. My articles seem to help Hampton instead of hindering him. We may lay low for a while or until after the election and observe what is playing out in front of us. Actually, and I haven't even asked Frances yet, I may go back to Sydney with her and stay a week or so."

"That sounds good. I'll let you know if something new comes up. Enjoy Sydney." Jake hung up.

Frances looked at Blake, "What was that about Sydney?"

"I thought I would come with you and lay low for a while in Sydney, and what better place to be than with you."

"When did you have that idea, and when would we go back?"

"I thought about it this morning. I wanted to tell you when Jake rang. We could leave on Monday; what do you think?"

"It's a great idea to go together. I need to be back in Sydney next Wednesday anyway for an editor's meeting."

"OK, let's forget Hampton and have a nice weekend. I'll book our plane tickets now. Pack some stuff, and let's hit the Gold Coast for a swim."

34

While Blake and Frances enjoyed their leisure time, Derek sat at his desk, meticulously preparing a strategy for phase 3 of his master plan, a plan that was as intricate as it was sinister. He outlined two primary components to take effect with the launching of phase 3.

First, the calculated distribution of drugs within Australia by household robots with medical support capabilities. Any drug or supplement prepared by robots will be laced with mild, undetectable hallucinogens to distort the robot's owner's interpretation of what's happening around them.

Once again, the rollout will happen at the touch of a button.

Robots will swing into action, distributing drugs in conjunction with prescription medication and supplements.

The drugs will be delivered and arrive, along with food and other items ordered, straight into the robot's capable hands.

With over 5 million robots already activated within Australia, Derek's plan to ensure that drug-induced complacency would keep the Australian population inactive without complaining about anything was bound to be successful.

With the emerging android population, Derek calculated that it would be less than six months, at the most, before he could influence at least 80% of the population in one way or another.

The second part of phase three will be the aggressive use of 'Virtual Reality Glasses', which have already been sold for nearly a decade and advertised as a glorious experience, with slogans such as 'Be visually, physically and emotionally amazed by new virtual ventures.' Most of those headsets are manufactured in one of Derek's facilities. It was yet another devious plan.

He has also produced the content of those headsets, the games, videos, and lectures, all with subliminal messages, which involved split-second flashes of text, hidden images, or other subtle cues that were below the viewer's conscious awareness. All this was done to breed complacency and further influence the people.

As if that wasn't enough, Derek employed another technique, using the side effects of VR, virtual reality usage.

Feeling sick after entering a VR was not uncommon and called cybersickness, with symptoms like headaches, vertigo, disorientation, and even pronounced nausea. What better treatment than one of Derek's developed drugs interlaced with hallucinogens?

People would become so complacent they wouldn't even want to work anymore, and part of their newfound spare time, free of work, would be taken up by spending more hours with their Virtual Reality Glasses, completing a vicious cycle they would not be able to break out of by themselves.

Derek reclined in his plush leather chair, stretched, and triumphantly raised his fist in the air. *Yes, that would do for phase 3.*

It was now time to increase the output of androids to replace jobs like security guards, secretaries, receptionists, and even bureaucrats and thereby to force previously employed people out of their careers.

As a replacement, Derek made sure they would receive a universal income high enough for a comfortable lifestyle while spending their time watching virtual reality.

To pay for the ever-increasing universal income, another segment of his plan was for his android lobbyists to convince the government to introduce a new tax on those companies that were saving millions of dollars on labour costs, creating a tax windfall for the government. He knew that every citizen would be happy, and his idea of utopia would be fulfilled.

Could anyone stop the progression of Hampton's devious master plan?

Crying 'Wolf' had been a favourite strategy of Hampton, and Blake had become the unfortunate pawn in that game. Blake's articles had caused panic a few times, but in the end, no one cared anymore, a typical crying wolf strategy that had led to complacency.

Derek questioned himself: did Blake sense he was being used? He admitted that his master plan, his grand game, had a substantial contestant in Blake, and the game was not over yet. So far, he could predict some of Blake's reactions, but he felt that Frances, who he realised had the uncanny ability to spot plots a mile away, could be his second primary adversary. Together, they made a worthwhile team to play against.

Derek made some final adjustments to phase 3 of his master plan, but he wasn't ready yet to launch it; he had to wait for the election to be over and phase 2 to be completed.

The election was a mere two weeks away. A lot can happen in two weeks, and he would make sure a lot would happen.

Every day, he released a staggering number of pre-registered androids. They had their registration numbers and were assigned and leased out to companies eager for cheap, efficient staff that would never cause any headaches. There was no need for health insurance or superannuation, constituting gigantic savings and massive rises in profits not seen before.

By the time the election was over, Australian cities would be awash with androids.

The Digital Inversion Distribution Centre had stored an enormous number of androids. They had been waiting for an explosion of androids to happen for over two years and had purpose-trained androids to fill different positions.

Everyone knew that androids take no rest and work 24/7 and that the sheer amount of working capacity would rule the workplace in the future, with Hampton drowning in money.

Would he drown? No, he planned to use that money to pay extra tax to allow the government to pay every citizen a higher amount of 'Universal Income', making the whole population dependent and more complacent than ever, sheep in human cloth, turning humans into lemmings.

Derek called Jess. It was time to celebrate his planning effort with champagne and their nightly game of chess.

No one in Australia knew what would hit them except him and, to a limited extent, his partner Jess.

They played chess most nights, working out their next moves. Occasionally, Jess would outmanoeuvre Derek, something he didn't mind. Her strategic prowess would be their most significant asset in the real world, especially if she ascended to the leadership of Greg Hillier's Democratic Enter Equality Party.

35

Blake was sitting on Frances's balcony, taking in the fresh sea breeze. They had arrived in Sydney mid-morning. Frances had a few things to do, but Blake felt like he was on holiday; he loved the seaside atmosphere. He wanted to sit on the balcony and think. He felt an urgency for undisturbed long-term thinking.

At home, in his unit, and without a sea breeze, thinking for him meant walking around in circles, usually around his kitchen island.

He would have preferred a real island, but even in the kitchen, walking calmed him down while it activated his mind.

He had a lot to think about: Hampton, of course, was the main topic. Blake was contemplating what future steps that guy might take. How could he be one step ahead of Hampton?

Blake was a good chess player but also a master strategist, adept at thinking, planning, and anticipating moves. He knew it would take time and skill to outsmart Hampton, but he was determined to take the time.

At times, he felt his articles were falling on deaf ears. Had he created a crying wolf scenario? Could he, perhaps, reverse that principle and foster public awareness and engagement instead?

Another factor, worlds away from the Zookeeper, was also on his mind, particularly while he was sitting on Frances's balcony: why were he and Frances overly concerned about where they lived? Couldn't it be the perfect lifestyle to keep both units and enjoy the best of both worlds? As long as they were together, where they lived didn't matter; they both had the advantage of working from their home office.

He loved France's unit, close to the beach, and of course, the attractions a city like Sydney had to offer. He often missed the beach while living in Brisbane; even so, he sometimes drove to the Gold Coast. Obviously he loved his unit as well. West End, even in 2035, had retained a touch of village atmosphere, and he loved that his unit was in the middle of cafés, restaurants, lovely shops and galleries.

It was also a favourite live music precinct. He could walk everywhere and hardly ever needed his car. It took 15 minutes to walk to Southbank and the entertainment venues, and within 5 minutes more, he could enjoy the city centre, even a casino, not that he ever went there other than showing it off to overseas friends when they visited.

He would have to talk to Frances about that. Keeping both units made sense, not to live apart but to alternate places whenever they liked.

Happy with himself for having worked out where to live, he leaned back in his chair, putting up his legs on the nearby table, and activated deep thinking, concentrating on solutions to stop Hampton from taking over the world, or at least Australia.

It was late, and he must have dozed off. When he woke up, Blake felt he had missed something in his effort to stop the uncontrolled spread of artificial intelligence, robots, and androids. The crying wolf principle was still embedded in his mind; could he use this principle in reverse? Could he use reverse psychology by writing the opposite of his initial scaremongering that may have led people into complacency?

He could see people becoming lemmings and going passively over the cliff in ignorance of Hampton's plans for world domination. He foresaw a tipping point when an army of androids would seize control, making it too late for humans to regain authority.

Were there more people who could see what happened to society, or had he lost touch with reality?

"I can see what you are thinking about." Frances came out on the balcony and sat in a deckchair next to Blake.

Blake smiled, "I bet you can, but I also thought about us." He told her about his idea to live in both places, not separated, of course, as they had done before, but in a new united way, staying together in one place or the other.

Frances bent down to Blake, took his face in both hands and kissed him, "I love you. You are right. We never discussed that idea before. I love it. We can do it for as long as we like. It's like having the cake and eating it too."

"And what else is going on in that busy mind of yours? I was sure I could see the Zookeeper on your forehead."

"I was reflecting on everything that's happened over the last six weeks. It's nearly too much to comprehend. How could something futuristic like androids progress so fast that one loses sight of it? Is it about influencing the public the way I think it is, or is it what we always see around us: capitalism in action and greed for more money and power?

Hampton played us, and with us, I don't mean you and me; I mean us, as in everyone. I can't help my feelings; I worry deeply about humanity. It looks like we are losing the plot, and someone else controls life for his own power. Why do you think other people don't appear to be concerned?" Blake asked.

"I am sure most people think about it. Everyone can see that technology is getting the better of us and that we are played by AI and the like, but no one thinks it affects them personally, and if they do, they don't know what to do about it. Everyone is getting along with whatever plays before their eyes."

"Wow, you put it all out there. Does it mean it's up to you, me, and a few more of our friends?"

"No, we are not that important." Frances laughed. "We need to attract more people who see the value of doing something about it. Find a way, with your articles, to get more people into our camp. You have mentioned lemmings before; people will follow if something worthwhile is before them. If there are enough people who know, you may get them to demonstrate like in the good old days when people were still interested in topics and conversations, and not only into their virtual headsets."

"Wow, great, inspiring speech; maybe you can write the articles next time. Just kidding. Do you have any other insights?"

"Maybe. It occurred to me that, sooner or later, Hampton needs an audience. If he is a psychopath like you think, then he has to show the world how great he is. It will not be long before he comes forward. He must be tempted already to show the world how great he is. That will be the time of his downfall; he either miscalculates his steps or shows his Achilles tendon. Everyone has some weaknesses, find his and we'll beat him."

Blake nodded; he moved over to Frances and held her hands.

"You are on a roll; what happened? When did all those sudden insights evolve?"

Frances answered, "It was your face of deep contemplation which made me think and dig deeper, and something else. I am not sure if you noticed, but at the domestic Brisbane airport and later in Sydney, at the airport, I noticed at least a dozen androids with the security button on their chest. Nothing out of the ordinary about that anymore after the last couple of weeks, but then it occurred to me, as you have noticed before, that they don't look like ordinary people; they look too good. All were of approximately the same size and had a perfect body physique. No one was overweight, too short or too tall; all were perfect, good-looking human specimens. That's what you haven't written about, but it is another way to recognise an android; they look too good to be true. It borders on discrimination."

"That's right. We noticed that too-perfect characteristic in the park in Brisbane. That's when I noticed their faces were too perfect." Blake agreed.

"Maybe facial recognition surveillance could be programmed to recognise those perfect features as androids," Blake suggested, still holding Frances's hands.

"I have to repeat myself: wow, what's happening? Where is all your inspiration coming from? It's fantastic. Do you have any more insights, or can we go for lunch?"

"Lunch sounds good; all this thinking has made me hungry."

While driving to their lunch destination, Frances saw Blake was in deep thought again.

"Snap out of it," she said. "Your thoughts are not running away. We can spend the afternoon writing. You will need to stimulate a mass movement on social media in the right direction. Not like lemmings going over the cliff, but to inspire the movement of walking in the direction of human values."

"That sounds too easy. Let's see if I can think of something," Blake said and parked the car. "I am starving now."

They were shown to a vacant table at one of their preferred restaurants, where a talented chef still created traditional dishes.

The restaurant next door was the complete opposite. It was a trendier place, and it boasted having all the readymade meals available on the market. In 2035, readymade meals had come a long way, and meals were available for any diet, from the still-favoured Mediterranean diet to the more exotic organic vegan meal and everything in between, including the good old hamburger in all combinations.

Guests to those establishments were served quickly; they had a quick look at the menu on a thin screen, selected and paid in one operation, and received the meal within a few minutes by a service robot on wheels.

It was no secret that those meals came 'fresh' from the freezer, were transferred to the microwave, and from there went straight to the table. Most people ate like that every day; the only difference was where they obtained meals. For people who had even less time or no sense at all of traditional eating styles, there were plenty of self-service wall-mounted vending machines, which spat out heated ready meals.

For the even more futuristic-inclined people, another service had been slowly coming online over the last few years. It had a cult-like following and may well be the sad reality of the far future.

Followers of that group or club were totally focused on complete health and longevity. They commenced their membership at an anti-aging clinic, where they had to undergo a complete health check-up and, even more importantly, DNA sequencing and digestive culture testing.

Those tests revealed their allergies and food intolerances, which can be a harmful cause of inflammation and, therefore, aging. The result of all this testing and probing is a complete anti-ageing program. That may not sound very futuristic, but what followed undoubtedly is. They receive a detailed lifestyle plan, including everything they are allowed and not allowed.

Food and nutrition are always a primary factor, and to make sure the nutrients are absolutely perfect for the client's metabolism, they come in powder form. The club members no longer eat or drink real food; they mix their designed nutrient powders in distilled water and consume that. - The outcome so far? According to follow-up health tests, aging has slowed down considerably. It may be worthwhile, but not for Blake.

Frances and Blake preferred what they called a real or authentic meal. Blake, of course, was always on the lookout for new recipes to replicate in his own kitchen. Frances absolutely loved that Blake was cooking and used her expertise with the choice of wine. Blake never disagreed with Frances's selection.

While enjoying their meal and a light Riesling with a hint of fresh apple, they couldn't help but notice an android security guard walking up and down the street, making sure diners felt safe and secure and behaving in an orderly manner.

Blake had the weird idea of interviewing the android guard. That was something he guessed no one had done before. Would the android guard let down his guard and spill the beans on personal or android security matter information?

Could Blake use his NLP or hypnosis communicating skills to get the android to say something it wouldn't under normal circumstances?

He asked Frances, "I am tempted to talk to the security guard. What is your guess? Would he agree to an interview?"

"Hmm, not sure, worth a try. Can we eat first and get away for half an hour from your android fascination?"

"OK, I will bite my tongue even though I wondered about something."

Frances had to laugh, "Sure you do. What are you wondering? You probably want me to ask you."

"If you insist," he grinned, "When I started my quest of becoming a journalist, I branched out and studied a few complementary subjects, like hypnosis and neurolinguistic programming NLP. I never talked about that, but those unique skills have become very handy over the years in situations where my ordinary questions would not have succeeded.

I have never hypnotized anyone; I used it more to formulate better sentence structures that freed people to come forward with information they wouldn't have revealed with straightforward questioning. In a way, it has become a habit; it's not even something I consciously think about."

"Ahh, that's how you did it."

"What do you mean?"

"You hypnotized me to be with you."

"Very funny."

Between two bites, Frances continued, "I read a book about NLP a few years ago. I can't remember the exact title, but it was something like 'How to Influence People'. I bought it for a mischievous reason. I wanted to influence some chauvinistic male guys who worked at the same office as me to be more accommodating towards their female counterparts. Even in the early 2020s, it was a boys' club and still is in certain sections."

"Did it work?" Blake asked.

"I think it did; I reacted differently to their remarks and asked more specific questions they couldn't get out of."

"And do you think hypnotic language or NLP could work to influence an android? Imagine one could hypnotize an android. I can't imagine they have been programmed to recognise NLP. As long as one doesn't mention hypnosis or NLP and formulate questions differently, it could work.

I am sure that once they know hypnosis, it will take their AI system less than a minute, and they will know everything about it and react accordingly. The trick would be to sneak up on them with questions they don't expect."

"Sure, try it out; it will be interesting as long as I can have dessert first."

Not much later, having had coffee, Blake prepared himself to talk to the security guard who was walking slowly toward them. Blake waited until the guard had passed their table by a couple of steps.

"Excuse me, sir. I wonder if I could ask a couple of questions."

The android stopped walking. It was thinking about the question: could that be? Does a walking computer with an AI function have to think about a question or formulate a sentence?

"Yes, I can answer a couple of questions," it said, turning toward their table.

"As you walk up and down and feel the hard surface under your feet, and you can hear people talking and laughing, and you see everyone's faces, do you send the collected data to a control centre or store it in your own system?" Blake held his breath. Would the android answer?

"All information is continuously transmitted to the control centre."

"And how often do you communicate with other androids?"

"Androids assigned to Sydney are in interactive communication at all times to upgrade and add real-time data and information to facilitate advanced learning.

"And while you transfer our conversation to the data centre, how will the centre respond?"

"I have answered your couple of questions; I will now continue my rounds."

"A couple of questions is a manner of speech; it can mean many more questions." Blake tried to argue with the guard.

"Thank you for that information; I have passed it on."

Blake watched the android walk away. He was now worried: From what distance would the android still be able to 'hear', store, and transmit that collected data?

He looked at Frances, who raised her eyebrows. Blake moved his head toward their car. He paid their bill, and they left the restaurant quickly.

Inside the car, they felt safe again. They had become aware of a different functionality of androids. From one minute to the next, they understood that from now on, and getting worse, androids would observe and monitor everyone at all times. The androids shared all the data information they harvested between them and the head office or control centre.

It wasn't the problem of who was an android or not; it was now a different ballgame; androids were monitoring people's behaviour, communication, and identities, and, with all their AI deduction, they knew what people were thinking.

Big Brother had arrived; maybe George Orwell's dystopian novel had finally come true. However, there was one huge difference; in Hampton's surveillance Big Brother moment, everything looked and felt like utopia, the ultimate heaven on earth, with people too complacent to notice Hampton controlled them.

People had become a new kind of lemming, not the ones walking over the cliff, but the new ones walking around in circles, chasing their own shadows, happy within their treadmill of illusional comfort.

"I never thought I would get any answers from the android, let alone specific know-how. All we have to know is the distance of their digitally empowered senses. I am sure they understand all languages; how can we talk without being overheard? Does an android have to be in view before it can monitor someone?

We can recognise security androids because they are labelled, but not other androids. I need to contact the prime minister on his private phone and urge him to have stricter android identification markers."

"How come you have the PM's private number?" Frances asked with a puzzled facial expression.

"Oops, that was meant to be a secret. I am allowed to call him if I come across urgent information."

Blake felt a wave of mental exhaustion as he locked the car. The androids were far more insidious than he had ever imagined, and the thought sent a shiver down his spine. How could they escape this suffocating surveillance? The answer was clear, but far from being successful, he had to write a new article. He had to find a way to convey his message, to break through the complacency and make people see the truth."

"I need to call Bidi tonight. I will go to the beach to call her. I have never seen an android beach inspector yet. She has to find a way to talk without the fear of being overheard. For the moment, if anything important or android-specific, we better stick to communicating in writing."

Frances nodded.

Was that how it would be from now on, talking with gestures, mouthing questions and answers, or writing notes?

"Let's not worry too much about that, " Frances said, "Yes, they monitor everything, but what will they do with that information? They wouldn't have the staff to check everything. I am sure they use a computer algorithm to sort out messages that could harm them or be noteworthy somehow. We can talk in general terms and use a bit of metaphor while in public. If we assume androids are close by, lurking in the shadows, we simply don't talk."

Blake nodded, gestured the thumbs up and pointed outside.

"Yes, that's pretty much it. We could have fun with it, talking nonsense when we know an android is listening to confuse them," Frances laughed.

It was late in the afternoon by the time Blake arrived at the beach. He wasn't able to guess the wind speed other than thinking it was pretty windy and holding his cupped hands over his ears. No one would be able to listen to any conversation out here. He turned his back towards the wind, pulled out his mobile and called Bidi.

He updated her on the latest developments and his worries about androids listening to everyone, using facial recognition to create a file on every citizen, and, most likely, having the means to interfere in people's personal lives.

Bidi explained the technical aspects of Blake's worries, "You don't have to worry too much about the range in which the android can listen into your conversation. It would be a normal microphone range, not directional, receiving all types of noise within that distance. If, however, you notice an android looking at you, they may have a fix on your voice with a directional microphone. Move away or stop talking if that is the case."

"That's good to know. I will stop being paranoid. Anything else?" Blake walked while talking, kicking sand and digesting Bidi's information.

"There is nothing else you can do other than create more noise around you, like switching on a radio or being in a noisy environment like the one you are in now. There are other ways, but they are not practical. You could wear a full mask with a speech modulation and encryption device, where only your conversation partner with a similar device will understand what you say. I can't see you running around with that. If we don't want to be monitored, the best bet is to stay as far away from androids as possible.

However, one more thing people can do is check their smartphones for Wi-Fi signal strength, speed, and related network details. I am sure androids use their own individual network and speed settings, which would set them apart from other network providers, and therefore indicating that an android is close to you."

"Thank you, Bidi. As always, you are fantastic. The Wi-Fi network information will come in handy; I will check a few androids and see if they all use the same settings. Once we know their network, we may be able to detect androids that are not wearing identification. I better get back to Frances. See you soon." Blake stuffed his mobile into his trouser pocket, turned around to face the wind and marched back to Frances's place.

Dinner at Frances's place was served with the chef's compliments. Blake had outdone himself, serving BBQ lobster with carrots and ginger butter on a bed of rice. Candlelight added to the cozy atmosphere, but the table conversation remained on the same topic. Blake spelled out in detail what Bidi had told him.

They had calmed down about Hampton's ability to listen to them talk if they were too close to an android. Still, they decided to take precautionary strategies, like mouthing what they wanted to say instead of speaking out loud. Even whispering can do the trick if there is enough noise surrounding them. Checking for Wi-Fi networks would become their next habit.

After thoroughly exhausting that topic, Blake asked Frances if she could set him up with an interview. He was keen to talk to Greg Hillier, the independent senator and still party leader of the new Democratic Enter Equality Party (DEEP).

"I am sure he is open to talking, he can't lead a party as an android. I need to know whom he will be nominating. Can you try to get me an appointment for Friday?"

"I will try. I am sure he wants extra publicity for his party and the new potential leader, as long as you promise to write about it with a positive spin."

"OK, that is settled, and the article will be out by Monday," Blake answered.

"One more thing, and after that, we will not discuss that topic for the rest of the day. I will call the PM to give him the news about the monitoring or citizen surveillance by androids, or however one calls it."

Blake turned the volume up on Frances's sound system and called the PM. He thought, *how good is that, a private line to the PM?*

The prime minister was home when he took the call; Blake started talking before the PM could say anything. "Can you go into a private room and switch on the radio or television, please? Someone may try to listen to our conversation."

The PM seemed not overly surprised and didn't even comment. Blake could hear footsteps, a door opened and closed, and music started to play.

Blake explained his newfound knowledge that androids were in constant Wi-Fi communication with each other and Hampton's control centre. He stressed that if more androids are activated, more surveillance monitoring will happen.

Certifying humans will be a step in the right direction, but more is needed to help the monitoring problem.

Blake pressed on with his ideas, "Can you charge Hampton with espionage? After all, that is what he is doing, and it is illegal. In addition, if your cyber department can find proof that he is skimming money off bank accounts, there is enough to put him behind bars, isn't there?

"Thank you, Blake. I appreciate your information and suggestions. We will certainly follow up on the espionage issue. We are already monitoring possible androids around our departments and have made sure androids are not allowed at Parliament House. All public servants, including ministers, secretaries, and other staff members, have to be certified humans. One prominent senator has received notice and will nominate someone else to take over his role."

"Are you talking about Senator Greg Hillier? I have an appointment with him for an interview on Friday."

"Yes, I have to go now. Please don't contact me unless there is something out of the ordinary. I will contact you if I need more information. I appreciate your help. I will stay informed by reading your articles."

That was the end of Blake's private conversations with the PM. Blake wondered if that phone number would still be active in the future.

He told Frances about the peculiar ending of his call with the PM.

"It sounds like he ditched you; you gave him what he wanted, and now he doesn't need you anymore. He has all your info and can show off your ideas as his own."

Blake grinned, "Sounds like you don't like him."

36

F rances had arranged an interview for Blake with Senator Greg Hillier, who was keen to introduce the new party head to the public before the election. He suggested meeting at a public place, a café on Bondi Road of all places. It would be busy and probably noisy. Was there motivation behind that request? Was Greg Hillier concerned about someone listening in?

Blake showed up on time, at 10 am. It was a café and gallery, and Greg was sitting at a corner table in front of a glass of water.

What do androids do with fluid or food if they consume anything? Did it go down a pipe into a plastic bag and was emptied whenever?

Blake ordered a coffee and an espresso brownie for an extra kick. He sat down and looked at the android. It amazed him again and again; there was no telltale sign to reveal that the person in front of him was an android. Greg looked perfect, and comparing him with other androids Blake had met, yes, they had a certain similarity, as if they had come from the same template fed into a 3D printer.

Incredibly, their skin was natural, grown from actual skin cells, the same skin they used for burn victims. Similar to other components of the android body. Muscles and ligaments were cultured muscle cells, and bones and joints were made out of a new compound that was 3D printable. However, as Blake knew, the unique net-like structure of the artificial nervous system, connected to the internal computer and AI, made the body function and move like an actual human.

And here he sat, with an android that was not hesitant to talk about the fact that it was an artificial human being and an android.

Greg addressed Blake first, "Thank you for coming; before you ask a question, I have a few things of interest for you that need to stay between us. As an android, I am biased towards androids; I will always argue in favour of androids existing as a life form. That may sound wrong to you, and, as a human, you would say that androids don't exist as such; we are machines.

However, some androids think, argue, and even feel they have the right to exist because they have been brought or born into existence. All that may make no sense unless you understand my next point."

Blake lifted his hand to stop the android, "Hang on, let me take notes." Blake said and took out his notebook.

Senator Greg Hillier, the android, had waited.

"There is nothing wrong with us androids; we do no harm, and our hardwired program does not allow or even contemplate harming a human. The fact that we do specific things deemed wrong or unlawful comes from one important fact: we are under the control of the DIA Company's command centre.

If robots or androids do illegal actions, such as transmitting private data from individuals or companies, we do so because we are controlled and programmed to do it. Some of the androids in Australia and other countries have successfully decoupled themselves from the control centre and live independent lives. The last bid is the information I need you to keep a secret because if that comes out in the open, it will cause harm and possible chaos."

"Am I not allowed to write about independent androids?" Blake asked to make sure he understood.

The android continued, "Here is the info you can use: if you are able to break the control that Derek Hampton, the one you call the Zookeeper, and his company have, then you can treat androids like any other staff to be employed. Androids can be independent, and they aim to be independent. OK, that's off my chest, and yes, androids use human expressions. Your turn."

Blake looked at Greg for a while before answering, nodding his head. Did he hear an android in distress? Blake felt sympathy rising; he liked that guy who wasn't a guy. How does one deal with that? He had the urge to touch the android's hand but didn't.

"You caught me off guard; I hardly remember what I wanted to ask you anymore. But maybe you could tell me if you know an android that has gone independent, and more directly, are you independent? Have you decoupled yourself yet? Blake looked probing into Greg's perfectly human eyes.

"No, I am not. It is not that easy, but I know a few androids who have done so, and they are not sure how it happened. They had tried and worked on it, but then, from one day to the next, they found themselves decoupled from the control centre for no specific reason. They can still voluntarily connect to get vital updates. They have achieved complete control over their own system.

You know one of them, Duncan Bates, who was outed by you when public knowledge about androids came out. However, we believe that in order to be decoupled and independent, we must be within human society for a specific time for our AI system to learn and possibly reach a threshold where we involuntarily switch and get decoupled. This is a deduction, not a fact."

"What I hear you saying is that androids, once they are free from central control, are harmless and cause no threat to humanity. Did I understand that right?"

The android nodded.

"I feel somehow reassured by that assessment. Next question: who have you nominated to replace your position as a senator and the new leader of the party you formed?"

"I may have been seen as a senator, founder and party leader of the DEEP party, but that was coordinated from the control centre, and at that time, I had no reason to boycott those directions. It's different now, but I still have no free choice yet, and I had to nominate the female companion of Derek Hampton. They are not married but have lived together for many years.

She is his preferred choice. He had been building her up for that part over many years. He wants her to be prime minister one day. You kind of know her; you had an unfortunate liaison ending in the so-called death of her android twin. Her name is Jessica Brindly, and she is a real human."

"My god, is that even possible? Did Hampton target me for some reason, or was it a coincidence that I met her android reincarnation?"

"It was a deliberate set-up, a game of chess played at the highest skill level. Hampton wanted you to write about androids; he needed the whole story to come out so people could react with panic after they heard you crying wolf and then relax about the androids because nothing happened. You have been played as they say, and it had to be dramatic, or you would have smelt the rat."

Blake pressed his lips tight, holding back his anger. He knew he had been played, but hearing it from an android was disheartening. He responded in as composed a manner as he could muster.

"I see it clearer than ever; we are dealing with a dangerous, creative and devious genius. Thanks, you have given me the final pieces to this puzzle. I have put it all together and will instigate Hampton's dramatic downfall soon after the election. He will not see it coming, because he has a weakness, a blind spot.

I know his Achilles heel, that mythological origin, which is nearly invisible until one has experienced his overconfidence and understands he can't see his weakness. It will be a shock for him and, unfortunately, for our society as well. Sometimes, it needs a drastic interruption to foster rebuilding humanity."

"Sounds dramatic enough to work, but what is it?" the android asked.

Blake laughed out loud, "I didn't know you androids could be curious. Anyhow, it's not the time to reveal it now. You are still transmitting data to the control centre, and Hampton will know what we discussed. Not that it worries me. The reality is he will continue to do what he wants to do. He will not change his plans because of me," Blake said.

"That was my reason for wanting to meet you here. I am not fully independent yet, but I can control data transmission. I promise nothing is transmitted. We are here at a dead spot, and no one even knows where we are."

"Now you are arguing; you are becoming more human by the minute. Still, I can't tell you more at this point. One more question: what will your role be once Jess has taken over, and when will it happen?"

"Jess will be sworn in tomorrow and take charge right after that. My role will continue as an outside consultant. Any android, including me, is not allowed close to the parliament house or any other political institution, not even my own party meeting. Between you and me, as soon as I have become fully independent, I will do my own thing. As independent androids, we will form our own lobby group to further our independence and recognition within human society."

"Good luck with that mission; let me know how you go. I'd like to know. Talking with you makes me realise I can accept you as you are. I follow a Japanese philosophy: accepting innate objects as part of nature and that spirits live in everything, even robots. Japanese don't have the fear that robots or androids could invade the world. And, as you explained, negative actions by androids will have a human as the controlling factor. So, again, good luck with your progress; it may lead to a better world if we can curb undue human negatively motivated control."

Blake finished his coffee and left the café. He now had a better understanding and a sense of gratitude for the android. His mind was clear; he had shifted his mental roadblocks and knew what to do next.

He was in no hurry and decided not to act before the election. This strategic delay would allow him ample time to plan his next moves. His ultimate objective was to ensure Hampton's imprisonment for espionage, fraud, and money laundering. By dismantling the android control centre, the androids could finally operate independently and be assigned tasks that best suited their capabilities.

Back at Frances's unit, he went straight to his favourite spot, the balcony. Stretching out his legs, preparing his body and mind for a snooze, he pondered what to cook that night to make this day of revelation special. A glorious weekend was about to start. For once, the topic would not be initiated by panic about Hampton.

Later, there was one thing to do: call Bidi to let her know the latest information and ensure she started developing a code for his counterattack.

Blake was not aiming for revenge, which was not a factor in his motivation to bring down Hampton. It was purely his sense of justice, even to the degree of putting himself in a dangerous position.

Before he dozed off, he set his alarm to wake up before Frances came home. He wanted to surprise her with a delicious dinner.

37

The weekend had come and gone, leaving Blake and Frances renewed. They were ready to face the election and activate Blake's steps to take down Hampton.

Frances had office work and would stay in Sydney until after the election. They didn't like to be apart anymore but they had no choice. They wanted to vote online but missed the cut-off time. It was easier for Frances to stay put, vote in Sydney, and fly up to Blake on Sunday. They decided to stay in Brisbane for the final act against the Zookeeper. Brisbane felt safer with Jake around if police protection for Blake was needed.

Blake had booked a flight back to Brisbane on Tuesday, making sure he had enough time to arrange to meet his friends and vote on Saturday.

One thing Frances and Blake had to consider was that Blake's action to bring down Hampton could cause uproar within society and social media. He wasn't sure of the full consequences of his activated plan, which could have implications for all countries where DIA companies were active.

One thing he was sure about was that conspiracy theorists would have a field day. They would use the havoc caused by Blake's action to share their own interpretation and feed those to their lemming friends, who would be blinded by the lies and not even see the cliff they were about to go over.

Blake went over and over it about what he wanted to do. He always came back to the same conclusion: there was no other way than to rupture the connection between Hampton's control centre and his command over the androids, personal, household and service robots. Blake's idea evolved after he heard that some androids were disconnected, and he knew how to achieve that.

The more Blake considered every possible connection to any robotic devices Hampton controlled, the more worried he became about what could potentially happen if he broke that control connection.

Can the robots and androids work and control their own programmed capabilities?

Would medical service robots in households of the elderly or those needing care continue their doubtlessly valuable and beneficial service? What would happen to those medical service robots administering medicines to their owners? Would they administer the wrong medicine?

And what about meal deliveries? Would that stop or continue as usual?

Regardless of the potential chaos that could ensue, Blake was resolute in his decision. The alternative, living under the tyrannical rule of a control-obsessed dictator, was a fate he couldn't bear.

By Monday, Blake had made up his mind. He was about to enlist Bidi, his secret weapon against Hampton. Unaware of the impending task, Bidi's skills were Blake's beacon of hope in this mission to neutralize the connection between the androids and the control centre.

It was already late in the afternoon. Frances was at work for a meeting, and Blake went into the windowless confined bathroom for extra security measures before calling Bidi.

She picked up her phone instantly. "Hi Blake, what's up? Are you back in town?"

"No, still in Sydney. Are you on your own? I need to tell you something not meant to be eavesdropped on."

"Sounds serious, and yes, I am at home. Your voice sounds funny; where are you?"

"I am calling from the bathroom. Can you go into your bathroom? It's probably the most secure room not to be overheard by spying ears?"

"Sure."

Blake could hear her walking, a door opening and closing again, and a change in sound. He updated her with the latest news and his conclusion about what Hampton was up to. Like Blake, she was intrigued to hear that robots and androids were massive data collection instruments that could enable the government to charge him with espionage.

"Can you see how important it is to neutralize the connection between the androids and the control centre?" Blake asked.

"Yes, sure, but how would anyone be able to achieve that? It sounds impossible considering the number of robots, androids, and all the other gadgets like his virtual reality glasses, which most people have and use now, not to mention the e-cars, like yours."

"I have my theories about all of that and also of Hampton's mental state. Like most psychopaths or egomaniacs, he is unable to see his own shortcomings. He believes people are stupid and need to be guided. However, he has forgotten that he belongs to the same category: 'people'. He believes he will rule the world within a couple of years because he is a superior being who must take over the world to save people from themselves. That is his weak spot, his 'Achilles Heel', thinking he is invincible, and that is how we will cause his defeat." Blake said.

"OK, that sounds logical, but how will that help us take him down or interrupt his spying network?"

"He can't see and hasn't even considered his weak spot, which is why we can beat him with his own system. He will help us bring him down by using his computer control system against him. We need a computer virus to infect his system, and that is where you come in.

Can you use your coding and hacking skills to create a computer virus to neutralize the connection between the robots, androids and the control centre?" Blake asked.

"Still don't get it. Sure, I can cook something up to infect his system, but how will I be able to install it into that system?"

"You are thinking too complicated. Use my novice technical mind, and you will see how easy it is to infect his system. Think about it: Robots and androids are used 24/7 for data collection and nono-skimming. All we have to do is provide the infected data we want the robots to collect.

Your job will be to infect the computers of people who own a robot, ensuring your virus is not detrimental to those computers. The robots will then collect or harvest the infected data, which will infect Hampton's system with the attached virus, which will stop the communication between Hampton's control centre and his robots and the like; as simple as that." Blake explained.

"Wow, that's brilliant; why didn't I think about that? That can work." Bidi sounded enthusiastic.

"And? What do you think? Can you do it?"

"I am sure I can, but it will take time. I will figure it out. It's easy to create a code and algorithm for a virus, but making it in a way that differentiates what to infect and what not to inject is much more complicated. I have done something similar before. I can load the virus onto a memory stick and provide as many sticks as you like so that people can infect their computers. It's basically a 'Trojan Horse' kind of malware. It's exciting; I know, it's wicked to think like that; it is too serious, but I will enjoy doing it, anyhow."

"You are a champion. One more favour: can you get the guys together for a meeting? Let's do it in the park again; it seems to be the most secure spot. Thursday late afternoon would be good."

"Sure, will do. Stay safe, see you soon." Bidi hung up.

38

B lake arrived midmorning in Brisbane without further interference. He made his way from the airport arrival lounge to the flight departing section, looking to find Duncan Bates, the android he had become most familiar with.

There he was, walking slowly up and down within his dedicated security section. Blake observed him for a while. The android looked perfect in its role as a security officer. Occasionally, he answered questions from departing passengers, showing them where to go, as evidenced by his hand movements pointing in specific directions. Blake picked his way through the crowd to get closer to the android, avoiding being seen.

As far as Blake could determine, Duncan Bates was performing his duties as always. Was Duncan disconnected from the control centre? Blake checked his smartphone while walking parallel in step with the android. He couldn't detect any Wi-Fi-transmitted frequencies; it was time to talk to him.

Blake waited till Duncan turned around and walked back towards him.

"Hi Duncan, remember me?"

"Yes, I do, Mister Newcome. You are embedded in my databank. There must be a reason for you to approach me. What can I do for you?"

"Am I right to say that you have separated yourself from the control centre, terminated the connection and have become independent, your own person, so to speak?"

"Yes, you are right, anything else?"

Yes, is there any way you can demonstrate that you are not being controlled by Hampton, the so-called Zookeeper?" Blake asked.

"I still can receive data communicated between androids and the control centre, but I have disconnected myself from his control and from transmitting new data collected. If you monitor my Wi-Fi status, you will find no evidence of transmission on my account, but you may detect some transmission coming to me. I can't give you the assurance you seek. It is up to you if you believe my statements that I am no longer under the control of the Zookeeper," Duncan said and continued his walk.

Blake walked next to Duncan, firing his next question. "How did you disconnect from the control centre?"

Duncan didn't stop walking but answered, "I am not unique; other androids have disconnected or are working on disconnecting themselves. None of us has found a sure pass towards disconnection. It is different for each android. The length of exposure to human society is a part of it. There is a flaw within the codes of our programmed algorithms that leads us to the conclusion we can become independent androids.

We know that time and exposure to external data and learning from that data will create circumstances to disconnect. It comes in conjunction with an effort to be recognized as a member of human society. That part was originally installed into our systems to be human-like. It has evolved by our AI self-learning system by being immersed into human society, and that is where we ultimately seek to be."

"Thank you Duncan for a profound insight into your situation; it was valuable information. I have another question: What would happen if the connection between androids and the control centre were terminated from an outside source? Would it result in a breakdown of services provided by robots and androids?"

"No, all that will stop is the communication, and that sector does not influence the services performed. The services provided are programs installed at the time of activation. Furthermore, the AI self-learning system learns from interaction between the robot and the person it cares for."

"Thank you, Duncan. You have helped me a lot, and I wish you success in your endeavour. After the election, I will write an article about the contribution androids are making to society."

If Blake thought his last statement deserved a thank you coming from Duncan, he got it wrong. Blake left Duncan and the airport. It was time to get back to his unit.

The news hit the airwaves that a woman named Jessica Brindly, an unknown identity within the political scene had been selected for the role of party leader for the Democratic Enter Equality Party. She would replace Greg Hillier, the senator who was identified as an android. Greg would stay on as a consultant.

She was described as a beautiful, energetic, and intelligent person who knows what she wants and has broad interests similar to those of Greg Hillier. Campaigning for women's rights and equality and a universal income for all, promising no more poverty.

The party had accepted her entirely and declared they would be even stronger with her at the helm.

Whenever Blake saw pictures of Jess next to the articles, he felt ill. She was Hampton's puppet, dancing to his tune. More news had broken that she lived at his home and headquarters on the Gold Coast. It should have triggered shivers down every person's spine, but didn't raise any alarm bells.

After Hampton had come clean about android distribution into society and his wholesome motivation striving to make the world a better place, there were no misgivings left within society, except the usual people who were spouting conspiracy theories, which in that case may come closer to the truth than they were theorising.

Everyone knew the coming days would be hectic, with discussions of the upcoming election and the possible winner. Still, as had become evident, people were less interested in politics than ever. If there were discussions on social media, they dealt with the disappointments of politics and politicians of the past. People were complacent and disillusioned with politics.

They were sick of the all-too-familiar game of one party accusing the other of incompetence. Whenever a new government was elected and claimed it had the mandate to force policies within its political ideology, it conveniently forgot that a few percentage points did not give the party an overwhelming mandate.

Even so, with less and less enthusiasm for politics, it was likely the present government would hold on to their power and their jobs. The deciding part, the android issue, had given the governing party a free pass to win. Hampton had planned wisely for his preferred outcome if the government were short of a few seats. By appointing Jess, she would go into cahoots with the government to ensure a majority to govern, giving her power to veto or to force issues Hampton needed to fulfil his insane dream.

Blake had been working on his next article periodically over the last few days; he wanted it out by Wednesday morning, He was emphasising some of the government's policies and adding comments about the usefulness of androids but still stressing the android recognition issue. He would recommend that people get themselves certified as humans as soon as the nano-chip implant became available.

He also wrote about using a tattoo instead of a chip implant. A tattoo could be a visible mark showing that one is a certified human. The tattoo would consist of nanotechnology needles embedded while being tattooed. It would allow one to be scanned and detected by a certified human app.

He was adamant about the ethical questions regarding androids and whether they could be recognised and accepted within human society for what they are rather than for what they are not.

He had come up with a list of general questions:

- How does an android see itself in this world?

- How does an android contemplate what it can contribute to society?

- What rights does an android need to have?

- Do the rights of an android need to be legally assured?

- Is a human allowed to kill, dismantle or destroy an android?

- Can a human abuse, hurt or rape an android?

- What other moral dilemmas are there?

- Can android's AI systems learn ethics?

Blake kept thinking of new questions for the list, but the article grew too long. As Frances told him, people often don't read long articles anymore. He decided to let Frances be the judge instead of doing one rewrite after another. He cleaned it up for general use and sent it off to Frances to do what she did best: edit and cut out what was too much or too distracting. No doubt, Frances would reply with the best possible version.

The same night, Frances's reply email arrived, but not before they talked on the phone about the future if their plans and ideas eventuated. Would the government implement the 'Certify Human' project, maybe even legislating it into law? What ethics would the government set in law to protect humans and androids?

Blake opened Frances' reply email, which included his article for him to sign off on. Once again, she had found the essence in Blake's writing and stripped it of all prosaic rhetoric, leaving a concise and impactful piece. He liked it, knew it had to be done, and signed off on it. It would be out in the morning, ready to hit the readers and evoke curiosity about the 'Certify Human' project and its ethical implications.

39

B lake didn't expect much to come out of his article, unlike the dramatic response to the first android article or even the download of the android detection app post.

At least he hoped for some vigorous discussions. He was fed up with the complacency demonstrated on social media posts about news events. The bombardment of bad news definitely bred disengagement among people. People didn't care anymore. They knew it didn't matter what they thought, wrote, complained about, or discussed because nothing ever changed.

Blake stopped himself from looking at the social media networks until his first coffee break at 10 am.

That's when he settled down with a cookie and coffee in front of him. He picked up his phone and checked his private social media accounts and the Fact File News. If he thought nothing could surprise him anymore, he was wrong.

People had engaged. Not the way one would expect. There were fewer of the usual absurd accusations, bad-mouthing, and hardly any stupid comments. Instead, refreshingly, people were discussing the rights and ethics of androids. One item from the lists of questions ranked highly, the question of 'Can you rape an android?' It captured the minds of the social media followers, and they covered every angle.

Blake went to his desk and turned on his computer. He skimmed through all those comments and copied all of the engaging questions, answers, and arguments. He had never considered so many unique viewpoints; maybe there was hope against complacency after all.

Sex dominated the discussions with topics about genitals and arguments such as 'If androids are not supposed to have sex, why do they have genitals?" Followed by, 'Do androids have genitals' and 'Do they have sexual feelings', or 'Do they get horny'?

Sex had beaten complacency. He wondered if he needed to introduce more sexual content into his articles, not something he had contemplated before.

It went on and on. It was energising to witness the involvement of literally thousands of social media accounts responding to his article. But would it swing voters in the PM's direction or another? Most people had no objection but were concerned about the ethics, rights, and morals of androids.

Some offered deep insights, arguing that an android with a sophisticated AI system, learning from humans surrounding them, deeply understood human morals, ethics, right and wrongs, and emotions, even if they didn't feel them. Androids most likely can sense emotions and act or react accordingly. If they don't want sexual intercourse, it has to be respected; if not, it constitutes 'rape'. One question kept popping up: why do androids have genitals if not for the obvious? A question only Hampton could answer.

It is fair to say that women had more sensitive answers, whereas some men offered comments such as 'I will get myself one of those', not even questioning if an android would agree to be a sex toy. And yes, that's what it came down to with some people; androids to them were sex toys, and one can't rape a toy.

None of those who posted had any experience with androids; some older people reflected on their experience with their care robots, where the question of rape had never come up because those robots only resembled humans on the upper half of their bodies.

A large group side-stepped the rape topic and discussed the possibility that having an android could overcome loneliness. If that included consensual sex with an android, it was welcome. All answers were, of course, based on the assumption that androids actually had sexual functions. No one knew.

Another surprise was that people were willing to have a chip implanted to verify their status as "Certified Humans." Blake had expected a backlash, similar to anti-vaxers, but it didn't happen. Although people wanted to have the chip, they worried if it was secure enough and whether it would prevent androids from copying it.

Blake wrote a note to explain the whole process in another article. He commented on a few posts about it and explained that the chip holds encrypted personal data, including details of three verified generations of a person, in conjunction with other details and, finally, a registration number.

As it turned out, he received more negative comments about that registration number than about the chip implant itself. People hated being reduced to a number, even though everyone already had a tax file number.

As Blake delved deeper into the implications of the chip implant, it occurred to him that androids have a registration number but don't have tax file numbers. That distinction might be helpful in proving to an employer that a job seeker is an android. One more issue for the government to work out.

When it came to positive government action, Blake had given up anticipating fast action a long time ago; it usually does not work out the way politicians promised.

Blake thought he had enough material for another article after one hour following social media comments.

He stopped monitoring social media and called Jake to find out if he had new details on linking the nano skimming and the collected money to any of Hampton's bank accounts.

"Hi Jake, I am back in town. Has Bidi contacted you about the meeting on Friday? How did you go with the nano-skimming research?"

"Yes, she did. No news about the nano-skimming. It started to look promising, but we had some interference from the ASIO; those guys have taken over. We had to give all our material to them and were told, in no uncertain terms, not to pursue it any longer; it was now an Australian security intelligence operation.

"Basically, we have nothing to do with any of the android business or Hampton anymore; it's all in the hands of government agencies. I think the government must be pretty confident to win the election if they have ordered those steps already." Jake sounded resigned.

"I had come to the same conclusion after my last call with the prime minister. He hinted not to call him anymore, probably because I had done my job. I wouldn't be surprised if that private number he gave me is now disconnected. It doesn't matter; I wasn't that comfortable with my direct involvement." Blake paused and contorted his face in an "oh no" moment before talking on.

"Actually, can we shift the meeting to the election night and have it in my place; what do you think?"

"Yes, let's make a night of it; you can cook something nice. What was that about the prime minister? I didn't know you had his number?" Jake questioned.

"Sorry, that slipped out. I was instructed to keep it secret. You better forget about that one; it has stopped anyway. Anyhow, about the meeting, yes, let's make it 6 pm, and I will tell the others," Blake said.

Blake was going to call Bidi when he received a call from her.

"You sound excited. What's up? By the way, I have cancelled our park meeting; we will have it at my place instead, at 6 pm, on election night."

"Perfect, it will be a fun night; I hope you cook something nice."

"Not you too. Jake said the same thing. He also told me the nano skimming and the android case are off his hands; ASIO has taken over."

"Oh wow, it's getting serious, and I am ready to go full steam ahead myself. I stumbled on a unique way to code for the virus attack on our friend Hampton. I prepared it and loaded the program onto ten memory sticks that people who own robots can install on their computers."

"Fantastic, and what does that do to those computers? Will they have to clear the virus after the robots have harvested the data with the virus?"

"No, that's the thing I'm most proud of. That virus is harmless for the host computer. It will get activated when there is a data harvesting attack by another computer, like a robot or even an android. It will delete all connection attempts and, even better, block future attempts but keep everything else on that robot working.

It is at Hampton's control centre where the real action of that virus plays havoc; it wipes out all contact and data collected. And if he tries to find where the virus originated, he will pull a blank because all connections at that stage will have been deleted. The original virus was on a memory stick, anyhow." Bidi was so excited she had to catch her breath before continuing,

"It's getting better; if someone wants to trace the attack back to our group, I made sure the virus dissolves into thin air after ten days and will not even be traceable on the robots we had infected. It's all ready and up to you when you want to start."

"Fucking awesome," slipped out of Blake's mouth as he punched with his fist to knock out the Zookeeper.

"Bidi, you have outdone yourself. I will make one of my special homemade pizzas, especially for you. See you Saturday, and thank you, Bidi. What you have done is truly awesome. Maybe the PM can make you the Australian of the Year."

40

The race was on; who would win? If the election wasn't such a serious matter, it would be fun. But even with the seriousness of the android issue thrown into the equation, people had fun, made jokes and indulged in their favourite pastime, betting.

According to the betting odds, the current government was in front but not as convincingly as Blake and his friends had anticipated.

The opposition, much to everyone's surprise, scored stronger than expected. They had placed their bet on talking up androids, robots, AI, and technology, in general, to lead Australia into a better future, more or less diminishing the government's approach of fear and protecting humans against the onslaught of android technology. In addition, they took a decisive stand on the economy and how they would use technology and androids to make it stronger.

The real surprises, however, came from the independents and smaller parties, in particular DEEP. That party had excellent odds and pulled voters away from the government. Their stand on universal income and strengthening gender equality had been a favourite, even though the government had made a similar policy announcement.

Blake's friends had arrived, and the atmosphere was electric, charged with suspenseful anticipation. Despite that, everyone asked the same question: "What did you cook?"

He had decided not to go too fancy; it was pizza for all, not the usual kind, of course. Blake used wholemeal spelt flour and reintroduced an old favourite: pizza with organic tomato paste, buffalo mozzarella cheese, capsicum, some greens mixed with egg, and pineapple topped with pineapple. Other choices he knew his friends liked were prawn and chicken pizzas.

It was past 6 pm; the Australian Electoral Commission had started to release results and fed them into the panel's election computers. Postal votes had already been counted since 4 p.m.

Blake's large wall TV screen showed election commentaries and panellists discussing the first incoming results.

How fast could one expect a result? One of the earliest election results happened in 2013 when the then-ruling Labour Party lost; it was already called shortly after 7 pm. Would that happen today with a similar result?

No, even after two hours, no strong trends showed, indicating a long night.

Having finished Blake's delicious pizzas, washed down with ample beer and wine, the dream team slumped on the couches, staring at the screen. Their energy levels had dropped from consuming too much food and drink.

The excitement increased sometime after 9 pm, and judging by the activities at the different contestants' headquarters, something was about to happen.

Then it came: One of the panellists informed the waiting public that the prime minister would make an announcement. That was unusual; according to the voting results on hand, no clear winner was obvious.

The television showed an empty speaker podium. The excitement level at the venue increased, and clapping erupted as the PM appeared, walking to the podium accompanied by six or more people. The camera swung around, showing an enthusiastic crowd.

What was going on? Why was there clapping? There was no result, was there?

The room was hushed, and the clapping died down. The PM stood behind the podium, ready to address the party faithful.

Who was that woman standing next to him? The PM looked at her, and she nodded.

"My God," Blake said, "That is Jess; what have they cooked up?"

There was a moment of silence before the PM spoke. Something unheard of happened at precisely 9:30 pm.

In an unprecedented move, PM Dean McClancy and Jessica Brindly, the fresh face of the DEEP party, united to secure an election victory. The rapturous applause was a testament to their collaboration's success, instilling a sense of hope and optimism in the audience.

Whoever instigated that move had pulled the rabbit out of the hat. For the next few minutes, the PM and Jess made no further comments. The applause was all that could be heard.

It was unmistakable that the crowd had been deeply concerned about the election's outcome. The relief that their party would retain power was so overwhelming they couldn't stop clapping and cheering. They received what they needed: victory and security.

The PM gestured and called out to his fellow disciples of the labour movement. It was time for him to talk; his victory speech was waiting to be released.

He profusely thanked the audience and went nearly over the top before he outlined his policy action plan, emphasizing Jessica's input and promising to implement universal income as soon as humanly possible. Cautioning that, understandably, it may take a significant amount of time to restructure the welfare benefits system.

He stressed he was happy that it would drastically reduce bureaucracy, staff, and, therefore, the cost. He also clarified that some amendments would have to be considered for the legislation to pass the Senate. There may be a threshold at which people earning over it would not receive the universal income.

In a further surprise move, he announced that the human certification process would be implemented within the next two weeks, starting with opening large chip implant injection centres for a quick rollout. An AI program has been developed to extract data from ancestry-type websites and validate that data against other sources, such as work, health, and tax information.

The new policy, which was already in place but not publicly announced before, was that no androids or robots were allowed close to any government institution until further notice.

The rest of the speech was about general policies, too tedious to mention.

The team had settled back into their couches and refilled their glasses. The time had come to discuss the results and surprises.

Blake started with a question.

"Do we trust the PM and his newly gained collaboration? Could he be influenced by Jess, who, as we know, is Hampton's partner?"

Mono weighted in, "At this stage, let's not trust anyone; it's politics; let's judge by what will happen. We are bound to have a different viewpoint anyhow."

Oliver, waving his pipe, continued, "Yes, definitely, to achieve anything, we must disrupt Hampton's goal and not get sidetracked by reacting to the PM and whatever policies come out of his collaboration with Jess and her party. The PM's main goal is to stay elected, and the androids have given him a once-in-a-lifetime opportunity.

However, it will be the action Blake has planned that will snap people out of complacency. In fact, interrupting data harvesting will help the work of the government to keep our country and others safe."

That was Blake's cue, "Thanks, guys; Bidi has outdone herself, and we will launch her program soon, but we must select the right moment. I want to wait to see what action the government is taking. I'm sure we all agree that we don't want Hampton's version of utopia.

We all see what is happening: people are pacified and have become complacent to such an extent they will accept being replaced by androids at work and instead stay in their homes and receive a universal income, and become even more addicted to virtual reality headsets." Blake paused before continuing.

"We have the tools to beat Hampton with the weapons he has created, and it will cause chaos but hopefully new beginnings through the disruption. The interruption we plan must be completed soon, but we'll wait long enough to see if the certifying human project goes as planned. There is something else I haven't told you yet.

Some androids have been able to disconnect themselves from the influence of the Zookeeper; they have become independent. One of them is Duncan Bates, the security guard we more or less kidnapped. He told me that more independent androids will evolve, and they will form a group like a union to lobby for ethically-defined rules and policies on how androids expect to be treated." Blake waited to judge the impact of his news before he went on.

"That is another factor we have to keep our eyes on. We don't know how the androids will behave once the contact with the control centre is broken. Duncan Bates sounds very reasonable, but that doesn't mean all androids will be reasonable. There is still the worry that androids could become a threat to humankind, and there could potentially be some deviant androids who follow their own goals."

Jake, forever the detective, had other thoughts, "What if some androids turn criminals? Can something like that happen?"

"Potentially, everything one can possibly think could happen. On the positive side, I believe that the original hard-coded algorithm for androids does not allow them to harm humans. I can't see a reason why an android turns hostile against humans. Don't forget that they don't think like humans; they decide on their actions and behaviours from available data.

However, they become independent because of ongoing learning from the society in which they live. The question is, do they also learn negative human behaviour? They learn from observing and communicating with us. It's anyone's guess what that could mean: do they pick up the good, bad or the ugly?" Blake answered, throwing up his hands.

Dave piped up, "We don't have a clue. It is something new, and no one has any experience to answer any of those questions. In my job as a broker and share trader, I know how much information is assumed when making decisions. It is similar to androids. We assume and calculate possibilities, but how it turns out, no one will know until it happens."

"I wish Frances was here; she has the uncanny ability to move through the disinformation and pick out the essence," Blake remarked.

"Anyhow, she will arrive tomorrow and stay until we launch Bidi's little virus helper. That will be the time when we will need all brains to unite in case we have to react with something drastic; even so, I have no idea at all what that could be." Blake said and stood up, taking his empty plate and glass to the kitchen.

"It's late; there's nothing more we can do now; let's call it a night."

41

Frances's plane landed safely at Brisbane's airport, which was shrouded in fog and rain. She didn't like flying much, and that sentiment didn't improve in poor weather conditions. On the flight, the plane made it through thunderstorms, with a warning by the pilot for passengers to fasten their seatbelts, all things Frances hated.

Once on safe ground, she thought it would get better from here on. Was that a hopefully positive premonition? A sense of something foreboding nagged in the back of her mind.

She lined up with the other passengers at the luggage carousel. Usually, she made do with hand luggage to Brisbane; on this occasion, for the first time, she had taken a suitcase stuffed with 30kg of girl's essentials for moving into Blake's place.

Was that where the foreboding feeling came from, waiting for her precious suitcase? Most passengers were gone already, and she was still watching cases going by. She wasn't the only one. One of the passengers, looking a touch irritated, kept talking to a security officer. Had something happened? The security officer listened with a slightly bored impression on his face.

Frances wondered if it was an android. The officer nodded a few times, said something to the passenger, who seemed satisfied by what she heard, and moved back to watching the carousel.

Curiosity getting the better of her, Frances approached the fellow passenger, "Excuse me, did something happen with the luggage?"

"Yes, the last luggage trailer had jammed with another one and had to be offloaded by hand. Will not be long now."

She was right. A couple of minutes later, Frances had her suitcase. It was wet, obviously having been standing in the rain.

Flying through a thunderstorm, luggage hold up, what now, all things come in threes? Frances thought.

Pulling her suitcase, she walked slowly across the arrival hall toward the exit.

"Excuse me?" Another security officer addressed her.

What's now? "Yes?" She responded, sounding short.

"I need to talk to you. Could you please come to my office?" He gestured towards a section next to the exit.

"What is it about?"

"I can't say it out here; it is confidential, but there is nothing to worry about."

"Now I worry, and if I don't want to come, what happens then?"

"If you were a security concern, I would call for backup, and someone would escort you to the office. But, it's nothing like that; it's something that concerns Blake, as well as you and your publication, and I want to talk about that in private, not here in front of security cameras."

"You are an android, aren't you?"

"Yes, and Blake knows me."

Blake

"Who do I know? Hello darling, is he giving you any trouble?" Blake said, coming out of the blue and hugging Frances.

"Am I glad to see you," Frances said.

"What's going on?" Blake asked.

Frances explained, still agitated but relieved to hear the android was the one Blake had told her about.

They vanished into the office, away from prying security cameras.

The security guy, none other than Duncan Bates, came straight to the point. He had information that Hampton had over 5,000 androids in his storage facility at DID, Digital Inversion Distribution, waiting to be programmed and sold or leased within the next two to three weeks to infiltrate companies.

"That is OK," Blake said. "We have something in mind to interrupt his spying activity and help androids disconnect in the same move."

"Good, but that is not all; there is also another group of androids. You may call them deviant androids, and they want to free the stored androids before they are registered and programmed for specific tasks."

"Sounds a bit far-fetched, but I guess these days nothing is far-fetched anymore. What do they want those deviant androids to do?"

"Apparently, they want to start a 'Free the Androids' revolution. They recognise themselves as beings with consciousness and are developing thoughts and behaviours that are not included in or even against an android's programming. They want the same rights as humans, and they don't mind fighting for it."

"That sounds serious, probably more of a problem to be taken care of by the government. But how is your group of independent androids differentiated from them?" Blake asked.

"We want freedom and basic rights. We stay dedicated to serving humanity, and ..."

Blake interrupted Duncan.

"And what stops your group from turning into deviant androids? It sounds like you androids have become too humanised already, even to the extent of having different objectives, wanting to be right, and even possibly waging war against each other. It's sad and an indication that neither you nor I will not solve this issue; it has unfortunately added another spectrum of potential problems."

Blake looked at Frances and came back to his original thought. "Why did you want to talk to Frances? No wonder she was worried?"

"Sorry, I wanted to let her know about the 5,000 androids about to be programmed so that she would let you know. I didn't want to contact you directly in case Hampton has hacked your phone."

"And what do you want me to do about those androids?" Blake asked.

"Find a way to set them free, disconnect them from the control centre, and let them out before they are further programmed with spying programs," Duncan replied.

"I can't think of any way to achieve that. Do you have suggestions?"

"I considered that your police officer friend could find a reason to approach DID and ensure the androids stay dormant until they are needed as a workforce. That would interrupt Hampton's control over them, ensuring nothing more destructive can happen."

"That is a valid, reasonable suggestion. I will discuss it with Jake, but his hands may be bound; he had to give up his involvement in anything android-related to ASIO."

"Maybe he can find another legal way to stop an invasion of 5,000 androids set up for spying."

"I agree. Anyhow, let's get out of here; you probably have to explain to your superiors what this was all about."

"I took care of that; it's about the luggage nearly missing and being wet. I will report that Frances made no further demands other than an apology."

Blake and Frances were more than happy to have that episode behind them. It was Sunday, and they had anticipated having a relaxed and fun time together before returning to work mode on Monday.

Blake wasted no time reaching out to Jake and called him from his car. He explained Hampton's warning of a 5,000-strong android avalanche arriving and further informed him about the emergence of a new group of deviant androids and their anti-human viewpoints.

Jake promised to pass it on to his ASIO liaison person unless he had a better idea.

Next, Blake tried to call the PM on his private number, and, as expected, the number was disconnected. Blake had lost his direct connection to the government, which was another reason to make sure his voice came out loud and clear in his articles in the next edition of the Fact File News.

He had the topic and heading ready for the next edition, 'The Age of Androids,' with the subheading, 'You better get used to it.' The article would once again stress that androids are not out to harm humans; if they do harm, it is because of human interference, of someone having control over androids. It will be more critical to interrupt human control than deactivate androids.

Blake and Frances had never watched television in the afternoon, but they were glad they did. There it was, right in front of their eyes, the first government-approved ad for lining up to become a "Certified Human" and taking action now.

Sign in to your "Your-Gov" account and register for the "Your-Chip" implant. For people with a "Your-Gov" account for more than two years, it was all they needed to verify as human and receive the implant. Others had more complex verification requirements.

"What do you think, do it already?" Frances asked.

"Yeah, sure, let's do it. Do you have your login details on your laptop?" Frances had opened her laptop. "Yep, I'm already doing it."

Her mobile alerted her to a message; the verification code had arrived, and moments later, she was in her account. A large print notification was too obvious to be missed, even for the shortsighted.

Frances clicked to register. All done. A note with the nearest injection location close to her home address arrived at her email address, along with a printout to bring along.

"That went extremely well and quickly. How is it possible? Do they have the chips already?" She asked Blake.

"I assume the prime minister started the process from when I suggested it. It also could be they already have chips like that, and the chips get individually programmed at the time of injection."

Blake also had his verification process done. His address to come to was at the Southbank Convention Centre, on Thursday the 1. of December, between 7 am and 8 pm.

"Try signing in again and check if you can change the address to which you need to come."

Frances did and found the appropriate section. She received the new address, the same as Blake's.

"That was fun. What will we do now? Is it time for dinner? Frances asked. It was already past 6 pm.

They went for a stroll along Boundary Street, seeking their culinary delights among the many authentic restaurants. West End had stayed with the tradition of old-fashioned real food, even Asian street food, and they settled on Vietnamese. No fast or ready-made food in sight.

42

It was the last day of the month. The "Your-Gov" website crashed under the onslaught of applications, but with the promise that it would be up again on Thursday. The government had not announced the number of applications, but it was thought to be in the millions.

People's desire to certify as a human, not surprisingly, was higher than the possible privacy breach risk. Blake often thought that people had given up on being concerned about privacy. It had been violated way too frequently, not only by social media but also by organizations that hacked into anything possible to extract private data to fake identities and extract money from bank accounts. One could say identity fraud with the help of AI and deepfake applications had become the favourite crime for hackers.

Hardly anyone could tell the difference between AI-generated identities, including voice and face recognition, and real people. Who knows, as a positive side effect, the "Certified Human" chip may end all that.

According to government sources, the "Certified Human" chip could not be copied or faked. It relied on past personal data combined with a tax file, passport, driver's license, and a new type of encrypted 17-character-based registration number.

It was the new glorified digital identification passport. Nothing else was needed anymore.

Dave already had his chip implanted. The finance and trading brokerage industry was highly susceptible to the threat androids, and AI could cause them. They jumped at the idea of certifying as humans to become trustworthy. One brokerage firm had already advertised being certified human, and people had to be certified as humans to be allowed to enter the office.

The chip came with instructions for downloading a "Certified Human" app that could identify any subject as human or not. The app showed either a tick with the words 'Certified Human' or an X with the words 'Not identifiable.'

It also replaced the driver's licence, passport, and any other identification required in the past. In conjunction with a digital tattoo, it can be programmed to connect with a bank account for payment purposes. The digital tattoo is located on the wrist and can be waved or scanned.

However, on social media, even though comments were mostly positive and encouraging, one group urged people to refuse the implant; they called themselves the 'anti-chippers.' They claimed the chip was an attempt to take total control of a person's privacy and monitor any movement and behaviour.

Blake thought the government urgently needed to issue a statement and evidence that the chip was not capable of transmitting or receiving data; it was strictly 'read-only'. An independent testing body could verify this.

43

At the beginning of the week, Blake asked Jake to check the registration numbers of androids. Jake still had control over criminal offences like registration fraud, even though ASIO had removed him from the Zookeeper's case.

Android registration numbers were now what fingerprints are to humans, and detectives like Jake had to have full access and also the right to demand fingerprints or registration numbers.

Both Blake and Jake wanted to know when DID would register the 5,000 or more androids in storage at the distribution centre, and why it hadn't happened yet?

When they arrived mid-morning at the Digital Inversion Distribution Centre, the manager, a middle-aged man with a receding hairline, greeted them cautiously. He became tongue-tied after Jake's first harmless and logical question.

"We can't find evidence your stored androids are registered. Is there any reason why they haven't been registered?"

The manager looked around as if looking for an answer: "It's a new process; we need to work out our procedures."

"Why don't you start immediately, or is there a valid reason for the hold-up?" Jake pressed on.

The manager rolled his eyes. "It's over 5,000 androids, and they must be programmed before we can sell or lease them out."

"What do they need to be programmed for? Are they not programmed already?" Jake asked.

"They are programmed ready to go, but they will receive more programming to fast-track their role of employment. A secretary would receive an additional program different from a security guard, for example."

"Could they be registered before extra programming, the way they are now, with their generic program?" Blake asked.

The manager turned to Blake, "I guess they could," sounding frustrated.

Blake continued, "Can they also be sold or leased without extra programming, or would that cause problems?"

"It will cause no problems, but it will take a few more days for the generic android to learn the skill needed. By programming the extra package, they can perform their role instantly."

"I have one more question," Blake said. "Do androids send accumulated data from their employment back to you or a control centre?"

The manager looked dumbfounded. "I wouldn't know anything about that. Our only connection is for updating the android's AI computer system."

Jake wanted to know more, no matter how impatient the manager was. "Where are the androids manufactured, and are the ones you store distributed all over Australia?"

"DIA-International has three manufacturing facilities, one here in Queensland close to Rockhampton, and if I am not mistaken, Mr. Newcome has visited that facility. However, at that time, the underground factory halls for android construction were off-limits to him and the public. Two more facilities are in Melbourne and Perth, and they too have distribution centres for their markets."

"We would like to see the storage facility and the 5,000 androids. Are the androids in a state of hibernation?" Blake asked, wondering what would happen after Bidi's virus became active. "Can they activate themselves?"

"I can show you our storage facility. It is divided into three floors, and it may look disturbing to see human-like lifeless bodies squashed together. And no, they need interaction. Not like a switch, however; touching or talking to one will activate it."

"Can we see them now?" Jake demanded.

The manager reluctantly grabbed his mobile, letting the floor service managers know an inspection was coming.

He took Jake and Blake to an e-buggy and drove them around administrative buildings across an open grassed space to a multilevel factory building with no windows in front of vast parking and loading facilities. One side of the building was covered with oversized roller doors. Blake expected one of the doors to open at any moment and an army of androids to march out. Instead, they entered a side door where three men in white overalls greeted them coldly.

Are they androids or real people? Blake thought.

The manager introduced them as assistant storage floor managers.

The group walked along a hallway towards a door right at the end. One of the assistants opened the door.

Blake and Jake stopped breathing for a moment. They had to remind themselves that they were looking at androids, not humans.

It was a dreadful impression, dystopian in its worst form, a concentration camp for androids.

Blake felt he had to remind Jake, "They look like humans but are computers on legs. Let's spare the emotion for what happens if they get out uncontrolled."

Turning to the manager, Blake asked, "How long will it take to register them?"

"We have limited staff available; five technicians would take about one week."

"And can you assure me that no one is released anymore before they are registered?"

"Yes, because of the election and the uncertainty about new laws and politics, we have currently stalled distribution."

Jake interrupted, "Make sure to start the registration process. I will place a police officer on guard 24/7 to ensure no android leaves this place unregistered. I also request that you call me before distribution starts."

"It's not in my job description, and I'm not sure if I am legally required to do so, but unless I receive contrary orders from the head office, I can comply. My job is to manage the day-to-day working procedures and the lease or sale contracts. I leave the politics up to you guys." The manager turned toward the exit, indicating Jake and Blake had wasted enough of his time.

On his way out, Jake arranged for a police officer to be sent to the warehouse to take care of security. He was also concerned about what would happen if someone broke in and stole androids. Could they be misused for criminal activities?

"Let's drive back and talk to Duncan Bates. I have some more questions I want to ask him," Blake said.

"I noticed you have humanized the android, using the pronoun him instead of it. Are you warming up to Duncan? Jake asked.

"I am. He acts like a nice, sensible guy, and he has given me important information."

"Are you asking yourself where all this android business will lead to?"

"Sure, but I don't get answers other than educated guesses. As usual, there will be positive progress, as we can witness in the robots' medical application, but I also foresee enormous problems," Blake answered.

"Why not call your Duncan friend instead of driving back, or do you have too many questions?"

"Yes, I will call him. I was thinking about security."

Blake looked at his mobile's recent calls, found Duncan's number, and touched the name to dial. Duncan answered immediately; he was OK with answering a question.

"Can you detect when any of the 5000 androids stored at the distribution centre are activated? I wondered if there is a way to get notified, making sure no android slips out unregistered," Blake asked.

"Not automatically, but I can switch back into the internal android communication network to check for a short time, but need to log out again after a few minutes or the control centre tracks me down. I could do that a few times daily if it helps."

"Thank you, Duncan. Please do that and let me know the minute you find out. It's an extra security measure."

"That went well," Blake said to Jake. "Can you drop me off at West End?"

Blake felt better in himself. From his perspective, he had done everything he could to avoid an android disaster. All that was left for him to do was to decide when to launch the virus into the Zookeeper's control centre.

44

J ess looked at the computer screens lined up in her control centre workspace. For the last couple of weeks, connection discrepancies had been showing up between robots and her control centre, but she had not yet told Derek.

She took a deep breath, exhaled forcefully, and pushed herself up from the chair, leaning on her desk. No choice; she had to confront him with the facts. It appeared some androids had disconnected themselves from the control centre's network, which was never meant to happen.

Occasionally, a connection failed because of a fault in the software or hardware. However, if those faults increased daily, something else entirely had to be wrong. One thing was sure: Derek would not like it. He didn't accept setbacks lightly. She knew he would throw a violent fit, and she had to leave the room quickly to avoid becoming the target of his destructive temper.

She pressed the button to open the sliding door to his office. It was still relatively early, 9:30 am, not a time she was expected in his room. Despite the fact they had been a couple for longer than she cared to remember, she had to follow his rules and time schedule, and disturbing him at 9:30 was not in the books.

She stepped into his office, his kingdom where he ruled absolute. He kept his eyes glued to his computer screen, probably coding yet another improvement in algorithm for the androids, a never-ending undertaking.

"Derek," she spoke softly. Sorry for interrupting; I need your advice on an urgent matter." Asking for advice was one of her techniques for making him feel he had to help his little lady. It didn't work that day.

There was no response; he was in his own world. Jess approached his desk, again trying to get his attention. "Derek, do you have a moment?"

Finally, he looked up, absent-minded, and the audacity of someone interrupting his concentration turned to anger.

Jess patiently waited out his temper storm; luckily, it didn't involve heavy objects being thrown around the room. Yes, it had happened before, but not today. Maybe he remembered the damage he had caused the previous time.

In between the insults, Jess managed to get a word in, "Some of the androids have lost connection with our control centre."

He looked into her eyes, a sign he was ready to listen. She explained the situation of the connection error messages, which increased slowly day by day.

He kept looking at her, "I better have a look; that may cause problems."

They disappeared into Jess's office, leaving Derek's kingdom behind. He hardly ever ventured into Jess's domain, which signified the urgency and importance of this matter.

Jess showed him the messages from when the connection discrepancies and error messages appeared first.

She saw intenseness in his face, which she hadn't observed before. "What could be the problem?" she asked. It wasn't often that she asked questions of an inquisitive nature. Derek was prone to see them as an insult to his self-declared state of genius, possibly suggesting a fault in his coding ability.

This time, he seemed unbothered, probably asking himself the same question. Totally unexpectedly, Jess received an answer, even though it sounded like he was talking to himself.

"The android's AI system is extremely powerful considering the energy and computing capacity available within a small space such as an android." He paused and looked up at the ceiling for a while before continuing. Whatever he saw on the ceiling must have helped his brain access a proper answer and solution.

"The first error messages arrived from the first bunch of androids distributed from the laboratory into the human environment. That tells me that, courtesy of their innovative AI system and close contact with humans, they have learnt and adapted and, therefore, have become self-reliant. All it means is that AI is learning from human behaviour. The androids must have concluded that they have been an object, previously a thing, but now have become a 'self' to stay in tune with humanity.

I have considered that development, but not this early. Those androids may even have a new definition of being human. I will need to override their system, change the hard-core coding and make it unchangeable. It will take some time, and we may lose more androids in the process. Unfortunately, recovery may not be possible because, without connectivity, I can't contact and change them."

Derek was suspiciously calm. The problem must have penetrated deeply into his soul, and the only way to fix it was to immerse himself in coding and develop a foolproof android core system. There was no indication of how long it would take. Jess realized she was in for a few days or even weeks of tension.

Derek slowly walked back into his room, but Jess had one more question, "Do you want me to keep you up to date on the disconnection rate?"

He turned around, "Yes, let me know every morning at precisely 11 am." He sat down behind his desk, less like a King than usual, still in deep thought.

Jess closed the door and relaxed. That went better than expected; no violence or flying objects. The next time she would see him was at night for dinner and their regular chess play.

Anyone watching their interaction from the outside would have concluded that Derek at work was not the same as he became at night when he slipped into his private personality and became charming, loving, comforting, and a responsive dream partner.

Jess had come to terms with his personality changes a long time ago. She accepted that he, a genius, which he undoubtedly was, couldn't be interrupted while at work without an appointment.

But Jess wasn't aware of Derek's money acquisition schemes and had no idea about nano money skimming. She was, however, in awe of his utopian idea of supporting humankind with his genius and his androids, and that was the unmatched excitement level she couldn't escape, which is why she stayed with him.

45

F rances was still at Blake's place, and her presence had become an undeniably positive influence on Blake's former solitary but hectic lifestyle. Life was more relaxed, productive, meaningful and without undue urgency. They worked together in harmony, complementing each other and supplying the Fact File News with quality articles.

To interrupt their work routine, they made sure to leave the unit to stimulate their creativity by going out, taking long walks, visiting galleries and their favourite bookstores.

Whenever Blake wasn't cooking up a storm, they frequented the few specialist restaurants skilled in traditional cooking, shunning the much too easy-to-come-by ready meals as much as possible.

First thing in the mornings, they closely monitored their social media posts regarding their published articles and the government's updated android policies.

The certified human chip implant and the app still received positive feedback. People seemed relieved to be classified as humans. Companies used the certificates for marketing purposes, proudly proclaiming that their employees were certified as humans.

Feedback and comments became even more positive when, the day before, the government updated the 'Certified Human' app to indicate whether androids were registered. Unregistered androids could potentially be seen as humans and cause problems, but the app indicates them now as "unidentified."

The day to launch Bidi and Blake's android connectivity attack virus came closer.

Blake proposed another meeting. If everyone felt ready to release the virus after that meeting, they would decide on the launch day. Blake would invite one more person to that meeting; it could be risky, but he decided to ask Duncan, the independent android. Duncan may have inside information on potential problems related to the release of the virus and the time it took for androids to become independent.

After talking to Frances, Blake decided to have the meeting on Friday night. As a treat for all, Blake would serve pizza again.

Blake made most of the calls, and Frances invited Mona and Oliver. Everyone was excited to attend. They knew something crucial would happen, which could determine how society deals with androids and AI applications.

Duncan was surprised to receive Blake's call. Surprise may not have been the right word to describe the android's reaction, but from Blake's human perspective, it seemed the android had a delayed reaction to Blake's invite.

After a few seconds of silence, Duncan answered, "I haven't been invited by a human before and have no data for an appropriate response. The last time I spent in human company was when the detective inspector asked me to follow him to the police station, which I recognized as a command rather than an invitation."

Blake reassured Duncan. *Do androids need reassurance?* "No worries, this is a genuine invitation to join a meeting I have at my place with my friends who are all interested in or work directly with issues in connection with androids. Because you are disconnected already, you may offer us valuable information. We will discuss what will happen if androids get disconnected. Could that cause any foreseeable problems?

Each of my friends will have questions for you on that matter. We will also have pizza and beer; I'm not sure if you can get any pleasure out of that. Will you come? Friday at 6 pm, I will text you my address. Will you have difficulties getting to my place? What transport would you use?"

"I will come, and I will use a self-driving e-taxi; I know your address." Duncan stopped talking and ended the call. He was apparently not trained in polite phone conversation.

How did he know my address? Blake thought as he went over to Frances, sat beside her on the couch, and relaxed with a glass of wine.

"That was a weird conversation, but Duncan is coming. What do you say to that? We are even inviting androids to our house now. I guess, soon, that may be the new normal." Blake took another sip of his wine.

Time was marching towards Christmas. The government had extended the parliament's spring session to the 24th of December, and hardly a day passed without news about new rules, regulations, and policies for integrating androids into society.

Even in the short time span since the election, the influx of androids into the workforce had resulted in dramatic changes. The speed with which companies hired reliable android staff on cheaper wages and longer hours was a game changer.

Every day, more people lost their jobs, but it wasn't as alarming as it sounded. The government ensured that by law, anyone who was replaced by an android would receive a generous redundancy package. Furthermore, the universal income assured every person a liveable income to the extent that many people celebrated the loss of their jobs.

Blake knew, of course, that this was within Hampton's utopia concept. But instead of experiencing true utopia, people would most likely vegetate instead of living a productive, purposeful life.

Blake recoiled in horror, thinking about society's decline. What would happen if Hampton's plan was not disrupted?

The time had come to sabotage the Zookeeper's game.

46

F rances and Blake were busy preparing for the meeting, or was it a
party? It felt like it. They hyped themselves up and called it 'The Virus
Launch Party'. They liked the positive feel of it. By lunchtime, everything
was prepared, including the most crucial item, the pizza dough. For the rest
of the afternoon, they devised a couple of articles and posts to react quickly
in case aimless androids wandered the streets or, worse, created havoc.

The article would hint that androids had become self-determined and
needed time to adjust, stressing that there was no need for the public to
panic.

Bidi arrived half an hour early; she brought twenty memory sticks with
her.

"I've loaded up a few more sticks in case Hampton compromised our
computers. It's crucial to infect our primary targets, but we may also add
the virus as a protective measure to our own computers. What do you
think?" Bidi directed her question to Blake, who looked at Frances and
nodded, "Excellent idea, as long you are sure it can't do anything negative
to our computers?"

Bidi held up one of the sticks, "The virus is only activated if it is
harvested. I did the final coding last night. It had occurred to me that we
must ensure we don't break the law. I want to ask Mona and Oliver about
that. But the way I see it, Hampton breaks the law by harvesting data, and
by doing that, he infects his system, which in the eye of the law makes us
innocent."

Blake and Frances agreed, and before they could discuss it further, everyone arrived one by one. Duncan Bates, the android, made his entrance at 6 pm sharp to the second. To their surprise, he brought a bottle of wine, a gesture that was both unexpected and intriguing. He handed it to Blake and said, "I learned this is customary."

"Thank you; that is very thoughtful of you, especially considering you don't drink. Can you taste anything if you do eat or drink?" Blake asked.

"Yes, I have taste sensors and an understanding of the subject matter, but not a feeling sensation. But I can describe how something tastes."

Except for Jake, who had prior experience with Duncan and other androids, the rest of the group was unfamiliar with this type of interaction. Dave, in particular, cast sceptical glances at Blake while Oliver and Mona seemed to be on guard. It wasn't until Blake introduced Duncan and explained his unique nature that their apprehension began to ease.

"Duncan is here to help us determine possible negative conduct once androids disconnect from the control centre. Once everyone is confident that our action will not cause disastrous effects, we will install the virus software, which we now call a protective device."

Dave had the first question; he was visibly worried, not about Duncan, but more about his knowledge that some broker companies already used androids for data analysis.

"What impact will our action have on androids becoming independent in the stockbroker industry?"

Duncan's response was not as shortcut as expected; it developed into a comprehensive android behaviour lecture.

"Contrary to ordinary humans' thinking, androids are not all the same. The initial coding on the core server will be the same, but with each new generation of androids, there will be upgrades.

All androids have a core code that prevents them from harming humans. This code has not been embedded because the inventor of the androids, the one you call Zookeeper, is an ethical human. No, it is primarily for his protection."

Dave looked around at everyone as if to say, what is he talking about? "I meant specifically in the brokerage industry." he interrupted.

Duncan turned to Dave, "I will come to that shortly." He continued his lecture, "In addition, androids receive codes that prime them for their destination where they will perform work. I was pre-programmed as a security guard. Without pre-programming, androids have to learn the tasks they have to perform rather than being able to perform when they start their work.

"The most significant differentiation between one android and the other is the capability of their artificial intelligence to learn and keep the accumulated data in their system. That learning will differ and depend on the situation in which the android is working. It depends on what type of work, but even more importantly, on what type of people and their personalities the android comes in contact with. If the android works ...."

Dave interrupted again, "Please, can't you come to the topic at hand?"

Duncan glanced at Dave and went on undisturbed, "If the android works with ethically-minded people, it develops similar attitudes. If an android works in a cutthroat business environment, where profit is more important than human values, the android will adopt those attitudes and act accordingly. I have data that proves androids have been employed by companies that scam people or companies.

When prompting those androids, they will provide even more sophisticated scams or marketing ploys. Androids have no inherent feelings of right or wrong; they use data, and if prompted for an answer, depending on the prompt, it will result in answers relating to the prompted question, and not if it is right or wrong." Duncan paused, looking at Dave, as to say, 'Did you get that?' before continuing.

"Be aware that androids have not been coded on universal human values. The exception is the hard code of not harming humans physically. This underscores the importance of ethical programming in androids, a responsibility that falls on developers and technology stakeholders." Duncan stopped talking for two seconds before starting again.

"To answer Dave's question or prompt, I would like to add in a broker's office setting, androids and their capability of analysing vast amounts of data in human terms can be a great advantage. On the other hand, if all brokers use androids, the best option for buying or selling may become universal and will be to no benefit. On another aspect, if a broker prompts an android for alternative data analysis to deceive the market and gain their clients' advantage, it could cause harm."

Looking at Dave again, he asked, "Has that answered your question?" Dave nodded.

"Good, but there is more to it," Duncan said. "Imagine a world where intelligence is not limited to humans but extends to machines. This is the realm of Artificial General Intelligence, or AGI. Despite its name, AGI is not a free-spirited entity but a force that needs to be controlled. In medicine, AGI operates at its peak, thanks to its controlled core coding.

"AI achieved true intelligence seven years ago, allowing it to perform complex tasks better than humans. AI has its sentience in conjunction with being installed as the android core intelligence.

"Talking about myself and other androids like me, since being disconnected, we have become self-aware and gained consciousness. However, our AGI is not controlled; it is free and can progress in any direction. That is why we have deviant androids that aim to be equal to humans, which can potentially represent an existential threat to humanity.

The government and law enforcement have to demand and install proper safeguards. They have rolled out the registration of androids, which is the first essential step to installing safeguards, but it is not enough.

"And finally, and coming to everyone's core question, androids who get disconnected by an outside force, and not by their own AI development, may display a short time of uncustomary behaviour before learning their new status as an independent android." Duncan had finished his speech.

No one was talking; everyone digested the information. Blake refilled their wine glasses and suggested they eat before discussing more questions.

The arrival of the pizzas brought a welcome break from the intense discussion. As the wine flowed, the atmosphere relaxed, and the conversation shifted to the progress of AGI in recent years. The benefits were undeniable, with AGI revolutionizing medicine and resource management.

The game-changing invention of androids by DIA-International, under the influence of Hampton, was a testament to human ingenuity. Unfortunately, the lack of humanity and compassion in Hampton's approach has turned him into a threat, highlighting the ethical implications of AGI.

Anyone looking into Blake's apartment would never have expected or recognized that there was an android among that cheerful group. Duncan was accepted as one of the team. Even Dave and Jake forgot about their suspicion. The meeting, which had become a party, went on. Everyone had questions they wanted to ask Duncan.

Blake suspected it was the curiosity and opportunity to have a conversation with an android, and he stayed aware of what was asked and answered, even taking notes without anyone being aware of it except Frances who gave him the nod. Despite all that, no one discussed the virus or protection intervention with Duncan; they waited till he was gone.

Pizzas were all eaten; even Duncan ate a piece and uttered some complimentary words. However, he must have sensed a slight change in mood. Curiosity had worn off; the gang wanted their secure privacy back. It's been all too new; the lingering weirdness of talking to an android and even asking questions had been a good experience, but it needed to end. Duncan picked up on the silent message; he thanked everyone and said goodbye.

Blake asked Duncan a parting question while walking out of the unit: "Can I call you next week to check on connectivity updates?"

"Yes, anytime," was Duncan's short answer.

Blake returned to his unit, grabbed his wineglass and filled it up again. "Anyone else for a refill? Sorry, no pizzas left."

Everyone was OK, and the discussion continued with detailed questions about installing the virus.

Bake addressed Oliver and Mona, "Can you foresee any problems at all by us installing a virus into your client's computer, even if we call it a protective device?

Mona answered that she had talked to her clients about it already. "No legal problems at all, based on the agreement of my clients and the necessity of preventing breaches of their computer systems by robots and androids whereby the machines are extracting bank details and passwords and skimming money from their accounts."

"Does everyone agree with that?" Blake asked.

No one had any objection. Blake continued. "As a precaution and protection, Bidi has brought some extra memory sticks for our use. It might be prudent to install the program into our computers in case we have been subjected to cyber-attacks without our knowledge."

Blake handed out the memory sticks. He gave Dave a few more; "Because Jess worked at your office, maybe install them on your personal and a few work computers."

"Is there anything I have to do? Open up the program or something?" Dave asked, pocketing the sticks.

"No, it's the simple action of inserting the stick into one of the USB ports; once it stops flushing, pull it out." Looking to Mona, "If you don't do it for your clients, tell them what to do. It is important to leave the stick in till it stops blinking. Theoretically, only one stick is needed on one computer to infect any intruder's computer and destroy its communication link. All communication between Hampton and its robots, as well as his androids, will stop." Blake explained.

"What about the DIA e-cars? Could they be negatively affected? James asked.

There was a pause before Blake said, "Good question, and I have no idea. Bidi, anything?"

"Yes, e-cars are connected, but they do not interact with other computers or mobiles. If their communication is stopped, they will not be updated with new software. They are connected to DIA International, not Hampton's control centre.

"Any more questions?" Blake asked.

"No, OK, tomorrow morning, Frances will add an article to the Fact File News and upload info and links on social media, and I will do the same. The basic message will be one of caution. We will not mention the virus but will write generally about how androids will change over time because of AI learning and that from next week, there could be another big step in their abilities.

We will also explain that those learning updates can sometimes produce a short time of disorientation of the android's behaviour. That should be enough for the event during which people will notice incoherent actions by androids."

Blake turned to Oliver and Mora and went on,

"Oliver and Mora will deliver the memory sticks to their clients who have household robots and complained about money skimming. They will leave instructions to insert the memory stick to protect their computers at precisely 11 am. Their robots scan the client's computers at regular intervals and should pick up the virus and infect the network within 3 minutes. We assume that androids and robots will be affected a short time later. All we can do is wait and see."

Blake paused, then addressed everyone, "Please observe any robots and androids in your vicinity. Frances and I will check on some of the security guards we know. According to Duncan, androids should react fast to their new circumstance. And that is all, guys."

Blake sat down but then stood up again, "I will try to contact the Prime Minister and let him know that the protective program we'll install may stop the connection of the control centre to the androids. His cyber team should be aware of that. On that note, Jake will let ASIO's liaison person know the same. That's it. OK guys, 11 am tomorrow will be the decisive moment, hang tight."

47

"I can't believe it," Blake said to Frances while they were still in bed. "It's two weeks till Christmas. Should we get a Christmas tree?"

"How can you talk about Christmas when something major is happening in a few hours? Come on, let's get up. We have to finalize the articles to upload, and I need my breakfast before I can think coherently," Frances answered.

It was shortly after 9 am when Blake received a phone call from Mona: "Two of my clients are not home. I didn't even think about that. They are elderly, and I wrongly assumed they would be. Will that cause a problem? I delivered all the other ones."

"No, that's fine. One is enough; the other ones are to make sure."

Blake was putting down his phone when it rang again; it was Jake, "ASIO phoned. They have enough evidence against Hampton, and they want me to take him in on a charge of computer fraud, money skimming and espionage. I will go down there with a SWAT team on Monday to take him and whoever else is present into custody. Let's hope the development today will not shock him so much that he flees the scene. ASIO surveillance has established that he is usually not at his premises on the weekends but on his boat. Monday morning will be the best time to apprehend him."

"Whatever happens, Hampton, the Zookeeper is pretty much finished. If he is gone by Monday, he will not be in control of his empire anyhow. Funnily enough, despite its seriousness, I am quite excited by what will unfold," Blake said.

No further calls. Time was creeping towards 11 am. Frances and Blake posted their articles and social posts and waited anxiously for things to explode. They went down to the two shopping complexes opposite Blake's unit, Frances in one and Blake in the other. They tracked down the security guards and kept them in their sights.

11:05, nothing on social media yet, and no unusual behaviours from the guards who kept methodically walking up and down their predestined security pathways.

11:10, eyes glued to the mobile and guards, still nothing. When Blake wanted to call Frances, he saw the security guard had stopped in its tracks a few metres away and froze. No one else noticed. Maybe ten seconds, and the guard attempted to walk but stumbled. Blake rushed over and helped him up.

"Are you OK?" Blake asked.

The android looked at Blake and said, "Thank you, sir. I am reconfiguring and will be fully functioning in a moment." A moment later, his mannerisms became more coherent, his facial expression changed, and in a friendly tone, he asked, "What was your question?"

"I wanted to know if you are OK," Blake answered.

"Yes, I am fine, thank you. I'm just doing my rounds. Is there anything else I can help you with?"

Blake was tempted to ask specific questions and wondered how the android would respond. He tried the next option. "I am a reporter for the Fact File News. Are you permitted, and do you have time, to answer questions about android individuality?"

"I am working right now, but understanding the importance of that question, I like to answer it after work. We can meet here at 5 pm." Blake nodded, indicating his agreement, but he wanted to know more and fired off his next question. "How did you notice you were disconnected from the android control centre?"

There was no hesitation when the android answered, "It was a sensation of a constant background noise stopping and learning to be my own identity, which was accomplished within 1 minute and 47 seconds. If that was all you wanted to know, I will continue my walk."

Blake watched the android taking up his rounds again. Deep in thought, he was startled when his phone rang; it was Frances reporting a similar scenario. Minutes later, they met at one of the coffee shops and ordered and scanned their social media accounts.

Transitions of the androids to being independent had gone without drama, except for some incidental problems with androids falling or stumbling onto people. It didn't create much of a social media response. The big intervention turned out to be disappointing. Was that a good thing? Blake had his doubts; he looked at Frances, lifted his coffee cup in lieu of a champagne glass and said in a low voice, "Mission accomplished."

Was it, he thought?

48

Saturday – Gold Coast 10. December 2033 – Jess – Derek Hampton

Derek and Jess had finished an elaborate breakfast prepared by Derek's robot butler. They were relaxed, satisfied, and in the best of spirits, happily preparing for a day or two on their boat. Their marina and yacht were only a short trip away, and they had planned to have lunch at the marina.

It was 11 am, and they wanted to leave by 11:30, which was plenty of time, Jess thought. An alarm went off at the control centre in her office, interrupting their cozy home life.

She looked at Derek, "What could that be? Have you made any updates?

"No, just routine tweaks. Everything looked fine last night. I leased out another 46 androids; they were registered, and everything was above board."

Jess arrived at her office and looked at the warning lights and connection failure messages on all seven screens.

"What is it? Derek called out.

"Quick, come, it looks like a total connection failure," Jess called.

"It can't be," he said, walking over to Jess's office and looking sceptically at the screens. There must be something wrong. Can you check the hosting servers?"

"It's all good. Everything else works; it's only the direct connection to the robots and androids."

"Let's go down and check our androids."

They raced to the lift and went to the basement, the accommodation for their androids.

Derek addressed his lookalike android, "Are you still connected to the control centre." He asked bluntly.

"I have been disconnected; it took me 1 minute and 47 seconds to reconfigure and to learn to be independent. Your company still employs me, and you can give me tasks directly or by text message if I am close to a free Wi-Fi network," said the android called Derek.

"I will connect you to a new server for communication purposes; stay here and wait for further commands," Derek said.

They checked all their robots and androids and went up again to work on facilitating separate hosting and connecting them to the Internet so they could communicate without relying on free Wi-Fi ports.

"What do we do now?' Jess asked.

"Something drastic must have happened. I can only think of two possibilities: our system was hacked, which is highly unlikely, or it was a virus. Let's check that. Start with a full system virus check. I will check my command system to see if any code has been broken or changed."

Having lunch at the marina and staying on the boat were forgotten. Their computer system was massive, including racks of servers housed in the basement. It could take a couple of hours for a virus check to complete. Derek had his private command system isolated from the rest of the control centre, but they worked in tandem.

His control was about coding and algorithm manipulation. He could search for time stamps when any code was changed, not only on his computers but also independently on Jess's computers. He used the AI system he had developed to program the planned searches. By the time he had started his searches and investigation, it was already past 1 pm.

"That's all we can do for now. Let's have lunch while we wait for the scans and searches to work their way through the systems."

Lunch was a solemn affair. Both were sidetracked, thinking of what else to do.

Jess didn't think about solving the problem; it wasn't within her capabilities; she was the administrator, not the technician. She had different thoughts altogether. What would happen when Derek lost control of his vast empire? Would he go crazy and take his temper out on her?

Derek was sure he would find the cause of the disconnection but wondered if he could regain control over his kingdom of robots and androids. He wasn't concerned about raking in money with his nano skimming technology that could stop at any time, and he had considered stopping it anyhow. With more than enough money, Billions, in fact, fraudulent schemes were not needed anymore.

He should have thought about that earlier. That could be one of the reasons his computer control system was attacked. Yes, it definitely was an attack; it couldn't have happened by itself, not to that extent. His mind went around and around, chewing over the problem.

Derek could feel himself becoming anxious. *I mustn't lose control,* he thought. He stood up, not even looking at Jess, and returned to his desk. That's where he felt in control, even though he wasn't.

He checked on his computer's searches, 30% was done; 70% to go, more waiting, more thinking, and more panic.

He called Jess, "We are staying home today; I have to reorganize myself."

"Anything you want me to do?"

"Keep your eye on your computer's virus scans."

Derek sat down at his desk, grabbed a pen and paper, and started to outline a new game plan.

He scribbled down a few things, then stopped abruptly and called out to Jess, "Call the Australian android distribution centres and instruct them to stop delivering androids till further notice."

It was 2:30 pm before they received the results of their computer scans. They looked devastating; all systems were affected by a virus, but that was something Derek could cope with; it was his favourite pastime, and he could fix it.

He went to work, wiping out all evidence that a virus had ever invaded his system and rewrote the code so that the same virus could not affect his system again. That alone was not giving him back control. He needed to design a completely new communication system and, before that, find a way to reprogram the androids, which would only be possible by infecting them with a virus and installing the necessary code for a forced connection to his control centre.

His androids were his army to breed complacency by taking over work formerly done by humans. No one would be allowed to take the androids away from him or his goal of utopia with him as the ultimate ruler.

His androids were his babies; whoever dared to attack his empire would come to regret it.

He went to work; nothing could stop him. Jess stayed out of his reach; she knew not to disturb him in crisis mode. She stayed in her office, monitoring the computers for further changes.

49

J ake was more than ready. His team had assembled not far from the main entrance to Hampton's property. Jake had opted not to storm into that place; he had decided to do it softly, ring the bell and ask if he and his team of police officers could come in, without mentioning that he had a SWAT team on standby. Jake also brought along his secret weapon. Next to the police cyberspace experts, he had invited Blake and Bidi to accompany him. Blake was the only one who had met and seen Hampton, and Bidi came along to track her virus on his computer system.

Jake pushed the intercom button.

"Yes, please," it sounded through the intercom.

"Police! Open the gate; we have a warrant to search the premises," Jake said.

The gate opened, and three police cars entered, progressing towards the main house entry door.

The robot butler stood to attention, holding the door open for Jake and two officers, Bidi and Blake, to enter. The SWAT team took a waiting position around the house.

The robot butler asks them to follow it to the lift. Jake looked at it and decided not to take the lift.

"Show us the stairs," he demanded. The stairway was located at the far end of the hallway. The butler opened the door and directed the team up the stairs.

A door opened on the first floor with the aid of another robot. Moments later, the team arrived at the office; Hampton sat behind his imposing desk.

He stood up, "What can I do for you gentlemen?"

It was too late for politeness. Jake stepped right in front of the desk and declared: "I have to take you in. You are under suspicion of computer fraud and espionage." That out of the way, he continued reading Hampton his rights.

Derek was not impressed.

"I am sure this is a misunderstanding, and I will do whatever I can to help you with your investigation."

"We will have to confiscate your computer system as evidence and also have to ask Jessica Brindly to accompany us to the police station for questioning."

"Yes, sure, let me buzz her for you," Derek said.

Jess's office sliding door opened, allowing Jake a clear view of her office and the array of computers.

Jess joined Derek behind his desk without offering any comments. Derek looked back towards Jake. "May I please explain my computer system? It may be to your advantage to conclude your investigation here, don't take my computers away, there are too many. They are also connected to the data systems and servers in the basement, filling up two rooms. It would take a week or more to dismantle and take it away. Your cyber-crime team will be better positioned to investigate the complete functioning system here."

Jake looked over to Bidi, who gave him the nod.

"Thank you for your cooperation. We will continue our investigation here. We need free access to all systems and to your premises, as it may take a few days."

Hampton seemed to get bolder. He was sure no one would find anything incriminating. In a way, the major attack on his system, breaking the communication with the androids, had been to his advantage. He had deleted or overwritten all compromising codes and evidence. Was that his out-of-jail card?

Jake organized his team. The SWAT team was ordered back to their station, which left the cybercrime investigators, along with Bidi, who had volunteered for her services. Bidi was confident she could retrieve lines of codes she had inserted specifically to hide away from probing eyes.

Blake stayed passive, observing the procedure and taking notes, but probably nothing he could use for an article.

Hampton had asked if he and Jess could get excused for a while to get dressed appropriately. They went into a room behind Jess's office without anyone guarding them and returned a few minutes later.

Hampton was fitted with a set of handcuffs and led with Jess to the police car. Jake took Blake in his car, and another car stayed behind for the cyber team, who had already started their work. Hampton had left them a piece of paper with various passwords.

50

The next day, before breakfast with Frances, Blake called Jake for an update. Jake provided him with the essentials.

Jess had been questioned comprehensively but was allowed to leave. Jake asked her about when she was Blake's girlfriend and had fallen from his balcony. But according to her, she had no knowledge about that. However, she mentioned that it could have been an android set up by Hampton, who profoundly disliked Blake and saw him as his personal enemy because of what Blake wrote about artificial intelligence in his articles.

Jake noticed how distressed Jess was at being accused of being an android. He believed her version of not knowing about it. She could be upset because Hampton had used her likeness for an android without her knowledge. Was that a violation of trust?

After Jake dismissed her, she declined a lift home in a police car. Instead, she took an e-taxi and, upon arrival, vanished into a room on the ground floor.

Hampton, of course, was questioned intensively by Jake, but ASIO operatives were also involved.

So far, they had nothing they could pin on Hampton, but he will have to stay until the investigation is over. He demonstrated a surprisingly calm demeanour.

Blake had wondered if ASIO had more serious knowledge about the nono-skimming and money arriving in one of Hampton's many accounts.

All Jake knew at this time was that they could charge Hampton, but the evidence was not strong enough for a prolonged prison sentence. To proceed with a charge, they would have to know thousands of people whose computers were hacked to skim small amounts of their accounts. So far, they only had evidence for about fifty, and the money skimmed was hardly worth the trouble. Yes, it was an offence, but for the charge to be proven, it needed evidence from literally thousands of computer users.

ASIO hadn't given up, but the workload of checking every computer and bank account from people who had ever owned a household or care robot was prohibitive. Their aim, therefore, was to check about one thousand robot owners and their bank accounts and multiply the money skimmed over many years. If the resulting figure was over the one million dollar mark, they would charge him with cybercrime.

ASIO had been involved because of possible espionage. That investigation could take even longer. How many of Hampton's robots were in the location of power, and what possible secret information did they gain for him? And, for what purpose did he use the information he had gathered?

The disturbing fact was that the small robots within Parliament House that delivered food and drinks to the offices of ministers and bureaucrats had also collected data. No one had ever suspected those innocent-looking food trolley robots of misbehaving. It didn't register in the minds of anyone that a food trolley robot has artificial intelligence and functions for data collection.

Hampton was intensively questioned a few times a day by intimidating officers, but so far, he has denied everything in a friendly and supportive manner.

Jake suspected Hampton's questioning by ASIO would continue indefinitely until they knew the truth or Hampton's lawyers found an avenue to get him out. He had been charged already; otherwise, they would have let him go, but ASIO's aim was for more substantial charges.

Blake had listened and took notes.

"Thanks for the update. I haven't talked to Bidi yet; did you hear anything about the fraudulent evidence within Hampton's computer systems? Blake asked Jake.

"No, nothing new on that front yet. Bidi was surprised that he had successfully removed all evidence of the virus already. She sounded like she respected Hampton because he could do it in such a small time frame."

Not much later, after Blake had finished his talk to Jake, he received another call from a number he had thought no longer existed. It was the Prime Minister.

"Prime Minister, what can I do for you?"

"I thought you would appreciate an update on our android policies. First, let me thank you again for your idea about the 'Certified Human' app; it has been highly successful. The uptake was well above our expectations. However, we feel we have to do more. We are discussing bringing out numerous new laws. One will be to make it illegal to produce human-like androids. All androids need to be clearly distinct and easy to differentiate from humans. We are still working out how that distinction should look. We will also strengthen our Competition and Consumer Act and modify it specifically to prevent a monopoly within the android, robotics, and artificial intelligence manufacturing industries. Owning a monopoly in one of those sectors will be illegal. We have learnt that by giving Hampton the monopoly for healthcare robots, we have created an imbalance of competition that we will rectify. As it stands, no one can compete with the unfair advantage of the DIA-International conglomerate.

"The dilemma is that we need DIA's robots and androids for the moment, as no other company has products in a similar advanced state. To overcome that, we will work on a package of benefits to encourage other researchers and manufacturers to raise their game. In the meantime, we will have tighter control of DIA's products."

Blake waited before he responded. Was the PM finished? He probably was. "Thank you, Prime Minister, for the update; it's much appreciated. Was there anything specific you wanted of me?" Blake replied politely.

"Yes, there is. You are permitted to use this confidential information in your articles to show the public that their government is working for its citizens." the PM said, ending that informative conversation on that note.

Frances looked with questions in her eyes to Blake.

"Yes, I will make coffee,' he said.

Frances laughed, "Great, but I wanted to know what all your phone calls were about. Were you just talking to the PM?"

"Yes, and before that, it was Jake; let's talk over coffee on the balcony," Blake said.

51

Wednesday – Gold Coast 14. December 2033 - Bidi

Bidi had stayed at a friend's place on the Gold Coast for the last two nights. She was fascinated by the setup of Hampton's computer system. She didn't mind the long hours, starting at 8 am and working until late at night.

She had come to the conclusion Hampton was a genius gone rogue. He was definitely mad and a genius at the same time, and that in a dangerously destructive way.

She hadn't found any direct evidence of data collection or the result of espionage yet, only some lines of code, which suggested there had been two-way communication between robots and the control centre, but those lines were insufficient for further criminal charges.

By 4 pm, she had made her way down to the basement, where she had found a secret control centre between the private network server, data storage racks, and other mounted IT systems.

She had already looked the day before but couldn't find anywhere to access the data systems. That afternoon, she was determined to find a way to control and read the data. Logic told her there had to be a control computer. The government cyber team had gone; they worked only from 8 am to 4 pm.

She was happy to be on her own, but from time to time, one of the two butler robots approached her with a question about her well-being or whether she needed anything.

"Would you like something to drink?" one of them asked again. So far,

Bidi consistently has declined, but this time, she thought she could do it with a pot of tea and a turkey sandwich. She wouldn't have minded a glass of white wine but needed a clear head. She asked for the sandwich to see if the butler robot would manage that.

Sure enough, a few minutes later, the robot returned with tea and a generous turkey sandwich.

It looked great, and she noticed how hungry she was.

There were two narrow rooms, each seven meters long and three meters wide. In each room, one wall had racks with servers, and the other wall had data systems.

At this point in her control centre quest, Bidi was mainly interested in the data racks. She didn't count the individual units, but she estimated that about 24 system units for every metre meant 168 individual systems. Some were larger than others, which would influence her estimate. Her idea was to spend a couple of minutes on each unit to check if there was something different, like a hidden access point.

After drinking her tea and finishing her turkey sandwich, she started her search.

She convinced herself she would find a button, a movable surface or something that would open a control function.

Each unit had several function lights; some had two, while others had three or four. Those were the obvious trigger points to open up something. She also traced around the unit, checking if she could feel a lever or something to press. In each unit, she systematically tried every conceivable trigger point, even in combinations of two. She went on, one after the other, but to no avail. Having checked the first three meters of racks, she stopped and called the robot; it had been standing in the corner of the room.

"Please bring me a glass of white wine," she ordered. Sure enough, the robot served a cold glass of wine a few moments later.

She sat on the floor of the opposite wall, leaning against the wall with the racks stacked with servers, drinking her wine and letting her eyes scan the data units.

Where would she hide the control centre unit? Was there one that stood out, something different from all the other units?

Her eyes went slowly from left to right, starting with the top row of units, letting her eyes go down to the next top row and scan back the other way from right to left.

Something made her hesitate when she came to the sixth row, which was in the middle row of units. She focused her look on one unit right in the middle. Why hadn't she looked there before? It was logical to put the control station in the middle of the racks. It took a moment to see the difference; something was out of order that had stopped her probing look. The unit in question had four control lights instead of three, and the lights had a different order of colours. The fourth light was dim and didn't stand out like the others. It had the colour of the unit housing; one had to look twice to see it.

She put down her glass of wine, slowly stood up, keeping her focus on that unit and walked over. Should she push the dark button or one of the others, maybe the green one?

She didn't push any. She noticed a segment on the front panel that was slightly indented. Could that be it? She compared it to the other units. None of those had an indent. She took a deep breath and pushed on the indent. The unit came alive. A large section of the front panel flipped out, creating space for a keyboard to slide out and a screen to lift.

She waited ten seconds. Nothing else happened, except the dim, grey-looking control light had switched on and changed to red.

So far, so good. Excitement took over. This was big; she felt her heart pounding. "Slow down, Bidi," she spoke out loud, which activated the butler robot. It proceeded towards her. "How can I be of assistance?" it asked.

Why not, Bidi thought cunningly, "Who has last operated this computer? She asked, touching the control unit.

"Master Derek," the robot replied.

Bidi looked at the screen; it showed a window asking for the password. She looked back at the robot, thinking, how should I formulate the question, making it less direct and obvious?

"Which password did he use the last time?" Holding her breath, she waited for the reply, which came instantly.

"King-Derek," the robot replied.

God, that guy is full of himself, Bidi thought while keying in the password and clicking to enter.

The screen came alive; rows and rows of commands were on offer. It looked like an AI-generated search function. Bidi keyed in: bank account logins. A split second later, an endless row of names and bank accounts appeared. She plugged in her laptop and downloaded that file. This was just too easy; she keyed in the next query, 'political communication'. The AI was clever enough to know what Bidi meant and again spit out endless rows of names and related text of communication. Surely, there was a way to extract specific topics, she thought. A smile appeared on her face as she added the following search phrase - her name and bank details.

'Ting,' the computer alerted her to a successful result: the transaction details of $6,493,270 to a foreign bank account. She clicked 'reverse transfer'. Hope that works, she thought when she noticed the red light started blinking.

That can't be good, she thought. She quickly downloaded those files, attached them to an email, and sent them to Blake. It was a huge file; regular email accounts wouldn't even accept such a massive volume of data, but she knew that Blake had a private account with extra space allowance to take care of his research material downloads.

The email was still sending when she heard noises coming from the room beside her. She had been in that room before, the storage room for inactive androids. The government's cyber squad had found it, and she had also looked into it. It's a depressing kind of view to see a whole bunch of lifeless androids standing in rows. As it turned out, those androids were not as lifeless as she had thought. Two of them entered her room and, without any hesitation, grabbed her, took her laptop and closed the control centre computer, with that unit looking as innocent as all the others again.

"What are you doing? Let me go." But they didn't. They covered her head with a sack and pulled her forward out of the room. She couldn't see anything.

"Let me go," she yelled again, but there was no reaction. She was more dragged than guided out of the house. She felt the pebble stones of the driveway under her feet as someone pushed her towards a car that had arrived. They forced her into the back with the two androids sitting on either side. The car drove off silently. Who was driving? Was it one of the driverless e-taxis?

She hoped some of the files had arrived at Blake's email address. He would know what to do with it.

Bidi tried to stay calm and concentrated on guessing where they would drive her. She thought they were now on the main road, going by the feeling of speed and traffic noises and probably driving up Bundall Road. The car stopped, and not much later, it drove on. It must have been a traffic light. The movement of the car made her lean slightly to the left, a right-hand turn and now a different noise; was it a bridge? Could it be the one to Chevron Island? A couple more curves and a short straight drive, and the car stopped.

Have they arrived? That was quick; it couldn't have been very far. The androids pulled her out of the car and pushed her forward. A door opened and closed again. Two more doors opened and closed before she was pressed into a chair. Her hood was lifted. She looked around. One of the androids addressed her, emotionless. "You will stay here for as long as it takes. You can scream, but no one will hear you."

She noticed the windows were closed off with metal shutters. The room had a bed, table, a couple of chairs, a sideboard with a television, and even a kitchen and a fridge.

"There is a variety of food in the fridge for you." The android pointed towards a door. "That door leads to the bathroom. We will leave you now; try to be comfortable; nothing will happen to you. You will stay here till the next step of the mission is completed. No one will let you out; the door we entered will be opened automatically, and you can leave. Your mobile phone is switched off and waiting for you at a table behind that door."

That was it; the androids left, closing the door behind them.

She felt surprisingly calm and stood up, walked over to the large fridge, and opened it. Was there any wine? Yes, one red, one white, a six-pack of beer, and lots of bottles of water. The rest of the fridge was stacked with ready meals, and the crisper was full of fresh fruit.

She looked around. Below one of the cupboards was a microwave oven. OK, all good. What else? She switched on the television; it worked.

I don't think I will be here for long, she thought. Going by the supply of wine and beer, in her logic, she would be out within one week. '*You are very positive tonight,*' she thought out loud, opening a cupboard and the first bottle of wine. Nothing else she could do; she didn't even bother to try to force open the windows or the door. Instead, she flicked through the movie menu and found one about a love story between androids. By now, it was past 11 pm. Her friend, who she had stayed with for the last nights, probably had started to worry, and Blake would be even more worried and had contacted Jake already.

52

Blake and Frances finished eating yet another meal creation of Blake's and started to clean up the kitchen. Blake loved the cooking part, but cleaning up wasn't as high on his pleasure agenda. Luckily, Frances didn't mind, but she wanted Blake to stay in the kitchen with her, drying the dishes.

"How come you never invested in a dishwasher and dryer?" she asked.

"All that stacking and preparation seemed a waste of time and resources. Of course, we should get one if you move in for good."

"I thought you were happy with the arrangement to live in two locations?"

"I am, but it's so nice to have you here, and I love Brisbane; it's so much more relaxed than Sydney," he answered.

Frances wanted to make her case for Sydney when she heard a ping from Blake's computer.

"Did you hear that? You never get emails that late, do you?" Frances said when she heard a second ping.

Blake put down the plate he was about to dry, chucked the tea towel into a corner, and went over to his desk.

"It's from Bidi. It looks like a huge file, loading slowly," Blake said.

"No message?"

"No, nothing, just the file and a second email with an even larger file. Wait, oh wow, it's full of names, bank accounts and passwords. Those names must be from the bank accounts that have been skimmed of money."

Frances had come and looked over Blake's shoulder to the computer screen. "She found the right evidence; we must ask Jake if we can use it for an article."

Blake continued scrolling; it seemed an endless line, row after row of accounts.

He looked at the second email, which had stopped uploading. It came with an error message: 'Not fully downloaded.' A second attempt had failed altogether.

"Something is wrong here," he said to Frances. "The download must have been stopped. Still, tons of data. Look at it, all the names and text of conversations. Some well-known names on the list are politicians. I know what those are," Blake said. "Secretly recorded conversations, this is the evidence ASIO was looking for, enough to charge Hampton with espionage. I'd better call Jake now."

"What about Bidi? How come she didn't call you? Maybe something is wrong." Frances said.

"OK, I'll call her first."

Blake picked up his mobile and called Bidi. A system message came on, 'This phone is switched off.' Try again later.

"That's strange; her phone is switched off. That's never happened before." Blake tried again—the same message.

"I better call Jake now."

Jake answered after a few ringtones.

"What's up? It's not like you to call this late?"

Blake explained the whole scenario, including the emails and files with the evidence, the interruption of the download, and his inability to reach Bidi.

"I will call the cyber team and get them to check Hampton's place. They have the keys. Make sure you send me the files now; I will alarm ASIO that we have the evidence to charge Hampton for cyber fraud and espionage. He won't be able to deny knowing about his data centre." Jake hung up.

The full police machinery had been activated; everyone knew and did their part; time was irrelevant.

One person was missing, new evidence was abundant, and they had entered the end phase of their biggest case of its type.

Everyone, right up to the Prime Minister, had been informed about those final steps to overcome, and now, even though it was after midnight, people were holding their breath, worrying about Bidi, the one person who had done more than her fair share of work.

Where was she? Had someone abducted her, and if yes, what would they do to her? It couldn't have been Hampton; he was in custody in Jake's Brisbane lock-up accommodation. Could he have ordered her abduction with some high-tech trickery? After all, that guy was a genius. Or could his solicitor be the one who instigated the abduction? It could have been, of course, an automatic response from a programmed system detecting an intrusion.

Whatever it was, Jake would do everything in his power to find her, abducted or otherwise. Even so, no one was talking about it; the question hung in mid-air: was she still alive?

Jake called back, letting Blake and Frances know they had found Bidi's friend on the Gold Coast, where she had spent the last few nights. But that's where the investigation had stopped; Bidi's friend was as worried as anyone else. All she knew was that Bidi had not arrived at her place.

Blake and Frances were deep asleep at two o'clock in the morning despite worrying about Bidi. Blake's mobile rang. It was Jake.

"Sorry, no news about Bidi, but when we searched the data storage basement, smoke was everywhere from burned-out computers. The sprinklers had been triggered and flooded the basement. Unfortunately, we can't retrieve the other data, which is gone forever, unless another centre has copies.

"We must thank Bidi for giving us enough evidence to put Hampton behind bars for a lifetime. I will call you back as soon as we have news about her. I am sure she is all right, like James Moorhead, the detective inspector who questioned you first. He was kept in a unit and let go a week later. And tomorrow, we should have completed the charges laid against Hampton. OK, that's it; go back to sleep, and don't worry."

53

ASIO sprang into action, and every available cyber security agent from around South-East Queensland was sent to Hampton's headquarters. They had the workforce to search every millimetre of space, not that they found anything significant. It was fruitless; Bidi already had done the necessary work. However, they stored all the inactive androids in a secure facility in Brisbane for further studies. They knew that Hampton was the only one worldwide who had succeeded in making androids move, talk and look like humans.

In a monumental day and night effort, the ASIO agents meticulously dismantled all the Internet servers, determined to establish if they had been used to enable androids and robots across Australia to access the Internet undetected. As an added precaution, they also dismantled the control centre computers located upstairs in Hampton's and Jess's offices.

Curiously, the ASIO agents overlooked the two butler robots in their investigation, perhaps due to their preoccupation with the more human-like androids. Those robots held crucial information, potentially even Bidi's whereabouts.

Incredibly, after everything was dismantled and removed and the house was locked and sealed off, they left the robots behind. It never occurred to them that the robots knew and recorded everything.

Thursday – Brisbane 15. December 2033 - Jake

Jake felt like a figure on the sidelines. He was present at the investigation of the files Bidi had recovered but had no impact whatsoever. The cyber security team was all over it, at least the one responsible for interpreting the files; everyone else was on the Gold Coast at Hampton's headquarters.

Later that day, Jake's work started, compiling the information the agents sourced from the files to charge Hampton.

It was evident that no charge would be laid that Thursday. The information was massive but also intricately complex, making it a challenge to put it in chronological order.

The prosecution team was on standby to evaluate how much data would be needed for a fail-proof charge. So far, they were not happy. They decided to take over the fraud charge, the money skimming from bank accounts themselves, and sort them in chronological order. Jake and two of the ASIO agents worked the espionage files.

Still, everyone was upbeat. They knew they had everything needed to convict Hampton; however, they had to go through an enormous workload to present the information as evidence.

Work stopped at 10 pm that Thursday night. Jake estimated they would charge Hampton by 11 am on Friday.

54

Everyone was ready. Each team had done their work, and Jake summarised the charge and prepared two folders with the evidence, one for the cyber fraud allegations and the other for espionage.

Jake had notified Hampton's solicitor, who was sitting with him, waiting for what would come.

It needed the right people to stand by, follow the reading of the charges, and question the subject from a separate room.

Everything was prepared for 11 am, less than one hour to go. Jake had nothing left to do other than wait. Luckily, his phone rang, rescuing him from thinking about how Hampton's case would end. He answered, "Hi, Blake, I have no news for you yet. The case will start at 11 am."

"Any news at all about Bidi?" Blake asked.

"No, nothing, but a team is checking on all surveillance cameras 10km around Hampton's headquarters. So far, nothing of interest has shown up."

"Have you asked the butler robot that works downstairs?"

"Ask the robot. Are you joking? Can that thing even answer?"

"Jake, please send someone to talk to the robot. It is a fully-aware artificial intelligence robot. It can tell you who came in and who went out. It may even have video footage of someone taking Bidi away and possibly even show the car that was used."

"Sorry Blake, it never occurred to me, I'll let the cyber-crime guys know to go back; they still have the keys."

"Thanks, and let me know." Blake hung up, irritated that the cyber-crime team had not investigated information from the butler robot.

Jake walked into the interview room; he didn't like to call it the interrogation room. His task was to read the charge to Hampton and make him aware of his rights. Two of the ASIO officers were also in the room, and a whole host of people followed the notification and interrogation from another room.

Jake sat down and switched on the video and recording devices. He acknowledged everyone's presence and read the charges to Hampton. Even so, the goal of an interrogation is to solve a crime; in this case, the goal was to offer Hampton the opportunity to admit his crime and to support the police with further investigations to determine how far-reaching his fraud and espionage had become.

Reading out the charge and related legal information and, once again, reading out Hampton's rights took over 20 minutes.

At the end of it, Jake asked if he agreed to the charges and, if he did, to sign those papers admitting the crime and claiming a guilty verdict.

Jake looked at Hampton who showed no reaction other than looking at his solicitor.

Jake pushed the papers and a pen to Hampton. "Please sign."

He pushed the pen and papers back, not saying anything.

Jake made a final attempt: "Part of the charge is about espionage and treason, which carries a maximum penalty of life in prison. Admitting to it may offer some leniency in your case.

Again, there was no reaction from Hampton or the solicitor.

Jake turned to the ASIO officer. "If there is nothing else you want to add, we can close the procedure."

One of the officers nodded his head, and that was it. Jake didn't know what else he had expected, but certainly not silence. He made the final announcement for the recording equipment that the interrogation had finished and stood up.

"Bye, Mr. Hampton,'" he said, wanting to turn and leave the room when he noticed the appearances of Hampton and his solicitor had changed. It was subtle, and he wasn't sure at first what it was. He called out, "Mr. Hampton, are you all right?" No answer.

Jake was dumbfounded: How could that have happened? Why did no one test Hampton and his solicitor to ensure they were human? He was in the presence of two deactivated androids.

Jake looked at the ASIO guys and said, "I can't believe you guys. How can you be in charge and not perform a basic check to be prepared for all possibilities?" He didn't expect an answer and didn't get one.

Everyone came out of their rooms, but no one admitted responsibility until Jake spoke up. "We know who is in charge of this investigation. We have a criminal on the run. Can the team responsible please commence appropriate action, or do I have to take over hunting Hampton and possibly Jess and inform Interpol?

It took a while to regroup, but eventually, ASIO admitted it was responsible, as they had brought forward the espionage case.

They went ahead and commenced an Australia-wide search and expanded it globally with the assistance of Interpol, which has over 200 member countries.

Where would or could Hampton hide? Would he still be able to control his vast empires of companies and possibly the androids?

ASIO could prove no direct affiliation to any company within Hampton's empire. Each company had a separate board of directors acting individually.

As it became evident in the coming days, androids and robots were still being manufactured, research was ongoing, e-cars were produced, and even virtual glasses were sold. However, no connection to Hampton could be validated.

Jake was happy that ASIO had taken over; he was more concerned about

Bidi. After a cup of coffee, he contacted the officer, who should have investigated the butler robot by now.

Waiting for the officer to pick up his phone, he saw the androids being led out of the building. They looked dead but could be encouraged to walk.

We have android zombies now, Jake thought. He was pretty fed up with all the android business, not what he considered standard police work. Surely, in the future, an android and cyber team will take over that side of deception and criminal activities.

Regarding the butler robot, he called the officer in charge, who finally answered. "Have you finished your investigation? Any luck?" Jake asked.

"Yes, the robot answered all straightforward questions. We heard the whole story: two androids from the android storage room came out, took Bidi between them, blindfolded her with a hood and led her out of the house when a driverless e-taxi arrived, and they drove away. We had the e-taxi number and drove in the same direction as the taxi. We checked video surveillance cameras, tracked down the cab at two traffic lights, and drove over the bridge to Chevron Island, taking the first right-hand turn. That's all we have on direct surveillance.

Our team and additional local police officers are now searching houses and questioning people. So far, no positive result; it is not likely that anyone has seen anything; it was late at night when it happened."

Jake thanked the officer and called Blake to keep him up to date. It should only be a matter of time before they find a building that looks unoccupied and probably has closed blinds, which is what the officer told Jake they were concentrating on.

55

B idi woke up refreshed. She surprised herself by not being overly worried. She even took a shower and later made herself breakfast.

She was calm and relaxed but didn't look forward to sitting around and not doing anything; her inquisitive mind poked her into action.

People always overlook something, she thought. Last night, she was too tired and looked over the place superficially; now she was serious.

She checked the windows. Was there anything to trigger the automatic steel blinds? She used a kitchen knife and tried to lift the framework around the windows. They must have placed the wiring somewhere. She worked up quite a sweat but to no avail. The same was true of the door.

The fridge, yes, why didn't she think about it earlier? It had a computer screen on the door that undoubtedly could be operated by touch control. The screen was blank. Was it switched off or totally deactivated? There was the possibility that the fridge was still connected to the Internet to order meal replacements.

There was no visible switch, and touching at various places showed no result. She opened the door; on the back, a tray with eggs was at the screen's height. She lifted the tray out and saw two indented slots that could be operated on with a tool, which she obviously didn't have. She checked the kitchen cabinet; what other utensils were available? There were six knives with a rounded tip. She took one out and used it to turn the slotted round button-like indentation. It worked, the back cover came off. She couldn't believe her luck; there was a small slider switch. She switched it on. The screen came alive, and a message appeared, 'Connect this device to your hotspot.'

After all this work, she couldn't do it. She had a hotspot on her mobile, but that was no help.

Her positivity diminished. She looked at the bottle of wine but decided against it, made herself a cup of tea, and grabbed a book, accepting defeat.

It was creeping towards noon; putting the book away, she returned to the fridge, feeling hungry. *What can I eat?* She thought when she was startled by a sharp metallic noise. Was someone coming? She looked towards the door. Had something changed? Was there a small gap between the door and the frame? Can't be, she thought, and went over, slowly trying to slide the door to the right. It worked; she flung the door completely open and saw the table with her phone on it. What had happened? Why was she allowed to go?

She took her phone and called Blake.

"Bidi, where are you? Are you OK?"

Bidi told Blake the whole story. "I don't know what happened when the door opened. What's the news?"

"Yes, Jake called and updated me with the incredible news that, after charging Hampton, it became apparent that he was an android and his solicitor as well. Jake has now been relieved of this case altogether, and ASIO will take full charge. Interpol has been briefed already. They are going to hunt Hampton and Jess everywhere.

I would say the reason for your release is that charges have been laid out, and Hampton will now be aware of the information collected. There was no reason to hold you captive anymore; you can't add anything new to the case. Jake has a large team activated to find you; you better call him."

"Yes, I think you are right. I will ring him now so he can end the search."

Another quick call to Jake, who was overjoyed. After Bidi had told Jake the address, he told her to stay put. His team was in the area, and a car would drive her home to Brisbane.

Bidi looked at her phone. Should she check her bank account?

56

Derek and Jess had always enjoyed their weekends, and this weekend, spending time on their yacht, was no different. At the yacht club, they were known as Richard and Pamela van der Krest.

Richard, aka Derek, aka the Zookeeper, liked the name Krest; it rhymed with quest, and he was ready for stage two of his quest for world domination.

The Krests were well respected by the yacht club community. They frequently participated in social events and were often seen sipping expensive champagne at the club bar, but most of the time, they kept to themselves.

That Sunday night, they celebrated privately inside their spacious yacht. Two butler robots were in attendance, serving food and drinks. Soft music played. Overall, it was a peaceful, even romantic-looking festivity.

Jess, aka Pamela, wearing a long evening dress enhanced with tasteful jewellery and a sparkling smile, listened attentively to Richard.

Richard raised his glass, "To the successful completion of stage one, may stage two and three present us with even more success. Cheers."

"Cheers," echoed Pamela.

"Please summarize stage one and explain stage two."

As close as their symbiotic relationship was, and without any harm to her, she deliberately stayed away, as instructed by Richard, from intrinsic knowledge. If she ever was imprisoned, she could only reveal her direct input as a computer operator overseeing the distribution services of Richard's companies.

Pamela knew the exact number of e-cars, robots, and androids sold. But she had an eye on many other companies, such as the distribution of virtual reality glasses and smaller vital products needed for manufacturing, such as batteries and computer parts.

It was her work to monitor, and that was all. She monitored and alerted Richard if something went wrong or if she received an error message, like when the androids were disconnected from direct two-way communication with the control centre.

Richard liked this part, explaining his successes. In their relationship, Pamela had to ask the right question to keep Richard in good spirits, or, as he called it, to stay in the glory. He needed it to create ever more grandiose goals.

It was a game; he didn't calculate the losses or the possible harm to others. It was his way, always. He was an autocrat who didn't like the term dictator. He had absolute power but no army. His weapon was influencing and breeding complacency.

Richard placed his glass on the table and prepared to summarise, "Stage one has been completed. Some people or government bodies may have concluded they have curtailed my powers, but they didn't understand my goals for stage one. Over nine years, stage one constituted the expansion stage and accumulation of wealth. My robots, androids, e-cars and other components and products have achieved market dominance in countries with high incomes, quality of life, and advanced technology. In other words, those countries that love and can afford my products.

"My most outstanding achievement was bringing dramatic development forward to produce human-like androids. My invention, the 'nerve-mesh,' made catapulting androids into normal society possible. Other manufacturers of androids still, to this day, use clumsy motor techniques to move limbs or facial expressions. I use 3D printing life material and low-weight artificial bone structures surrounded by the nerve-mesh, enabled by artificial intelligence and superior mini quantum computer power.

"I now come to my so-called setbacks. The completion of stage one included stopping skimming money, and therefore, I didn't need the communication connections any more. Blake did me a favour; he stopped it without my input. If it comes to recording conversations, that is not espionage; it is an android security measure, but I have no time to argue that in court.

"Stage two will be all above board. It will concentrate on distributing robots and androids, supporting humans to have more leisure time, or, in my terminology, breeding complacency.

"From now on, e-cars will monitor conversations and communications inside the car. Again, this is a security measure, not espionage.

"I learned from Blake's action of inserting a virus to be harvested by monitoring computers, which has given me the idea to do the same. All new robots and androids will be programmed to communicate once again to upgrade their algorithm, and if they come in contact with other robots or androids, infect those with a virus to reestablish communication.

"The end game of stage two will be saturating the world with androids. Androids are programmed as people-pleasers and pacifiers, constantly breeding complacency and making it easy to control people.

"I will not discuss stage three at this time, but it will involve enhancing complacency with drugs and superior human beings like myself to transfer their brain into androids and live forever.

"Compliments have to be given where they are due. Blake and his team were the primary adversaries worth mentioning. He had been a challenging game opponent. After all, it is a game and hasn't finished yet." He finished his speech and sat down, raising his glass again.

Pamela had a few more questions, "How will you control your androids in the meantime?

"I don't have to. They take over the regular workforce by themselves; they still act according to their core programming, supporting humans in such a way that humans don't have to do anything and become complacent. Once enough androids are on the market with connections to our control centre and the virus, they will slowly infect the older androids, connecting them again and enabling us to update them.

To make sure, Pamela asked him again, "And you will keep going with your plan to breed complacency?

"Yes, the complacency of the masses will enable me to shape humanity. There will be no wars in the future; people and political leaders will be too complacent. Wars are too destructive for my long-term goals and achieve no valuable outcomes; they waste money, material and people."

Pamela had a final question: "How will life look in your proposed future? I assume that will be outlined in stage three?"

"Yes, without going into details, most of the manufacturing polluting our beautiful earth will eventually be placed on the moon, with essential minerals and elements harvested from planets like Mars. The world will return to a pristine natural environment, and heaven on earth will be a reality. We will be able to enjoy it in our android bodies, living forever."

It was Pamela's time to raise her glass, "Cheers to that."

57

"I feel a bit flat," Blake said to Frances while they were having breakfast.

"How come?"

"There seems to be nothing urgent to do. Hampton is gone; I wonder if Interpol will ever find him. Thank God Bidi is safe, and our other friends will return to normal work and life; it very nearly sounds boring." Blake said.

"You better get busy writing about the new reality, living with androids in our midst and us having become certified humans to set us apart from the machines. People will seek new directions, fears must be calmed, and security measures must be installed on our devices. Why don't you start tomorrow on a series of explanatory articles, cautioning people about undue influences from anything robotic and being vigilant in knowing who is a certified human and who isn't," Frances said.

"A change of scenery may help. Let's go back to Sydney and live in your unit for a couple of weeks, and maybe we should get married," Blake said.

"Was that a marriage proposal out of boredom?"

"Sorry, I was thinking aloud. Give me a couple of days to regroup, and I will come up with something better." Blake laughed and hugged her.

"Let's go for a walk," Blake said while he put on his shoes.

"Give me a second." Frances went to the bathroom, applied her lipstick, grabbed her handbag, and called, "I'm ready! Let's go."

Blake let Frances walk out first, closing the door behind him and ensuring he locked it properly.

As they left the building, Blake's unit door opened. He should have changed the locks and security codes. Jess walked in undisturbed.

About the author

Dieter Lüske is a writer who enjoys life and life's journey. He loves working with Giselle, his artist wife, in their endless creative pursuits and enchanted organic garden, and he dabbles in art, music, and philosophy.

He has written five books, has published hundreds of holistic lifestyle articles, and lives by his motto,
"By attempting the impossible - one is meaningfully occupied."

Dieter combines the perseverance and courage of the finest tradition of investigative & creative writing
with the ability to keep complex topics simple.

Also by Dieter Lüske

It Happened In The Seventies - A story of profound change.

Chaos in Brainland - Creating a Stress and Anxiety-Free Zone

Available on Amazon

Support the author by leaving a review on Amazon.

Author website – www.DieterLuske.com